SERENDIPITY RANCH
and the Quilters of the Apocalypse

Creative Texts Publishers products are available at special discounts for bulk purchase for sale promotions, premiums, fund-raising, and educational needs. For details, write Creative Texts Publishers, PO Box 50, Barto, PA 19504, or visit www.creativetexts.com

SERENDIPITY RANCH AND THE QUILTERS OF THE APOLACLYPSE
Diana E. Anderson
Published by Creative Texts Publishers
PO Box 50
Barto, PA 19504
www.creativetexts.com

ISBN: 978-1-64738-085-4

SERENDIPITY RANCH

and the Quilters of the Apocalypse

by DIANA E. ANDERSON

CREATIVE TEXTS PUBLISHERS

Barto, Pennsylvania

Dedication

My original plan was to dedicate this book to all my quilting sisters and brothers, especially those in my local guild, the Card Tricks Chapter of the Arizona Quilters Guild. However, life tends to sneak up on us and change things around on us. So, I now have a two-part dedication.

I do dedicate this book to my quilting friends. No matter where I go, I find quilters to be a special kind of people – kind, generous, helpful, accepting, and loving. At a time in my life that my world was crashing around me, my quilting sisters kept me sane with their kindness, care, and love. This book is written in part to share my love and appreciation for all of you.

I also dedicate this book to the loving memory of my beloved husband Michael, who passed away last September. When you died, I didn't know how I was going to go on with life, let alone finish a book. You were my editor, my staunchest supporter and my most honest critic. In spite of losing you, though, I managed to pull myself together with the help of my quilting buddies and finish this book. I will miss you every minute of every day for the rest of my life and will love you forever. This book is to honor your memory. Until we meet again…

Acknowledgements

There are a number of people I would like to acknowledge for their help, inspiration, and encouragement in creating this book. First, I'd like to thank my friend Barbara Yetter, who challenged me to write a post-apocalyptic book about quilters. I did my best, Barbara, and I hope you like it!

I'd like to thank the members of my guild chapter, Card Tricks Chapter of the Arizona Quilters Guild, and the members of the Patriotic Piecers. You have all been so encouraging and such good friends. While my husband was home on hospice, you all went the extra mile for us, bringing meals, love, and friendship. In the awful days after his death, you sat with me, listened to me and let me cry on your shoulders. I love you all for that.

Finally, I'd like to acknowledge my publisher, Dan Edwards. Dan has never bugged me with deadlines and has always been so encouraging and positive. It is such a pleasure to work with you!

Table of Contents

Chapter One

March 14

Joel Matthews reached across the breakfast table to help himself to another serving of his wife's bacon potato casserole. Rachel smiled as she watched her husband enjoy his seconds.

"I'm glad you like it," she said. "I tried out a new recipe and I wasn't sure how good it would be since I used freeze-dried hash browns and cheese in it."

Joel looked at her in surprise. "Really? This is awesome, and I would never have guessed if you hadn't told me. Way to go, using freeze dried stuff to make fancy retreat food!"

Rachel laughed. "Well, since I'm not sure we will ever get to open a real quilters' retreat, I can at least play and pretend. And… I am afraid we will have to use our prepping skills one of these days, so if I can play at fancy breakfasts and learn to use some of our food storage at the same time, it's a good thing!"

Joel just laughed and shook his head. "After being married to you for almost 30 years, you would think there are no surprises left, but you surprise me every day. I agree with you, the stuff will probably hit the fan long before we ever get to open your dream retreat, but I appreciate your practicing the fancy breakfasts." Joel knew Rachel's dream had always been to open some kind of a bed and breakfast. After spending a week at a retreat for quilters a few years ago, her dream shifted slightly from just a bed and breakfast to having a quilters' retreat of her own. This expanded the bed and breakfast idea to hosting groups who would come spend a few days to learn new quilting techniques, work on improving skills, or just have the peace and quiet to complete works in progress. Unfortunately, even though both Rachel and Joel both worked, there never seemed to be enough money to buy the property they would need for such an endeavor. It didn't stop Rachel from practicing new meals, in the hopes she would someday be able to serve them to her guests. Seeing the wistful look on Rachel's face, he quickly changed the topic.

"What are you and Chris up to today? I heard you making some plans last night when I was talking to Scott." Scott and Christine Wilson were the Matthews' next-door neighbors and their best friends.

"Chris and I are going to check out the sale at the quilt shop. Chris wants to use the gift certificate Scott gave her for her birthday, and I need to pick up some fabric for a baby quilt for Jessie at church. Then, if we have any money left, we're going to have lunch at that little French café that just opened across the street from the shop. We won't be gone all day, though, because I have to be at work at three."

Joel looked up in surprise. "Why do you have to go in on a Saturday? I thought one of the perks of being a supervisor was having weekends off."

"Well, Toby is sick again, and so I am covering his shift. Ever since he was in the hospital with Covid last year, his health has been really fragile. I told him to just stay home and rest, and I'd cover today for him."

"Honey, you are such a good person. I'm surprised you haven't fired him yet for all of his attendance issues. I know he has to have used up all of his FMLA time by now."

"He has, but I couldn't fire him. He is a sweet guy, with a wife and two babies at home. He's a great employee, and it's not his fault he's been so sick. The customers love him, and he does a good job."

Joel sighed. "What time will you get off?"

"I'll close the deli as usual at nine, but then I'll have to clean up and restock for tomorrow. I should be home by about eleven."

"Okay. I'll try to wait up for you. I'll be over at Scott's for most of the day helping him work on his generator. If we get done early enough, we may go out to the range for a little lead therapy. Don't forget Scott and Chris are coming over after church tomorrow so we can try out my new grill."

Rachel looked surprised. "I'm glad you said something – I forgot! Do you need me to bring anything home from the store tonight?"

"No, if I need anything, I'll run up later and get it." He stood up and began clearing dishes off the table. "You go and get ready for your adventure with Chris. I've got this."

Rachel smiled as she turned to leave the room. "Thanks, honey. I'll see you before I head out."

~~~

Rachel and Joel met the summer after Joel graduated high school as Rachel was going into her senior year. Both had signed up for the same young adult program through their church, and the two hit it right off. While both kids were smart, neither one had any desire to go to college. Joel planned to join the Army and learn a trade, and Rachel wanted to be a homemaker. She loved to cook, sew, and do other domestic activities, and working outside the home had no appeal to her. Although her parents were not particularly happy with her plans, they did love Joel, and could tell the two kids belonged together.

They married the week after Rachel graduated from high school. A month later, Joel left for basic training. Over the next nine years, the couple traveled to various Army bases and Joel was deployed to the Middle East several times.

During that time, the couple had three children. Noah, the oldest, was now 26 and worked as a veterinary technician at an animal hospital across town. Rebecca was 25 and, after graduating from culinary school, was hired as a sous chef at a restaurant in a city about an hour away from her parents. She remained close to her mother, talking on the phone with her several times a week, but she was definitely Daddy's little girl. She would find lots of excuses to text or call Joel every day. Marcie, the youngest child, was 23 and married to Billy Walker. Billy worked in the accounting department of the local hospital, and Marcie was a homemaker. She and Billy were expecting Rachel and Joel's first grandchild in a few months and lived in a tiny apartment about four blocks from Rachel and Joel. Marcie was much like her mother, in that she loved being a housewife. Of course, her sister Rebecca teased her and called her job a domestic engineer. No matter what she was called, Marcie loved keeping her apartment spotless and taking care of Billy. She was delighted to live close enough to her mother that they could quilt or cook together.

After Joel got out of the Army, the couple settled in a small town in rural North Carolina. Joel learned to be an electrician in the Army and found a job with an electrical company after getting out. They purchased a house on a quaint street not far from Joel's job. Rachel loved their neighborhood. The kids' schools were a short walk from the house, their church was just down the street, and they had great neighbors. As Joel's skills grew, he left the electric company and formed his own company, which grew and became very successful. A few years after they bought their house, the family next door to them moved away and the Wilsons bought the house. Scott Wilson was still in the Navy when he and his family moved in. After he retired from the Navy, he went to work as the executive chef for the restaurant downtown where Rebecca Matthews worked. His wife, Christine, worked as an inventory specialist at a local big box store. The Wilsons had one child, a daughter named Gwen who obtained a degree in hospitality and tourism in college and now worked at a travel agency downtown. Gwen and Rebecca quickly became best friends, and it didn't take long for their parents to become best friends as well.

~~~

Stepping out of the shower a few minutes later, Rachel stopped to glance in the mirror. "Not too bad for 47 and the mother of three," she thought. The reflection looking back at her had short blond hair, dark green eyes, and a petite figure. Working as the supervisor of the deli department of a local grocery store was often hard work, lifting cases of meats and cheeses and standing on her feet all day. Fortunately, it helped keep her in shape. She quickly pulled on jeans and a tee shirt and fluffed her hair. Half an hour later, she and Chris were climbing into Rachel's jeep, headed for their favorite fabric store. Both Chris and Rachel were avid quilters, very active in their local Quilt Guild, and happiest when they were surrounded by piles of fabrics. She and Chris both taught occasional classes at the quilt shop and it was definitely a happy place for both of them.

~~~

Chris Wilson literally met her husband Scott by accident. She was involved in a minor fender bender in her hometown of Norfolk, Virginia, and her car door jammed, trapping her in the front seat. Suddenly, a sailor was yanking at her door and helped her escape. The sailor would not take "no" for an answer and drove her home after she talked to the police and her car was towed away. Within two weeks, the sailor – Scott – and Chris were a couple. They married less than a year later. Chris often retold the story of the accident and usually joked that she had no idea her guardian angel was a handsome 6'2" black man wearing sailor's dungarees. At almost 5'11" with black hair, dark brown eyes, and a lithe figure, Chris and Scott made a striking couple. They were also some of the kindest, most humble people one would ever want to meet, and very active in their church. It was obvious to anyone who

saw them that the two were soulmates and still deeply in love, even after 28 years of marriage.
```
```
The quilt shop was a little busier than usual because of the sale, but Rachel and Chris braved the crowds. The shop was having a spectacular sale on batiks, and since she couldn't decide between several vibrant colors, Rachel decided to get a yard or two of each. While Rachel was looking at all of the batiks, she happened to see Mary and Trina, two of her quilting buddies. Mary worked at the shop and Trina was Mary's sister-in-law and best friend. As the two were pretty much inseparable, Rachel wasn't surprised to see them both at the shop together. She waved, and the two women came over to her, carrying several bolts of fabric.

"Look at this, Rachel, isn't this beautiful?" said Mary, showing Rachel a bolt of fabric featuring butterflies on a blue and cream background with silver metallic threads interspersed in the pattern. "We just got this line of fabrics in this morning. I think this ought to be your next quilt."

"Oh, Mary, that is gorgeous! That would look really pretty in that star pattern you were showing us the other day."

"Look at the other fabrics that go with the butterflies," Trina said, holding out several other bolts. I really like this one with the darker blue and the silver swirls."

Chris came over to see what Rachel, Mary, and Trina were looking at. "That is gorgeous! I want some of that, too. It would be perfect for the quilt I plan to make Gwen for her birthday," Chris said.

Rachel started laughing. "I was just thinking it would be perfect for Rebecca's birthday! Let's make both girls matching quilts. That ought to tickle them and remind them of the days when they were kids and wanted everything the same."

Chris smiled at the memory of their two little girls, one with fair skin, blue eyes, and blond hair, the other with dark skin, brown eyes, and dark hair, telling everyone they were twins. The good thing was the girls – now grown – were still as close as sisters and spent as much time as they could together.

"What are you grinning about?" Rachel asked.

"I was just thinking about Gwen and Rebecca telling people they were twins. I'm so glad our girls are still close."

"Well, if the girls take after their mamas, they ought to be close! I don't think I've ever seen either one of you in here without the other one," Mary chuckled. "Are you both coming to my class next week? We're going to do the double wedding ring pattern with a star added."

"I wish I could, but I have to work," Rachel answered. "And, before you say it, I can't quit the job, because then I couldn't come here and spend a bajillion dollars to feed my fabric addiction!"

The four women laughed. Mary went to help another customer, and Trina left to check out other fabrics. Rachel and Chris spent time looking for the perfect accent fabrics, and then had to find background fabric to go with Rachel's batiks. They finally got around to selecting a couple of yards of pastel fabrics for Rachel's baby quilt. After spending several hours looking at fabrics and checking out all of the new quilting tools and toys, Rachel and Chris put their many purchases in Rachel's jeep and walked across the street to the new French café, La Petite Bouchée.

"Wow, I'm surprised it's this busy," Rachel remarked, as a server showed them to their seats and handed them menus.

The two ladies browsed the menus for a minute, and Chris commented, "It all looks so good. Do you know what you want?"

"Oh, I know exactly what I want. I'm going to get the crab quiche with a balsamic reduction, and a small salad."

"That sounds wonderful. I think I'll get the same thing."

The two women placed their orders and sat in comfortable silence, sipping at their iced tea, and looking around the small restaurant. "You know, if I ever opened my dream quilters' retreat, it would be so much fun to be able to serve food like some of the things on the menu here… I'd call the menu comfort gourmet food."

"You and your quilters' retreat! I like that idea, though- comfort food with a gourmet twist – Scott could have fun with that. What else would you have on the menu?"

"Definitely would have to have barbecue – you know how Joel likes his ribs and pulled pork! I'd want some really good steaks, maybe some lobster, stuffed shrimp, crab, maybe some game meats, too, like stuffed venison roast or elk. Lots of great veggies like roasted asparagus and stuffed zucchini. I'd make some surprise type things, like shrimp strudel with a roasted tomato sauce, and stuffed pork chops. Plus, I'd want to use a lot of the freeze-dried stuff to help people learn how good they can be if fixed right."

Chris laughed. "Instead of a quilters' retreat, you ought to open a bug-out retreat so we all have some place to go when the apocalypse gets here."

Rachel smiled and nodded, "You know, maybe we could combine both and just call it the Bug Out Retreat."

"No, we should call it the Apocalypse Retreat, where you can check in, but operational security won't let you check out!" giggled Chris.

Laughing, Rachel answered, "We could call ourselves the *Quilters of the Apocalypse!*" Her smile faded. "With the way the economy is going, though, there is no way we could afford to do that. At least, not unless we rob a bank or win the lottery."

Chris nudged Rachel's arm. "I don't think we'd get much if we robbed the bank here in town, plus I'm not sure they'd let us quilt in jail. As for winning the lottery, how many lottery tickets have you bought lately?"

Rachel laughed, and said, "Well, none actually. I guess if we want to win, we have to buy a ticket, right?"

Chris replied, "I hear the Powerball is up over $750 million this week. Maybe you ought to stop and get a ticket on the way home!"

Rachel grinned. "Yeah, like I ever win anything. But. . . I suppose that's the only way it will ever happen. If I do win anything, I can use it to buy more fabric, I guess. That would thrill Joel, I'm sure. He already loves how the guest room is now my quilting room. You know there are two things you can never have enough of . . . fabric and ammo. He takes care of the ammo, and I get the fabric!"

"And don't forget, you have your quilt room happy place, but he has most of the basement for his reloading and ammo storage and stuff. I'm glad Scott is a chef - the kitchen is his happy place, and so it doesn't bother him at all that the third bedroom is my sewing room. As long as I stay out of his kitchen and don't mess with his knives, he's a happy camper. At least he didn't completely take over the basement. He left me lots of room for all of our prepping supplies. Which reminds me," she said digging in her purse and pulling out a sheet of paper. "I made a list of some things we need to use soon before they expire, and also a few ideas for some things we need to buy and add to our stocks."

SERENDIPITY RANCH

One of the many things that bonded the two couples was a belief that hard times were coming, and they needed to be prepared. The four did not have a specific disaster in mind but considering all of the threats the country faced over the last few years, they felt sure trouble was coming. The Covid pandemic finally had resolved, but China, North Korea, Iran, and Russia were still threats. There had been several cease fires in the on-going war between Russia and Ukraine, but every few weeks, fighting erupted again, and each time, the fears that Russia would push the battle into a NATO country emerged, sparking fears of a nuclear confrontation and World War Three. The huge migration across the southern border led to major issues across the country, and they felt the increased focus on the American military's "woke-ness" left the United States vulnerable. Hard-earned tax dollars were being spent on frivolous things such as gender studies in far-away countries and measuring cow flatulence, while there were thousands of veterans sleeping under bridges and children going to bed hungry. The recent failure of several American banks put both couples on edge, as of all of the potential disasters they could face, the disaster the group thought was most likely was a collapse of the United States' economy. Both couples felt the need to ready themselves and their families for when that happened. The two families were both avowed preppers and shared their preparations. Because Chris worked for a big box store as an inventory management specialist, she was responsible for maintaining the inventory of all of their combined supplies. Rachel kept track of the finances, accounting for every penny that both couples spent on preps. That kept the guys from going crazy buying too many guns, gadgets, and accessories. In addition to tracking inventory and finances, the two also kept a record of skills. The two couples took many classes throughout the year to learn things like first aid, cooking on a wood stove, and how to set up perimeter security systems, and Rachel tracked their competency. Once a month, the four sat down together to review their supplies and make decisions on what they need and how much they were willing to spend. It was a good system, and it gave both families a sense of security in a very insecure world.

Chapter Two

March 19

Chris, Scott, Joel, and Rachel were sitting in the Matthews' living room. Rachel was anxiously clutching the Powerball tickets in her hand. "Only a few more minutes and they'll announce the winning number. I'm so nervous, but I don't know why. I never win anything." Rachel said.

"Calm down, honey," Joel said, putting his arm around her shoulder. "If we win, that would be beyond amazing, but if we don't, all we've lost is the twelve dollars you spent on tickets. Life will go on, and we'll keep on dreaming about the Quilters of the Apocalypse Retreat." Joel gave Rachel a squeeze, and she grinned at him.

Suddenly, Rachel stood up and turned towards the others. "I have something to say before they announce the results. Scott and Chris, you are our very best friends, and we love you both. We are closer to you two than we were with our families. If we win today, we will be sharing the winnings with you both." Chris and Scott began to talk, but Rachel put her hand up. "No arguments. Joel and I talked it over. If we win, we will ALL win. We want you both to be a part of whatever we do with the winnings, so no further discussion! Besides, I probably wouldn't have even thought to buy the tickets if Chris hadn't goaded me into it! Now, if I win anything, it probably will be barely enough for the four of us to go grab a burger, but the important thing is that we share it with you guys."

Chris smiled affectionately at Rachel. "We love you guys, too."

Suddenly, the newscaster came on TV to announce the winning numbers. Rachel sat back down and said, "Everyone be quiet, let's hear the numbers." Chris grabbed a pen and paper and began to write the numbers down as they were announced.

"*...and the winning numbers are 9, 18, 42, 51 and 62. The Powerball is 13.*"

Rachel quickly scanned the tickets in her hand. Suddenly, she let out a scream. "Oh my gosh, oh, my gosh, oh, my gosh!" she kept saying.

"What is it, honey?" Joel asked. "You're scaring me, are you okay?"

Rachel turned to Joel, tears pouring down her face. In a shaky voice, she said, "We won."

She held out the winning ticket to Joel, while Chris and Scott looked over his shoulder.

"Oh, come on, Rachel. You had me going there for a minute. Good acting, I've got to admit," Joel said, shaking his head and laughing.

Rachel just looked at Joel and shoved the tickets in his face. Joel looked at the tickets and his face became pale. "Holy cow, you're right! The Powerball was for $750 million dollars! And we all just won that!" While Chris and Scott looked on, wide-eyed, Joel flipped the ticket over and read the information on the back. "Here, Rachel, take the pen and sign the ticket right away. It's a bearer document until its signed, and we don't want someone to steal it and take our money. Then, I'll put it in the safe. Tomorrow, we'll take it to Greensboro and claim our money."

Scott finally found his voice. "This is absolutely amazing! You know that you'll need to get an attorney, a tax advisor, and a financial advisor right away. You know Stacey Bennett at church? She is a corporate attorney, and she's handled a few things for me and the restaurant. She was really good. I'll bet she'd be willing to help you. Do you want me to call her?"

Rachel nodded. "Is Stacey the blonde lady, about 35 or so? She usually sits up front with old Mrs. Dupree?"

Scott answered, "Yes, that's her. Mrs. Dupree is Stacey's neighbor."

Rachel nodded. "Okay, yes, please call her. I'm too shaky right now to have a clear conversation."

As Scott stepped away to call the attorney, Rachel paced back and forth, shaking her head with a look of shock on her face. "I can't believe it!" she repeated over and over. Finally, Joel stood and taking her by the hand, sat Rachel down on the couch. Chris came over to sit next to her and took her other hand.

"See, aren't you glad I told you to buy a ticket?" Chris joked. "I am so excited for you," she started to say.

"For US," Rachel interrupted. "You are just as much a winner of this prize as we are." She laughed. "Now we just need to figure out how to get the money and what we're going to spend it on."

"Let's not make any fast decisions, honey," Joel interjected. "First, we need to go to Greensboro and become the official winners. Then, when we get back, once we know the prize is real and how much we'll get and when, then we can take time to plan out what we are going to do. Does everyone agree with that?"

"That's exactly the advice Stacey just gave us," said Scott as he walked back into the room. "Stacey is very excited for us and says she will be glad to do whatever she can to help us." Scott shook his head. "I can't believe all of this. You guys are too much. I mean, yeah, we are best friends, but to share a prize like this.... Chris, we sure picked the right family to move next to, didn't we!"

Laughing, Joel answered, "Oh, and we were sure we weren't going to like you when you first moved in."

Frowning, Scott asked, "Because we're black?"

Joel burst out laughing, "Heck, no. I don't care about that, but you were Navy! I wasn't sure Army and Navy were going to get along." Everyone laughed, and he continued, "but in spite of that, you guys turned out to be all right." He got very serious for a moment. "I can't think of anyone we would rather share this with than the two of you, and I mean that from the bottom of my heart. I am closer to the two of you than I was with my brother, and that's saying a lot."

Scott reached over and grabbed Joel's hand. "Joel, as far as I am concerned, you ARE my brother. I know I speak for Chris as well, when I say that you two are the best friends we've ever had. You know that has to be true, since we plan to spend the apocalypse together, after all."

Rachel piped up. "Okay, guys, enough of the love fest. Geeze, next you're going to start singing Kumbaya or something!" Chris giggled, and Rachel continued, "Let's plan on having a formal meeting tomorrow evening when we get back from Greensboro. Scott, will you call Stacey again and see if she can attend? I mean, as long as everything goes the way we want it to go in Greensboro tomorrow. Now we all need to call in sick to work tomorrow and clear our calendars for the next day or two until we know what we're doing. One more thing. Let's not tell a soul, not even the kids, until after we claim the prize just in case it is all a mistake, and we really didn't win. Once we find out its all real, then we'll have all of the kids over to let them know."

~~~

The next evening, the two couples and Stacey Bennett sat at the Matthews' dining room table. The trip to Greensboro was both exciting and exhausting. Happily, the Powerball office validated Rachel's ticket as the winning ticket, confirming she won the $750 million dollar prize. They also provided the group with a pile of paperwork to be completed and returned as quickly as possible in order for the prize money to be released. While at the office, they had to decide on taking a lump sum payment or taking payments over time. The four unanimously agreed that they wanted the lump sum in spite of the fact they would have to pay almost half in taxes, leaving them with a balance somewhere in the neighborhood of $400 million. They also had to sign several documents to be sure the Lottery Commission did not release their names or personal information. The stack of papers they brought home were mostly tax forms, as well as copies of the laws regarding lottery winnings.

Rachel was the last to be seated at the table, after serving everyone coffee and tea. Once seated, she took a deep breath and looked around the table. She picked up a fresh legal pad and a pen and handed them to Chris. "Chris, your handwriting is so much neater than mine. Will you take notes, please?"

"Sure," Chris said, taking the pen and pad.

Rachel looked around the table. "Let's get started. Joel, I am still pretty frazzled. Will you do the honors of running this meeting and keeping us on track?"

Joel nodded. "Of course, but before we go any further, Stacey, I know we know you from church, but we don't know you all that well. Can you tell us a little bit about yourself?"

Stacey smiled at the group. "I am happy to. I am 41 years old, and I am a widow with no kids. Bennett is my married name, my maiden name was Stone. My husband was a police officer and was murdered three weeks after our wedding by a killer who was let out of jail on bond the same day he shot my husband. I was so incensed at the legal system, I decided to go to law school. I graduated at the top of my class from Duke University School of Law and spent eight years working for the District Attorney as a prosecutor. A few years ago, I was really burned out from struggling to prosecute criminals, only to see so many of them go free from liberal judges. I quit the DA's office and accepted an offer to work as a corporate attorney for my current firm. My parents both died several years ago, Mom from cancer and my dad a few months later, I think from a broken heart. I have one brother, Will Stone , who is in the Army on active duty. Like I said, no kids, no boyfriend, and no other encumbrances. I don't even have a pet!"

Scott laughed. "Well, now you have us!"

Joel continued, "Thanks, Stacey, we are glad to have you on board with us. Getting back to business, here's the plan as I see it. Let me go through it, and then it will be open to discussion. Stacey, please feel free to add anything you think is important. First, Stacey thinks we need to form a corporation in order to better manage the money and to take advantage of tax breaks and such. So, we need to come up with a name for our corporation so it can be registered. We'll have to make some decisions as to corporate officers and such. I would also like to suggest we put Stacey on our corporate board of directors." He looked around to see everyone nodding agreement.

"Then, the next thing we should do is pay off all of our bills – for all of us. Scott and Chris, we'll need a list of all of your major bills like car payments, mortgage, that kind of thing. We'll do the same for all of the kids. Next, we have some big decisions to make. Rachel, how serious are you about running some kind of Quilters' Retreat? We will probably have somewhere around $350 million to work with after taxes and federal withholding, paying bills, and allotting out expenses for the corporation and Stacey's salary. We can afford more than just a simple retreat if you want."

Rachel thought for a moment, and then answered, "I was thinking, what if we try to find some kind of a recreational farm or ranch? That would serve two purposes – it would be the retreat I've always wanted to have, but it would be a perfect place for us to hunker down in the event of some kind of TEOTWAWKI event. It would give us room for animals and crops that we wouldn't have with just a retreat. Plus, it would give plenty of room for you and Scott to do all of the outdoor things you love – we could even offer that to guests."

Stacey raised her hand. "Can you tell me what you mean by TEOTWAWKI event?"

Joel smiled. "I guess since you are officially our attorney, and you have to keep stuff confidential, it doesn't violate operational security to tell you we all are preppers. TEOTWAWKI stands for "the end of the world as we know it", and we strongly believe our nation, if not the world, is quickly headed towards some kind of apocalyptic event such as an economic crash, war, or other life-changing event. Most everything we do is to be able to not only survive such an event, but for us, our families and select friends to thrive afterwards. We would really appreciate you keeping this confidential. When the event happens, if people know that we are 'prepared', they will try to take from us, and we don't want that to happen."

"Thank you for that explanation. I, too, am a prepper by your definition, because I believe we are about to have a major economic crash. I don't want to spend your time at this meeting discussing my SHTF beliefs." She smiled and winked. "See, I know some acronyms, too! I would like to discuss this further with you all at some later time. Let's get back to the suggestion about a recreational farm or ranch."

"I'm glad to know you understand our perspective, Stacey! I think the ranch is a great idea." Scott said. "We could have a world class restaurant as part of the services we offer. We could maybe have a range and horseback riding, too."

"It would be nice to have a place with enough land that Rachel and I could have a good-sized vegetable garden," Chris added.

"Oh, that would be nice, since we hardly have any space now. We could grow stuff to use in the kitchen, and maybe even have a separate herb garden," Rachel replied. "I'd also like the retreat area to be big enough to have comfortable classrooms, and enough space for the equipment we would need to do both quilting and embroidery, and we'd need to have lots of space for fabric and supply storage."

"These are all great ideas. Are we all agreed that we will look for a recreational farm or ranch?" Joel continued. The others nodded agreement. "Okay. Then at some point soon, we need to identify all of the characteristics we would want to see in a place like that. I mean, how many people, what kind of amenities, all of that." He looked down at his notes. "We've already discussed creating a corporation with the five of us as the principles. I think that's a great idea, since that way funds aren't coming directly from anyone's pocket, and we can just buy what we need. We can pay ourselves a salary for the work we are doing. Next on my list, I recommend we buy an RV so we can travel around to find the perfect property. We can get one big enough so all of us can travel together. And, before you ask," he said, looking at Rachel, "I think we should buy instead of rent, as that will eliminate worries over getting it returned, plus if we buy, we can have it set up exactly the way we want it to be. We can always use it for extra space for someone to stay in or for traveling later on." He looked around and could see everyone nodding their agreement. "Last for tonight, we need to figure out some basic responsibilities for each of us. I would like to recommend that Rachel be the CEO of our corporation, since after all, she bought the winning ticket! I also think that Chris, because she is so organized, ought to be our secretary. Scott, you and I can be the grunts. Once we know what we are looking for, we'll all need to start looking at ads for ranches and farms for sale, and I will volunteer Scott and myself to begin looking for a good RV."

"Let's talk a little bit about this recreational ranch idea," Chris suggested. "I think it would be a great idea to offer things like hunting, shooting, horseback riding, and other outdoor type activities. Of course, it goes almost without saying that we would be able to offer Rachel's dream quilting retreats. You know that quilting is extremely important to both Rachel and me, and the thought that we would be able to spend more time quilting, with all the supplies, equipment, and tools we could possibly imagine sounds like a fairy tale! How much fun would it be to be able to have a whole bunch of women come quilt – and they could bring their husbands who could enjoy the hunting and fishing and other stuff!"

Rachel jumped in. "I love that – we could even have a group of men come quilt and their wives could go hunting and such. You guys would love that, right?"

Joel rolled his eyes and Scott snickered. "Anyway," Rachel continued, "We would have to increase our fabric stock, I'm sure, and it would be a great excuse for us to buy a computerized longarm quilting machine!"

Stacey looked puzzled. "A what kind of machine?"

Rachel explained, "A long arm quilting machine. It is a special sewing machine that runs on a computer and does all the fancy top-stitching to hold the quilt together. In the olden days, women used to do that stitching by hand, but now the computer will do it all. It's a lot easier than trying to do it on a standard sewing machine like Chris and I do now."

"Thanks for the explanation." She smiled and added, "I can see that I'm going to wind up with a new hobby if I hang out with you guys!"

"Hey, now, let's not go crazy here" said Scott, laughing. "But you've given me an idea. I would assume your quilt retreat would help teach people to quilt. Also, we will all be learning how to run a ranch and learning basic skills that could be considered survival skills. What if there was a way we could use our ranch to teach people basic skills that would be needed in an apocalyptic type setting? Of course, we would have to be careful how we worded things for our own OPSEC, but that would really expand our own philosophy of why we prep."

"I think I have the perfect name for this corporation," Stacey interjected. My dad was in the Coast Guard, and their motto is 'Semper Paratus', which means "always ready". I think you should be "Paratus, Inc."

"I love that idea," said Rachel. "I think we should use 'Semper Paratus' as our motto, too. I can see we're going to have to make us a quilt with "Semper Paratus" on it to hang in the entryway of whatever ranch we wind up with!"

"Okay, guys, let's vote. All in favor of Paratus, Inc. as our name?" asked Joel. All hands went up. "All in favor of Rachel as CEO, Chris as secretary, and Stacey as our corporate attorney?" Again, all hands went up.

Joel looked thoughtful for a moment. "How about each of you make a list of the characteristics we want to see in our ranch, and then we'll get together to compile the lists. We'll also need to get input from any of the kids that want to be a part of this adventure. Stacey, how long will it take you to get us put together and legal as a corporation?"

"We should be good to go in about a week to ten days," she answered.

"Great! We ought to spend the next week getting things ready. We have bills to pay off as soon as our funds are released, we've got to talk to our kids about all of this, and we need to start thinking about what we'll do about our houses here. I suggest we invite all of our kids here tomorrow for a barbeque, and then we can let them know about their parents' new status at that time, and also see how they feel about participating. Stacey, we want you to come, too, if you can."

"Joel, that's a great idea," Rachel replied. "I also think we need to come up with an offer for Stacey to think about, giving her a salary to work with us full time so she doesn't have to juggle us and a job. I suspect we are going to keep her pretty busy." Everyone was nodding agreement, so Rachel turned to Stacey. "Will you help us come up with an offer? That is, if you are even willing to do that?"

Stacey, smiling, said, "I'd love to do that. I know we're just getting to know each other, but I feel like you all are family already. I'm looking forward to getting to know the kids better tomorrow. One other thing. Don't forget that you need to come up with an idea of salaries for each of you as well."

Rachel nodded thoughtfully. "Good point. And something else. I do think we need to consider how we are going to use some of our winnings for charity. We need to think if there are special causes we want to support, and how we will do that. I do feel pretty strongly that wherever we settle, we need to support the local community however we can. Let's adjourn for now and think about it. Chris, you need to call Gwen, and I need to call the kids. Let's plan on having them over around four tomorrow, and we will tell them then. Tonight, we'll just tell them we are making a major change in our lives and let them worry about it all night!"

Chris snickered, "Yes, it's good for the kids to worry a little bit, after all the worrying they've caused us over the years!"

Chapter Three

March 21

The next afternoon, Scott and Joel had the barbecue grill heating up and Rachel and Chris were busy in the kitchen getting food ready.

"How did Gwen act when you invited her?" Rachel asked Chris.

"Oh, she wanted to know if we were okay and if we were getting a divorce!" Gwen answered, laughing. "I told her, no, Mom and Dad are staying together, but we are going to make a big change. Then she asked if I was pregnant. Can you imagine? I almost told her maybe, but I didn't want to jinx anything, so I told her, no, but our family might expand a little." She laughed. "Boy, did that confuse her. I hope she's not too mad, but I didn't tell her."

Rachel grinned. "I went through the same thing with my kids. Rebecca is convinced one of us is sick, Noah is worried we are going bankrupt, and Marcie, well, she was the least curious, and just said she trusted me when I said we were all okay. Are we being mean to want to surprise them like this?"

"Nah, it's good for them to be shaken up once in a while." Just then, Stacey walked into the kitchen.

"I made a cake for dessert, I hope that's all right," she said, placing a large cake carrier on the table.

"That's wonderful, thank you," Chris answered. "We were just talking about keeping our kids in suspense. I can't wait to see what their reactions are when we tell them our news."

Stacy grinned. "I'll bet they will be more than a little excited, once they get over being mad for making them stew all night, worried about what's going on."

"I hope they aren't too upset that we didn't tell them outright, but this is way more fun for us," Chris snickered. "I think I hear voices out front. The kids must be here," she said. A few minutes later, Rebecca and Gwen both entered the kitchen, giving Chris and Rachel big hugs.

"Mom, what's going on, are you all okay?" Rebecca asked.

"We're fine," Rachel answered, "We'll let you know what's going on when everyone is here. Meanwhile, you both remember Stacey from church, right?"

"Hi, Stacey," said Gwen. "It's nice to see you again. Do you know what these guys are up to?"

Stacey grinned, "I do, but I've been sworn to secrecy, and not even chocolate or bacon will get the answer out of me!"

More voices filled the living room as Marcie, Billy, and Noah arrived. Rachel shepherded everyone outside, and then called for everyone's attention.

"Alright, everyone, settle down and get comfortable. I know we made you all pretty worried last night, but we had our reasons. Joel, Chris, Scott, Stacey, are we ready to tell them?"

Rebecca spoke up. "Quit playing games and tell us what's happening!"

Rachel laughed. "Okay, here's the story in a nutshell. We won the Powerball, so we are going to buy a huge ranch and open a recreational facility – like an expanded bed and breakfast with horses and cows and a shooting range."

Chris added, "Don't forget the quilting stuff and the chickens!"

There was dead silence for a minute, and then suddenly, everyone was talking at once.

"Is this some kind of a joke? I was really worried about you guys, and now you tell us some kind of goofy story?" Rebecca shouted.

"It's not goofy, and it's not a story," Joel answered. "Look, here is the paperwork to prove it. Stacey is here because she is joining our endeavor as our attorney." Rebecca and Gwen looked at the papers and handed them to Noah.

"You're serious," Rebecca said in a hushed voice.

Joel smiled at his daughter. "Yes, dear, we are serious." Suddenly, all the kids were talking at once, excited, shocked, and so happy for their parents. Joel raised his voice a bit. "Now, if you will all hush for a minute, let us tell you exactly what we are planning and what we need from you. First of all, we want to pay off all of your major bills – student loans, car payments, all of that. We also want to invite all of you to be a part of our new adventure. Rebecca, we hope to have a restaurant in our facility, and so we would hope you'd join us as a chef. Gwen, you've got a lot of knowledge regarding tourism and guest relations. We would hope to have you use your knowledge to help run the recreational side of the ranch. Noah, we'll have a lot of livestock, and could certainly use your veterinary skills there. Billy, you know we'll need accounting help. Marcie, well, you're going to be a bit busy in a few months when the baby gets here, but we want you to be a part of this too." What do you all think?"

The kids all looked at each other, stunned. Rebecca was the first to speak. "I'm all in. Since I work for Uncle Scott right now, I guess he'll accept my resignation when the time is right to go help you."

Scott grinned and nodded. "Yep, we'll both resign together. Guess we need to think about training some replacements!"

Gwen chimed in next. "I need to give a 30-day notice at work, so you'll need to give me plenty of advance notice so I can be ready when you need me. This is so amazing!"

Marcie looked at Billy, then at her father. "Dad, I know Billy hates his job right now because of all the politics at the hospital, so I'm sure he'll want to help." Billy nodded. "I'm not sure what I can do since I really don't have any skills, but I want to help too, at least, as much as I can with a new baby on the way!"

Joel smiled at her, "Honey, you have lots of skills. We'll just have to see which ones fit best with the ranch! Noah, you're awfully quiet, what do you think?"

Noah hesitated a moment before answering. "Work right now is pretty tumultuous. Dr. Lydia is in the middle of filing for a divorce after finding out Dr. Peter, her husband, is having an affair with one of the vet techs, and so she is planning to leave their practice to open her own place once the divorce is final, and she asked me to work for her. Also, you know I am dating Liz Torres, another one of the vet techs, who will also be going to work with Dr Lydia, and I'm not sure I want to move away from her. I think we might be getting kind of serious."

Rachel put her arm around her son. "I have an idea for that – maybe Dr. Lydia and Liz would be interested in working with us? If we have livestock, we're going to need a vet, and maybe we can help her get a practice set up somewhere else. Would you consider that?"

Noah answered his mom with a big grin. "That would be wonderful. I really want to be a part of your adventure and having Liz and Dr. Lydia along would make it perfect." He looked thoughtful for a minute. "If they are interested. When can we talk to them?"

Joel answered, "Soon, son, like in a day or two. Let us get a few things taken care of first. Now, we don't want you all to say anything to anyone about this just yet. The last thing we want is for people to be lined up at the door wanting a handout."

Once everyone had eaten, Joel and Scott went into the garage and brought out a large white board. "While we're enjoying Stacey's chocolate cake, let's all start listing some of the features we want our ranch to have. You call them out and Scott and I will write them on this board. Then we'll try to lump them into categories."

Rachel raised her hand. "I'll go first. I think we want to have housing for at least 20 guests, but not much more than 50 or 60. We'll need to have either a hotel, a resort, or some kind of guesthouse arrangements. I really don't want to have to build something from scratch."

While Joel was busy writing, Chris spoke up. "The ranch needs to have enough structural storage space for everything we need to run the ranch, but also for all of the preps we will be stocking."

"It also needs to have space for a fabulous kitchen and dining area," Rebecca chipped in.

Noah added, "Plenty of pastures and fields for livestock. It would be nice to have a building that could become an actual animal hospital."

Marcie added, "I'd like to see a safe area where kids – our kids and guest kids – could play. Also, we need to have enough space for all of us to live without being right on top of our guests." Marcie paused a minute. "It would also be fun to have a little shop to sell souvenirs and little things the guests might need."

Rachel continued, "It needs to be at least 10 miles from any town and way farther than that from any cities, but easy enough for our guests to get to, meaning it needs to be on a paved and maintained road. I suppose if we had to, we could get a bus and pick guests up from a central point, but I think it would be better for them to be able to come straight to us. We will also need to have a lot of acreage. I am thinking not only about all of the recreational activities we might want to offer like hunting or shooting or horseback riding, but also as our bug-out location, we don't want a lot of near neighbors."

Joel laughed. "I think this will be a bug-in location, honey, since we'll already be there when the you-know-what hits the fan! I agree on the acreage. I'd love to have something big enough that we could have a good-sized range, and still have lots of area for crops, livestock, and lots of natural areas for wild game to live. I would love for the ranch to be self-sufficient – able to produce everything we need without having to rely on commercial suppliers or utilities. So, solar or hydro power, wells, septic systems, all stuff we can control."

Scott nodded. "I agree. I don't have an issue with being hooked up to the grid, but I'd want lots of backups in case the grid failed, and not just the electric grid, but also like you said, wells for water instead of relying on a tank or reservoir somewhere that could become compromised."

Joel laughed. "I wasn't even thinking about the water being poisoned, or something. I was thinking more for convenience, but you do have a point!"

"I think your tin foil hat is too tight," Chris said, laughing at Scott. "I'd like to see us have a lot of storage space so we can be more organized with our prep storage. Maybe even a mini warehouse. I'd also like to see us have a computerized system for tracking everything, both preps and the stuff we'll need for the business." She turned to her daughter. "Gwen, you're being awfully quiet. What would you like to see?"

Gwen smiled. "I agree with everything everyone's said. I'll add that I'd like to have a place that has some character. I don't want us to open another generic hotel-type place with the same kind of structures and interiors that most hotels have. We need something special, something that will stand out in people's memory and in our marketing materials."

Scott smiled. "That's thinking, Gwen! I would also like us to have some sort of small chapel on site. We are, after all, a Christian family, and it would be nice for us to have a place to give thanks for our many blessings. Stacey, any ideas?"

"Thanks, Scott. I'd like to see us find a place that has no liens or encumbrances on it that would make the sale complicated. Ideally, I'd like to see us purchase for cash and take possession right away. I would also like to recommend we avoid states that have really high commercial taxes, complicated zoning, or political climates that don't support the activities this ranch will offer. In other words, not being so politically correct, I think we need to avoid states that are anti-gun or anti-faith."

Laughing, Joel said, "Well said, Stacey. That rules out quite a few places. Anything else?" He looked around the group and saw everyone thinking hard. "We also need to think of what we want to do for charity.

Rachel and I have decided we are going to donate this house to the church. You know that ever since Reverend Arnold retired and moved to the retirement village, Reverend Willis and his family have been living in that same small apartment where Reverend Arnold was living. We think the church could use this house as a proper parsonage since it is only one block from the church, and they could save the money they've been using to pay rent on the apartment. We also plan to set up some kind of endowment for the church, but we need to talk more with Stacey about what that would involve. Are there any other charitable causes we want to support?"

Marcie raised her hand. "I'd like to see us support one of the veteran's support groups, like maybe the one we see on TV where they build homes for wounded soldiers?"

Scott jumped in. "Marcie, you're brilliant. Chris and I were wondering what to do with our house. Maybe we could donate it to an organization like that and it could be used to help a wounded vet."

Chris was nodding her head in agreement. "We should also see what the needs are in our new community, wherever we wind up. We might want to support a Boy Scout troop or the local animal rescue group or something like that."

"I like that idea," Joel answered. "Okay, let's just think on it for a few days. Tomorrow, a couple of us can go talk to Dr. Lydia to see if she wants in on this adventure. We'll put this list together and then maybe Chris and Rachel can start looking at the want ads while Joel and I go buy an RV."

~~~

A few weeks later, the group had purchased an RV and were getting ready to leave the next day to go look at properties. Joel, Rachel, Chris, Scott, and Stacey were sitting at the RV dining table going over everything they needed to have done before leaving in the morning. On this first trip, only Joel, Rachel and Chris were going, as Scott had work commitments he didn't feel good cancelling and Stacey had several court dates scheduled over the coming weeks.

Once everyone had a snack, Joel picked up the pile of papers in front of him. "Let's review our travel itinerary. Chris, you've done an amazing job finding a few really good places for us to check out. Let's go first to the one in the Ozarks. It has just under a thousand acres, with crop land already planted and a large house that might be suitable to housing guests. Asking price is $1.8 million, which seems a little low to me. The real estate lady said that if we don't like that one, she has quite a few more for us to check out. She asked if we could plan on staying there about four or five days to see what she has. If none of those work out, we will head to Kansas next. There's a large property, almost 2500 acres for sale, and it is $1.3 million. There are also a few other undeveloped properties that are zoned for what we want, and one that if we like it, we'll have to get the zoning department to change its current rating. Quite honestly, unless it is spectacular, I'm not sure I want to waste time with zoning issues."

Stacey nodded. "Zone changes can be tricky business, and depending on how the public perceives the change, can bias people against your business. You know, 'there's the company that stole grampa's land to build their ranch' sort of thing. I highly recommend we avoid doing anything that requires a major zone change."

"Thanks, Stacey, I think we all agree with that," Joel continued. "There's a ranch in Montana for sale that is over 3000 acres, but it isn't a recreational ranch, although we could probably still work with that. I would like to suggest we not bother going to Idaho to look at the property there, as according to my topo map, it is far too mountainous to be able to do much farming. Likewise, Chris, you found a great property in Colorado, but it is close to Denver, and I'm not sure we could abide the taxes or the politics there. I would recommend we keep the property in Arizona as a last resort if none of the other places work out. It is in the middle of the state, over 3000 acres and is bordered on three sides by national forests. I do worry, though, about availability of water there. I'm still waiting to hear back from the agent handling that ranch in Santa Fe, New Mexico. It sounds interesting at over 2,000 acres, but like Arizona, I am concerned about water. Plus, it is a little close to Santa Fe. I'm not sure if that will be a problem. If none of those properties work out, we will just have to continue to look. Meanwhile, though, we get to have a nice trip across country! Does everyone agree?"

Scott grinned. "It sounds like it will be a lot of work, but also a lot of fun. I wish I could be there with you all, but Rebecca and I are still training our replacements and I don't feel right backing out on that. If you find something really great, though, I will drop everything and fly to wherever you are to see it."

"I wish you were going, too," Joel added, "but we can get you on the phone any time and I know Chris will send you lots of pictures. I don't think we are just going to make an offer on the spot unless something is so incredibly perfect that our guts tell us not to leave without an offer." Joel handed a packet of papers to Scott. "Here's our itinerary, contact information for all of the real estate agents, maps, and a prospectus of each property. We will call you every day to go over what we've seen and get your opinion. Stacey, we won't even begin to consider an offer without talking to you first."

"I wish I could go as well, but I still have those two cases I need to finish before I officially leave the firm. Like Scott, though, if you find something perfect, call me and I will be there." The morning after she accepted the offered salary, she quit her job with the corporate law firm and began working full time for Paratus. Her boss, though, begged her to stay long enough to resolve two complicated cases she had been handling. Her fellow Paratus board members understood her need to complete her obligations to her clients and supported her decision. "I expect one case will be finished by the end of this week. It will probably take another week or two to finish the other one, and after that, I will be completely available to you as you need me," Stacey answered.

Chapter Four

Joel stretched as he stepped out of the RV into the early morning sunlight. Sitting on one of the lawn chairs they set up the night before, he thought back on the last two months as he sipped his coffee. Life had been a whirlwind of activity after their win was confirmed. Stacey helped the couples complete all of the forms for the Lottery Commission, and then helped them create their corporation. They were now Paratus, Incorporated, with Rachel as the Chief Executive Officer. Joel thought about how invaluable Stacey was helping them maneuver the intricacies of the fledgling corporation, including developing a charter, opening corporate bank accounts, establishing a budget, and purchasing the RV as corporate property. She was certainly earning not only the salary they agreed to pay her, but her place at the ranch if anything happened.

Chris and Rachel spent weeks looking through advertisements, calling real estate agents to set up viewings, and trying to identify possible properties to purchase. They decided to search across the middle of the country, starting in Missouri. Although they knew that every state probably had great properties, they wanted to avoid highly built-up states with large populations, as well as parts of states near the southern border. Extreme northern states were also ruled out due to the long, cold winters.

Paying off all of their combined bills was an amazing experience for everyone. As soon as the last bill was paid, Rachel and Chris both quit their jobs. Joel put his electrical company on the market and sold it very quickly to one of his competitors. Gwen, Rebecca, Billy, and Noah, although now debt-free, decided they would continue with their jobs until they were needed to start setting up the ranch. Joel and Rachel finished the paperwork deeding their house to the church. All of their belongings were placed in storage and Joel and Rachel were living in the RV for now. Scott and Chris would sign the final papers donating their house to the Tunnels to Towers Foundation as soon as Scott quit his job, and they were in the midst of packing up and storing their belongings, too. Scott was in the final stages of training his replacement at the restaurant, and soon he and Chris would also be temporarily living in the RV.

After meeting with the kids, Joel and Scott began looking for an RV that would hold all four of them plus Stacey in comfort as they traveled around the country searching for the perfect ranch. They found an amazing 45-foot Class A diesel pusher that easily slept 7, had 2 bathrooms, a 55" flat screen TV, and even a fireplace. Joel recalled with a laugh the expression on the salesman's face when he and Scott told him they would take the model they liked and pulled out a checkbook. The salesman and his manager were even more in shock as Joel calmly wrote out a check for the several hundred-thousand-dollar purchase price, refusing offers of financing.

As Joel sat enjoying his coffee and smiling at the memory of the salesman, Rachel stepped out of the RV. "What are you smiling about, honey?"

"I was just thinking about when Scott and I bought the RV, and how the salesman nearly had a heart attack. He and his manager were falling all over themselves to make sure they got all the extras we wanted like the bigger generator, the hitch in the back to tow the car, and the extra storage compartments. Then, they were confused when we said we wanted just a plain brown exterior, not the fancy chrome-bedazzled model. I wasn't about to explain to them that we wanted it as low key on the outside as possible, so we just let them think we were eccentric."

"Well, you are eccentric, dear! I'm just glad you didn't get it in camouflage – don't deny you thought about it."

"You know me well, Rachel. We probably would have, too, except it would have taken too long and we were anxious to get it as quickly as we could. Are you set for a new day of ranch-hunting? And where's Chris?"

"Chris is taking a shower, and yes, I'm ready. I am really disappointed that we didn't find anything in Missouri this past week. You would think of the sixteen properties we examined, at least one would have been a contender and would have had at least half of the things on our list. I thought Missouri was supposed to be prepper heaven, but if it is, we sure didn't find anything remotely heavenly."

"Now, Rach, what about that last one we looked at. Granted it was a little smaller than we wanted, and they wanted a lot more than we all thought it was worth, but the views from that one hill were pretty awesome."

"The views were great, but by next year that view would be of the new highway the state is planning to build. A six-lane highway that close rules it out for me."

Joel finished his coffee and stood up. "Well, at least we made it to Kansas without any problems. Maybe one of the ranches we are supposed to check out this week will be the one. Let's get breakfast in town before our realtor's appointment."

"Sounds good. Let Chris know. I'm going to sit out here and enjoy the sunshine and quiet for a few minutes. Do you have our list of must-haves?"

"It's inside. I'll get it for you."

Rachel looked through the list the group put together of all the items the ranch had to have to be a contender. "Nothing on this list is too extravagant or unrealistic," she thought. The two couples, their kids, and Stacey all helped create the list of must-haves, must-not-haves, and nice-to-haves. They hoped having a checklist would keep them from making a hasty purchase or not getting what they really wanted. Today, the Kansas realtor was going to show them three different properties. Based on the descriptions, one sounded really good, while the other two sounded a little iffy.

After a nice breakfast at a diner up the street from where the RV was parked, the three took off to meet the real estate agent at the first property. Although the road was a little rough and there were no particularly impressive views, it was a pleasant drive. Arriving at the property, though, the three were disappointed. The house was not nearly big enough to serve as a lodge, there were only a couple of outbuildings, most of them in poor repair, and most of the land they could see was open with very few trees. Still, they took a quick tour of the property. The only positive they saw on this site was a decent-sized creek with a swimming hole. The realtor explained this was the best of the three properties she was going to show them, and the group decided not to waste their time and the realtor's looking at the other two sites. They headed back to the campsite and left for Montana in the morning.

Although the ranch in Montana was impressive and would have been an excellent choice for a recreational ranch, there were several factors that all contributed towards deciding against it. First, the rancher who owned the property had already sold several large parcels of land adjoining the ranch. These properties were in the process of being zoned residential, and there were plans for a developer to build a housing development on one of them. The second factor was that the owner already had several offers for the ranch, and two of them were above the asking price, meaning the Paratus group would have to increase their offer by several hundred thousand dollars to stand a chance. The final negative factor was that the animals and equipment were not included in the sale price, and the separate asking price for them was just too much to consider. They thanked the owner and realtor for showing them the property and left immediately for Arizona.

The property in Arizona was amazing, but there were still problems. The biggest problem was water. Although they had a few wells, it is just so dry there that Joel felt they wouldn't be able to have what they needed for the ranch and for the guests. In addition, the property was close to a major north-south interstate. Joel had Scott on speakerphone to let him know of yet another disappointing site. "I know we want to be close to roads so our guests can get there, but that was just too close, and if something happened, it would be right on the way for the millions of people leaving Phoenix for cooler climates. I know we planned on going to Santa Fe, New Mexico, next, but I had a call from the real estate agent up there and he said the property we really wanted to look at just sold. They still have a couple of others, but they all sound like big compromises for stuff on our list."

Suddenly, Rachel sat up alertly and interrupted Joel. "Hey, guys, listen to this. I've been looking at listings online, and I just found a listing in Texas for a place that actually was a recreational ranch. It just came on the market today. The owner died and his family has no interest in running the place, so they are selling. The listing says it is an established recreational ranch in West Texas… listen to this" she said, as she began reading from her computer screen, " 'a 4,977-acre recreational ranch for sale in southwestern Texas, with reduced prices because the lodge and cabins need work. Sale price is 7.2 million. Ranch offers hunting, fishing, horseback riding, hiking, swimming, a shooting range, and other outdoor activities.

The lodge is over 7000 square feet with owners' living quarters on the main floor and 12 guest suites on the second floor. The ground floor also has a huge living room with a massive fireplace, a library, a commercial kitchen, a large dining room, a game room, a meeting room, and bathrooms. Full finished basement for storage with a secure armory. Outdoor recreation area includes swimming pool with a hot tub, picnic area with BBQ pits, kid's playground, and game area with horseshoes, a croquet course, and a baseball field.

"The property also has 18 guest cabins ranging from one to four bedrooms. There is a meat processing building with large walk-in cooler, a bunkhouse for ranch hands, and six barns (two for equipment/storage, one for horses, one for cattle, one for pigs, and one for assorted other livestock). 2500 acres of the property are fertile land, originally planted in hay, oats, corn, and alfalfa. The perimeter of entire ranch has an eight-foot game fence. The property has numerous improved gravel/dirt roads, an outdoor shooting range, 32 wells (mostly for irrigation, but the lodge has two large wells, each barn has well, and nine wells provide water for cabins and bunkhouse). Within walking distance of lodge and cabins is a 76-acre lake for fishing, small boating, and swimming. The lake has been stocked in the past. The terrain is conducive to hunting, hiking, and horseback riding. Rolling hills cover the northern end of the property, with the rest of the property being relatively flat. Although there are many acres cleared for growing crops, there are also large areas of forests, with mesquite, oak, and other hardwoods. The whole property is crossed with small creeks and springs. Wildlife includes deer, quail, turkey, feral hog, and dove. The property is being sold as is, and all items and animals on the property are included in the purchase price.'" Rachel paused to catch her breath. " I think we need to go check this place out. Let's call the listing agent and see if we can set up an appointment in the next few days. Let's see, her name is Janet Armstrong."

Scott chuckled. "See, maybe all of these disappointing sites were to get us ready for finding the perfect one."

"Well, this one sure sounds a lot more promising than the other ones we've looked at, but I'm not getting my hopes up until we actually see the place," Joel said.

"Well, aren't you the pragmatist," Rachel said. "I think this place sounds exactly what we're looking for. I'm going to be really disappointed if it isn't the one."

"I agree," Chris chimed in. "We've seen plenty of what we don't want. This place sounds wonderful."

"Well, girls, if it turns out to be not so great, don't be all moping and sulking and all. Remember we warned you," laughed Joel. Rachel rolled her eyes.

"Chris and I don't sulk. We just.... make sure the entire world knows we are displeased. So...don't disappoint us and you won't feel our displeasure."

Scott laughed over the phone. "Joel, you'd better keep those two princesses happy, or it sounds like ranch or no ranch, we'll both be sleeping in the RV!" Joel just shook his head as the princesses laughed.

Chapter Five

June 12

They drove all night following the directions the realtor provided. Around mid-morning, they arrived at the gate to the ranch. They parked, and got out, standing near the gate. Their first impression of the property was spectacular. On either side of the gate, stone pillars towered over eight feet high. The gate itself was decorative iron with swirls and a big letter S on each gate. Branching off the pillars on either side was an eight-foot stone fence topped with decorative spikes, extending as far as they could see. Beyond the gate, they saw a paved road bordered with pecan and oak trees winding into the property.

Joel pointed to the gate. "Look closer at that gate, guys. The way it swirls looks decorative, but nobody is getting through the gate or climbing it easily."

"What about the big letter S on each side?" said Chris.

Rachel chuckled. "Well, we'll just have to call it Serendipity Ranch if it works out- then we won't have to buy a new gate!"

After a few minutes, a dark green Land Rover pulled up, and a tall blonde woman exited the car. Instead of being dressed up as most of the real estate agents they had met were, she was wearing jeans, a denim shirt, and cowboy boots.

"Howdy, folks! I'm Janet. Welcome to Texas!" She smiled and held out her hand. After introductions, Janet suggested they take a few minutes before the tour for her to explain the situation with the ranch.

"Zach Spencer owned the ranch, which had already been in his family for three generations. Originally, it was a working ranch, but Mr. Spencer decided to convert to a recreational ranch. He built the cabins, pool, range, and other amenities to entertain guests. He was a pretty smart guy, though, and decided to keep the business side of the ranch flourishing just in case the recreational side didn't work out. He had a healthy herd of cattle, horses, sheep, goats, pigs, and poultry, and kept the lake stocked well. Of course, the guests did a lot of fishing, too, but he saw the wisdom in keeping all of the ranch's animals. He also maintained the crops- mostly wheat, oats, hay, and corn. I think he also had some cotton fields. I guess he used the crops, not only to feed his livestock, but also for sale to help keep the ranch going. His wife had a huge vegetable garden, too. Three years ago, Mrs. Spencer was killed when she was thrown from a horse. After that, Mr. Spencer lost his joy in running the ranch. He cancelled all of the guests, and essentially withdrew into himself. His ranch foreman continued to keep the ranch running, but Mr. Spencer didn't do anything but sign the checks. The Spencers had two daughters who both married and left home years ago, and neither daughter wanted to come to the ranch to take care of Mr. Spencer. They both offered him a place in their homes, but he refused. About six months ago, the foreman came up to the house one day and found Mr. Spencer unconscious on the living room floor. He had a massive stroke and died the next day. After the funeral, the two daughters went through the house and property and took anything they wanted to keep. They ordered the sale of everything else.

"Because there had not been any guests for almost three years, the guest cabins need work. The foreman focused on keeping the livestock and crops going but didn't have time to see to the lodge house or the cabins. I went through the house and a couple of the cabins yesterday when we accepted the contract on this property, and I have to warn you, it's pretty dusty and messy. Most of Mr. and Mrs. Spencer's personal items are still in the house."

Joel laughed. "A little dust won't throw us off. We are really anxious to see the property."

"In that case, follow me," Janet answered. "We'll drive up to the lodge and park there. After we tour the area around the lodge, we can use a couple of the four wheelers up there to ride around the property." Janet unlocked and opened the gates, and then hopped into her Land Rover. Joel, Rachel, and Chris followed her up the road about a third of a mile, finally coming around a bend to see the lodge house.

After parking the RV, the three stepped out to look at the lodge in wonder.

"It's beautiful," Rachel whispered.

In front of them was a huge two-story lodge. A large porch covered the front of the building, and the lower story was faced in stone. The second floor was faced with logs, with a huge Victorian stained-glass window over the main entrance. A green metal roof crowned the building, with several chimneys perched above the roof. The front door was painted red, with an inset stained-glass window and stained-glass lites on either side.

"The lodge was built in 1872 by Jeremiah Spencer, Zach Spencer's great grandfather. The window over the door is original to the house, although Mr. Spencer had it restored about 10 years ago. Likewise, the stained-glass in the front door is also original."

The four stepped up onto the porch and noted ceiling fans spaced along the length of the porch, with rocking chairs placed invitingly in groups. Upon entering the building, they found themselves in a large foyer. To the right was a large registration area with an office behind it. To the left, they saw the glass front of a small gift shop. Just past the gift shop was a hallway that Janet explained went to the housekeeping and storage areas. In front of them was a huge log arch. The arch led into a large open area two stories tall. Directly in front of them was a massive fireplace, flanked on either side by large windows and doors to the back porch. On the right, a large curving staircase led to the second floor, which surrounded the open area with a balcony. Below the stairwell was a large dining area with numerous tables and chairs. At the far end was the kitchen. To the left, a second curving staircase led to the balcony on that end of the house. Below the stairs, they could see a number of rooms.

"Gwen wanted a place with character – I'd say she got her wish with this place," Chris whispered to Rachel.

"Let's start out to the right," Janet said. "The way this dining room is set up right now will seat approximately 60 people at a time, although you could probably add a couple more tables and rearrange things some to fit more people. I believe it was licensed for 90 occupants at a time." They walked past the tables and into the kitchen.

"This kitchen hasn't been used in three years, but you can see Mr. Spencer did not spare any expenses with furnishing the kitchen. I understand one of you is a chef?" Janet asked.

"Yes, my husband is," Chris answered. She looked closely at the various appliances, making notes on a small pad. "My husband would be quite impressed with the way Mr. Spencer outfitted this kitchen, and it is set up very efficiently. Of course, it will take a while to get it clean and functional again."

Beyond the kitchen were several storage areas, a large walk-in cooler, and a huge walk-in freezer. Although the cooler was almost empty, the freezer still had many items on the shelves. After walking through the storage areas, they came to a door leading to the basement. The stairs were wide and well-lit. At the bottom of the stairs, they found a large warehouse full of sturdy shelving. Again, there were many boxes and cartons still on the shelves.

"You said all of the items in the buildings also come with the property?" Rachel asked.

Janet smiled. "Yes, everything on this property including all of the stock on the shelves, furniture, animals, vehicles, and anything else I've missed all come with the property."

Rachel looked at Joel and Chris and smiled. "That's great. Looks like he left a lot of paper products and staples on these shelves."

Janet laughed. "You haven't seen anything yet! Come with me."

She led them past the warehouse to a smaller hallway. A door on one side led to the laundry area. Several industrial sized washers and dryers were surrounded by linen carts and laundry baskets. Shelves along one wall held buckets of commercial laundry products. A door on the far side of the room led to a small room for clean linen storage. Again, sturdy shelves were full of all types of sheets, blankets, towels, and other linens.

Going back into the hallway, they saw a locked door on the other side of the hallway. Janet unlocked the door and turned on the light. Locked cages along three walls held an assortment of firearms, including rifles, shotguns, and handguns. A huge safe on the fourth wall held ammunition, and a reloading station was set up in the corner.

Joel could barely contain himself. "Geeze, this guy has almost as many guns as we do!" he said, laughing. "I can't believe the daughters didn't want any of these."

"The daughters each took one of the pearl-handled revolvers that belonged to Zach's grandfather. One lives in New York and the other lives in California, so neither one really was interested in anything except the historical and sentimental value of those revolvers. Come on, there's still so much more to see!"

Janet locked the armory and showed them the rest of the basement. In addition to a housekeeping area storing cleaning supplies, there was a large storage room with extra furniture and totes with seasonal supplies and outdoor equipment.

Going back up to the main floor, Janet showed them the rooms that were tucked under the balcony for the second floor. The first room was a game room with a large pool table, darts, and several large card tables. A bar was set up at one end of the room, dusty bottles of liquor still sitting on the shelves.

The next rooms were commercial men and women's restrooms. Past those was a small room with arcade games.

"I'm sure these games probably still have the coins in them. They had this area for the kids who came with their parents and needed entertainment. I understand it was a big hit with the teen crowd!" She guided them into the next large room. "This was an arts and crafts area to also entertain kids and probably mothers who weren't as interested in other ranch activities."

Rachel looked at Chris and smiled. "This would make a great quilting work area, wouldn't it?"

Chris nodded. "Oh yeah, with plenty of room lots of fabric and for a bunch of machines and we could probably get a long-arm in here too!"

"We could easily host quilting retreats here – with lots for the husbands to do while the wives are sewing."

Janet grinned at the two. "I knew we would get along! I quilt, too, and we could use a quilt retreat location in this area. But before you get too excited about this room, let me show you the conference room on the other side of the living area – it's way bigger than this and has more windows."

They all walked over to the conference room. "Janet, you are so right," Rachel exclaimed. "This would be a much better quilting area. Look, we could put in cabinets for supplies and fabric shelves over there, and a long arm would be great over by those windows. I'll bet we could fit 20 sewing stations in here, and that long wall would be great for setting up our design walls. We can make the other room a library area or something."

"Well, right next door is a small library. You could probably get more books and move it to the craft room, and yes, you could easily fit a longarm in that far corner by the windows." Janet explained.

Joel started laughing. "Okay, girls, we can plan the quilting retreats later. Let's finish up our tour now."

The library next door was a rather small room, paneled in dark wood panel with several very comfortable looking chairs, each with a good reading light, spread out around the room. Chris looked around, and observed, "You know, this room would make a nice chapel, don't you think?"

They finished up checking out the rest of the areas on the first floor, and then went upstairs to examine the twelve guest suites on the second floor. They were happy to see a small elevator tucked into one corner. Janet explained it was used for housekeeping staff to bring up cleaning supplies and take laundry to the basement and was also handy for bringing up guests' luggage. There was an open space without any rooms in front of the stained-glass window. Several comfortable chairs and tables offered a quiet sitting area overlooking the balcony to the living area below. The group then went back to the first floor.

"I thought there were living quarters for the owners here somewhere. Did we miss it?" Joel asked.

Janet blushed, and said, "I can't believe I forgot to show it to you. It's back here behind the reception area."

They went into the office behind the registration desk, and through another door which opened into a modest living room. A small kitchen was off to one side, and three doors led to a small guest bedroom, a guest bathroom, and the master suite. The master included a large walk-in closet, a nicely appointed although somewhat dirty master bath, and a small patio area. The patio area was surrounded by a stockade fence and included a hot tub.

After they finished touring the lodge, they went out the back doors to check out the cabins. Eighteen cabins circled a fenced swimming pool, several horseshoe pits, and a large barbecue area with picnic tables. Off to one side was a small, fenced playground. Beyond the playground they could see the ball field surrounded on two sides by bleachers. They found the cabins were in fair shape, with three having problems with broken water pipes and two with cracked windows.

Next, they toured the barns. Joel, Rachel, and Chris were pleasantly surprised to find all of the barns were clean and well-organized. The animals they could see all looked healthy and well cared for. After the barns, they toured the bunkhouse. Although it was neat, it was dusty and needed a thorough cleaning and airing out. In the field behind the bunkhouse, they saw a generous-sized greenhouse. The greenhouse was dark, though, and didn't look like anything was growing in it. As they were approaching the shed with the four wheelers, they saw someone approaching on a horse.

Janet waved to the approaching figure, and turned to the group, telling them, "That's Jeff Miller. He's been the foreman here for the last 22 years. The daughters talked him into staying on until they can sell the ranch. He says he'll retire when that happens."

Jeff dismounted from his horse and walked over to the group.

"Howdy, folks, Janet. I'm Jeff Miller, ranch foreman. You hoping to buy this ranch?"

"Hi, Jeff. I'm Joel Matthews, my wife Rachel Matthews, and our friend, Chris Wilson. We are sure thinking about buying this ranch!"

"Well, you picked the best agent to help you. Janet is a good little gal and will take good care of you. Y'all need anything? If not, I'm headed over to do some work with the horses."

"Thanks, Jeff. If these folks have questions, can we come find you later?" Janet asked.

"Of course, I'm happy to help." Jeff smiled and waved as he walked his horse towards the barn.

"Let's grab a couple of four-wheelers and go check out the grounds," Janet said, as she opened the shed.

"I think Chris and I will stay behind so we can talk and give Scott a call. You two go on." Rachel said, as she pulled her cell phone from her pocket. She and Chris headed over to the picnic tables as Joel and Janet headed out.

"What do you think, Chris?"

"I think we need to call Scott and find the checkbook! This place has everything we were looking for, and more! I think it's perfect." Chris grabbed Rachel's cell phone. "You're taking too long to call Scott. Let me!" Rachel laughed as Chris dialed the phone. Scott answered on the first ring and Chris put him on speaker.

"Well, what do you think? Is it nice? Do you like it?" Scott said.

"Gee, Scott, you're not anxious or anything, are you? It is absolutely amazing, and you are going to love it. Joel is off riding around the property, but Janet and I have seen what we need to see, and it is exactly what we are looking for."

"Tell me about the kitchen – will I like it? Does it need a lot of work?"

Rachel laughed. "Scott, honey, you will love it! It needs a good cleaning, and we need to check that all of the appliances work, but it is amazing. It has a lot of space, plenty of room for prep areas and for the fancy stuff you do. There's lots of storage, and big walk-ins and freezer space. The pots and pans and stuff that we saw out all look like they are in good condition. And, they even have a freeze dryer in the kitchen! You know we've wanted one of those for a long time!"

"Awesome. I wish I was there. Are we going to make an offer?"

Chris answered. "I hope so. We'll see when Joel gets back."

Rachel jumped in. "I still have some questions about utilities, and I want to talk to the foreman, too, but I am all for making an offer. I expect it will be a while before Joel gets back, so we are going to go find the foreman and ask him a few questions while we're waiting."

"Okay, girls, call me back as soon as you know something. I'll keep my fingers crossed that it works out. I've gotta go. Bye girls, love you, Chris."

"Love you too dear. Talk to you soon." Chris smiled as she disconnected the call. "Let's go find the foreman!"

Rachel and Chris quickly walked over to the horse barn and found Jeff cleaning a saddle.

"Hi, ladies. How can I help you?"

"We have a couple of questions that we hoped you could answer for us. First, I noticed the kitchen looks like it has gas stoves, but I didn't see any tanks or anything." Rachel said.

"We have two ten-thousand-gallon underground propane tanks. Both of them were filled right before Mr. Spencer passed away. I doubt all that much has been used since then."

Chris nodded and made a note on her pad. "Does the ranch have any back-up power, or is it all grid-tied electric?"

"The ranch is grid-tied, but we also have a solar farm and several wind turbines. That concrete block building just past the last barn houses the batteries and inverters and stuff. If the grid power goes out, we automatically switch to battery power. We've lost power out here a bunch of times, and we've never had any issues with back-up power."

Rachel looked puzzled. "Where are the solar panels? I don't see any on the roof?"

Jeff smiled. "No, there aren't any on the roof. We have a solar farm. Just past the cabins, there's a large field with solar panels mounted on racks. They move around to get the best exposure to the sun."

"Thanks for explaining that to me!" Rachel shook her head. "I don't think I ever heard of a solar farm before. What about sewer? Is the ranch tied to the city sewer system?"

Jeff laughed. "No, the ranch is all septic. Why do you think the ball field is so green?"

Chris looked surprised. "Wow, that must be a lot of septic. Do you ever have problems with it?"

"About seven years or so ago, we had a back-up. It seems the housekeepers at the time were flushing cleaning cloths and vinyl gloves. It took a bit of work to fix it, and they told us then that we should be sure to properly maintain it. Ever since then, we put a special product down several of the commodes every month, and we haven't had a problem since. You still need to be careful what gets flushed, but as long as you keep diapers, towels, and gloves out, you should be fine."

Chris jotted a note on her pad. "I didn't think about it, but I guess we'll need diaper pails for guests with babies."

"Good thinking," Rachel murmured. Turning back to Jeff, Rachel asked, "I noticed the greenhouse out there. Is there anything growing in it?"

"No, the greenhouse hasn't been used since Mrs. Spencer passed. She used to grow exotic flowers out there. After she was gone, Mr. Spencer just shut it up. It needs to be cleaned up a lot and fresh dirt and all brought in before it can be used. Probably still full of dead flowers, for all I know."

Rachel looked sad, so Chris asked, "Next question is how many livestock does the ranch have?"

"Oh, that's a good one. We have a large herd of cattle, about 300 head, give or take a few. There are 28 horses, not counting this one – he's my own horse, not the ranch's. There are somewhere around 200 chickens, about 30 turkeys, and lots of ducks on the lake. We have 22 goats, 14 sheep and 44 pigs. We also have four donkeys and two mules. I can't tell you how many barn cats we have because that number changes all the time. We have four dogs that I use to herd the livestock. You'll probably want to get more because the four we have are getting

40

pretty old. To feed all of these animals, we have hay, oats, and corn growing on about 50 acres. I also have two acres of wheat going. We have a lot more crop land, but most of it is planted in clover, buckwheat, millet, and vetch right now to keep the land viable for crops when we're ready."

Janet and Chris both looked surprised. Chris smiled at Jeff, and stated, "You are so knowledgeable about this ranch!"

Laughing, Jeff replied, "I ought to be – I've been the foreman here for over 22 years and worked as a ranch hand here for seven years before that. I know this place like the back of my hand."

"Jeff, I was wondering…" Rachel started. "If we were to buy this place, would you consider staying on as foreman? I mean, Janet told us you wanted to retire once the ranch is sold, but I am thinking that maybe we could work something out?"

Jeff looked thoughtful. "I would consider it if everything works out. At least, until you could bring in new folks. I could probably help train them, too, if necessary. Let's wait until we know you are buying the ranch, and then we can all sit down and negotiate, okay?"

Rachel gave a sigh of relief. "Thank you. I appreciate all of the information you've given us. One more question. With all the work you do here, do you live on the ranch?"

"Yes, I have a small apartment in the bunkhouse. It's not ideal, but since I am a widower and it's just me, it will do."

"I'm glad you're close. Thank you again for your help. I'm sure we'll be talking soon. Meanwhile, Chris and I are going to get out of your way and head over to check out the area where Mrs. Spencer had her garden."

"You won't find anything there except dirt and weeds, I suspect. Every year after she passed, we would till it and get it ready because Mr. Spencer said he was going to plant it, but he never did. We didn't till it this year, so it probably has a lot of weeds growing."

"Oh, well, we want to check it out anyway. Thanks for your help, Jeff," said Chris, as she and Rachel left the barn.

It was a short walk to the far side of the lodge where they saw the gate to the garden. As Jeff guessed, the area was full of weeds. "This is huge! It must be at least a half-acre," said Chris.

Rachel smiled. "Janet said it was ¾ acre. Think of all of the veggies and fruits we can grow here, and it's already fenced. We can put vines

41

on the fence... this is so perfect. I hope Joel doesn't see anything that spoils this."

Chris nodded agreement. "I think I hear the four-wheelers coming back. Let's go see what he found out."

A few minutes later, Janet and Joel rolled up. Joel got off his four-wheeler and came over to the two waiting women, shaking his head. "Oh, my gosh, you wouldn't believe how beautiful it is back there. We saw a lot of game running around- deer, elk, rabbits, all kinds of stuff. We saw some of the fields, the lake, and the solar set-up. The scenery is amazing. There are a lot of trails and many of the trails have gravel on them to make it easier to ride. We need to talk." He turned to Janet. "I know it is starting to get late, but can you give us a few minutes to talk? We'll get back to you in a few minutes."

"Of course," said Janet, smiling. "I'm going over to visit Jeff in the barn. Did I mention he is my uncle?"

Rachel and Chis laughed. "No, but that explains the glowing reference he gave you! We'll talk to you in a few minutes."

As Janet walked away, Joel, Rachel and Chris sat at one of the picnic tables. Chris pulled out her phone and called Scott while Rachel called Stacey, putting both on speaker. "Hi, Scott, Stacey, this is Joel. This place is exactly what we are looking for. I can see it will take some work to get us going. There are a few places the fence needs reinforcing. A few of the cabins need repair, and everything needs a heavy cleaning. We'll need to fix the parking lots, and the outdoor range needs a little work, too. We'll also need to find out about the livestock, how much there is and all..."

"We already know about the livestock and it is about what we were hoping to get," interrupted Rachel. "Jeff gave us numbers, and we can email them."

"That's great," Joel continued. "The wells all are functioning, and Janet can provide inspection paperwork for all of them. I know there are buried propane tanks, but I'm not sure how big."

"Two ten-thousand-gallon tanks," interrupted Chris.

"Okay, you ladies have all the answers. The asking price is 7.2 million. I propose we offer 6.8 million cash. I think that is a very fair price for everything we've seen today. What do you all think?"

Chris and Rachel were both nodding their agreement.

"I'm not there to see it, but Chris texted me a few pictures during the day, and it looks terrific. I trust all of you, and so my vote is yes," Scott said.

"As long as there are no liens or encumbrances on the property, I think it sounds perfect," Stacey added.

"I'll talk to Janet and make sure the property is free and clear," Rachel answered.

Joel looked at Rachel and Chris.

"This place is perfect, and we are the first to see it. Let's get an offer in so we can beat the rush.

Hopefully, a cash offer will entice the daughters into saying yes!" Rachel said.

"Yeah, what she said!" Chris answered laughing.

"Okay, let's go find Janet and make an offer!" said Joel.

~~~

A few minutes later, Joel, Chris, Rachel, and Janet were sitting at the dining table in the RV. Scott and Stacey were still on speaker on the cell phones. Joel began, "Janet, we want to thank you for your time today showing us this wonderful property. I speak for the five of us when I say this property is everything we hoped for and more. We would like to make an offer. Seven point two million would be a fair price if everything was in perfect working order. However, there is a considerable amount of work to be done, especially the cabins, range, and fence. We've discussed it and would like to make a cash offer of six point eight million dollars for the property and contents as is. Our only request is that we would like to take possession of the property as soon as possible if the owners accept our offer. Are you good with this?"

Janet beamed. "I am so glad. I had a feeling you were the right people for this place after I talked to Rachel on the phone. I will give the daughters' attorney a call right now and see what they say."

Janet stepped outside the RV, and they could hear her muted conversation with the attorney. They watched as she hung up and went to her car and pulled out a briefcase. A few minutes later, her cell phone rang, and she began speaking again. Finally, after what seemed like hours, but in fact was only seventeen minutes, she came back into the RV.

Rachel was so nervous, she almost burst into tears when she saw Janet was not smiling. Janet took a deep breath, then broke out into a huge grin. "They accept your offer!"

Everyone began cheering. Joel turned to the two cell phones and said, "Scott, Stacey, can you get yourself here tomorrow? I suspect we have a lot of paperwork to do, and we will need you here to do it!"

Grinning, Scott replied they would get a flight out tonight and be there by morning. Stacey agreed, telling Scott she would call him as soon as they hung up. After saying goodbye and hanging up both phones, Joel looked at Janet and asked, "Can we do the paperwork in the morning? Is there anything we need to do tonight? Do you want us to write you a check now?"

"Let's just do the offer paperwork tonight, and you can write me a check for the whole amount or just a down payment and give me the rest tomorrow."

"We'll just write the full check tonight. Rachel, you're the CEO, so will you do the honors?"

Rachel pulled out the checkbook and cautiously wrote the check. "I've never written a check for this much money! I can't believe this."

It only took ten minutes to complete the initial paperwork for the offer and for the group to get a receipt for their check. Chris' phone rang when they were just about done.

"Stacey will be with me tonight on the 11:45 flight. We'll be there early morning tomorrow!" Scott said, excitement in his voice.

After ending the call with Scott, Joel turned to the group. "I think we need to celebrate! Is there a steak house in town, Janet? We'd like you and your husband to join us for dinner," he exclaimed.

"That sounds wonderful. Let me give you directions and we will meet you there." After writing some short directions, Janet excused herself and left.

After quick showers in the RV, Joel, Rachel, and Chris were sitting in the RV living room parked in the restaurant lot waiting for Janet and her husband.

Rachel looked at Joel and Chris, and said, "I think one of the first things we need to do is decide on a plan for how we are going to proceed from here. We'll need to decide how the work is going to be divided up among ourselves and create a to-do list. Chris, since you are our corporation secretary, will you please take some notes?"

Chris smiled and pulled out her pad and pencil.

"First, we need a list of things to do back home. Our stuff is all packed up, but we'll need to ship it all out here. Then, Stacey needs to finish the details on transferring the titles on the two houses. We also need to let the kids know and see how soon they will be available to come out here. I think we ought to divvy up the responsibilities here so we can stay organized. Otherwise, we'll be stepping all over each other and won't get much done." Joel and Chris nodded agreement.

"Joel, will you oversee the animals, including getting vet services, the outbuildings, maintenance, and any construction?"

Joel nodded. "That's all right up my alley. I'll get busy on a to-do list for those areas."

Rachel smiled. "Thanks. Chris, how do you think Scott will feel about handling setting up food services, both for the restaurant and for staff on the ranch? He'll need to get the kitchen up to par, hire and train staff, and create menus and shopping lists."

"I think that will suit Scott perfectly. He can get Rebecca to help him with all of that."

"Perfect," Rachel replied. "Chris, I'd like you to be responsible for ordering and inventory of all of the items needed by the ranch. Once you know what's here, you'll need to create a shopping list for what we need. That includes things we will want to have on hand for prepping, too, not just the day-to-day stuff. I think we will all need to have input into the shopping list, and then, since you are the queen of shopping, you get to start ordering things! I also think that wherever we can, we need to shop locally."

Chris grinned. "That sounds more like fun than work, and I like your shop local idea."

Rachel continued, "I will take on responsibility for handling staff and finances. I will come up with a staffing plan for you all to approve, oversee interviews (although each of you will be the ones to select the people in your areas) and will put together a wage and benefit plan for you all to approve. I'll also put together a preliminary budget for discussion and approval when everyone is here. I'd also like to get the kids all involved as soon as possible. I know Rebecca said she would be here as soon as we needed her, and she will be Scott's sous chef. Gwen said she would have to give notice before she could come. I'd like to see Gwen be given the position of Guest Services manager. She

45

could oversee reservations, housekeeping, and guest activities. She could also help with our marketing plan."

Chris interjected, "I think she'd like that. She is so organized, and after all, it's what she went to college to learn."

Rachel smiled at her friend. "I know, and it's what she is so passionate about doing, too. I talked to Noah, Liz, and his boss, and all three are willing to relocate if we decide to build an animal hospital. Maybe the three of them can come out here after we get keys and work up a list of what we'd need to do to convert part of one of the barns into an animal hospital."

"I need to call Billy and ask him what he will need in the way of computers, programs, and all that to manage the accounts. We'll need to get him set up in an office where he can work without a lot of distractions. As for Marcie, what do you think about asking her if she would like to oversee activities for the younger kids. I know Marcie feels like she has nothing to offer, but she loves working with Sunday School and Vacation Bible School at church, so this might be a good fit for her. Plus, it wouldn't be anything she couldn't do with a baby around."

Seeing everyone agreeing with her, Rachel continued. "One last thing. I would love to offer positions to our friends Mary Garner and Trina Baker to help with the quilt retreat. I think both of them would be able to contribute a lot to the business."

Chris nodded, and Joel asked, "What about their families?"

Rachel replied, "Mary has three kids, all boys, but two are married with kids of their own. The third boy is an officer in the Navy on an aircraft carrier somewhere in the Atlantic. Mary's husband Alan raises and trains guard dogs, something he could continue to do here. Trina and her husband Chad don't have any kids. Chad is a mechanic at an auto dealership in town. I think both families offer skills we could use, plus it would be nice to have our friends near."

Joel nodded. "That sounds like a plan. I guess you'll need to talk to them and see how they feel about moving out here."

Just then, Janet and her husband knocked on the door to the RV. "Anyone hungry?" she called.

"We're coming!" Joel called out the window as Chris and Rachel beat him to the door.

Janet turned to her husband, "Chase, I'd like you to meet some new friends. Joel and Rachel Matthews, and Chris Wilson, this is my husband Chase Armstrong." After shaking hands, Joel suggested they hurry inside.

"The smell of steak is killing me! I'm starved," he exclaimed.

They had a leisurely dinner and got to know each other. They learned Chase was a contractor, but with the slow economy, he had not had much work lately. Finally, over coffee and dessert, Joel asked, "Do you mind if we talk a little business?"

Janet and Chase smiled and agreed.

"Good, thank you. I was thinking over dinner of all of the things we will need to do before we can open our ranch for business. We have cabins to be repaired, the bunkhouse needs renovation, we have fences to mend, and there are things to be done in the lodge, too. I was wondering, since you said business has been very slow for you, Chase, if you would be interested in being our general contractor for getting these repairs done for us?"

Chase looked surprised. "I think that would be awesome, but I have to ask, why me? You don't know anything about me or my work."

Joel smiled. "Chase, I have a really good feeling about you. I think I am a pretty good judge of character, and you just strike me as the right guy for us."

Rachel jumped in. "I agree. Janet has been wonderful with us, and we think you will be, too."

Chris added, "You have a strong handshake and look us all in the eye. That says a lot, and I agree with them."

"Well, then, I would be honored to take on this work. Janet, how long before the property actually belongs to these good people?"

Janet thought for a minute. "If your other folks get here in the morning, I can have the paperwork overnighted to the attorney. Then, once he sends it back, it will take two days to get the legal stuff taken care of, so we should have keys for you by Friday."

Rachel looked startled. "That soon? That is fantastic! Guys, we have a lot to do over the next three days!"

~~~

After making plans to meet Janet at her office in the morning, Joel drove the RV several blocks and checked them into a public campground. It took only a few minutes to get the RV hooked up and for Joel, Rachel, and Chris to take a short walk around the campground. Later that evening, while Joel and Chris sat watching TV, Rachel was busy at her desk in the RV.

"What are you doing, honey? Come relax with us." Joel called.

"No, I'm busy making lists for all of us of things we need to do. I want to get this written down before I forget some of it. It won't take me all that long."

"Well, just remember, it doesn't all have to be done tonight… except I know that you think it does, right?"

"It won't hurt to get a jump on it, and if I do this tonight, then I'll have time to do other stuff tomorrow!"

Joel rolled his eyes and Chris grinned.

"Quit laughing at me, guys! I know I can be a little OCD, but since I didn't bring enough quilting stuff with me, I have to do something, and watching TV and hearing about how bad the economy is and all of that is just depressing, so I'm going to stick to something that makes me feel better, okay?"

Joel got up and went over to Rachel, putting his arms around her. "We were just teasing, honey. Don't get upset. We'll leave you alone, but tomorrow, maybe we need to see if there's a quilting store in town, so you've got something else to have fun with."

Rachel grinned. "Yes, there is a quilt store on the same street as the steakhouse, up about three blocks. It's called "Strings Attached" and they open at nine tomorrow."

"Strings Attached?" asked Joel. "What kind of name for a store is that?"

Chris laughed. "Haven't you ever heard the saying that quilters come with strings attached, meaning all the little threads we get all over our clothes when we sew? I think it's a pretty clever name, actually. I'm looking forward to meeting Barbara, the shop owner, tomorrow."

Seeing Joel's surprised expression, Rachel explained, "Janet told us about the shop and its owner over dinner. Chris and I plan to check it out tomorrow while we're waiting for Scott and Stacey to get here."

Joel grinned. "Why do I think I've been played by you two? I'm going back to the TV."

An hour later, Rachel called out to Joel and Chris. "Do you two have time to listen to my list and tell me what I am missing?"

"Sure, honey, let me turn off the TV so we can hear you."

"All right. My list is not in any particular order of importance, but I tried to organize it in a timeline of sorts. Naturally, we can't do much until Friday when we get the keys, and so I would suggest we spend part of the next two days just getting to know the town and what's here. We will need to of course make friends at the quilt shop – that's a high priority for Chris and me! We'll also need to find the newspaper office, find out about local doctors and dentists, and make a list of churches we want to check out. We need to restock the groceries in the RV because we are almost out. We probably ought to plan on just staying here until Friday. I want to find out if there is any kind of cleaning service in town that we can hire starting next week to get the lodge clean. I also want to see if we can get an actual plat map of the property that's better than the map Janet gave us. We will probably want to hire a surveyor to make sure our fences are on the property lines."

"I haven't started working up a budget yet, but I did start on a staffing plan that we can look at tomorrow when Scott and Stacey are here. I also started writing help wanted ads for some of the positions, once you all approve those positions, that is. We also need to come up with an offer for Jeff Miller to keep him on as foreman. I think if we can get him enough help so he doesn't have the heavy burden he's got now, he may be willing to stay long enough for us to get settled. If he's willing to stay, we will need his input on things like how much tack we have for the horses, what kind of farming tools we have or will need, seeds, all of that kind of stuff.

"We'll need to figure out where we all want to live. The owner's suite is nice, but it would be a bit cramped for all of us to live there, so we will need to come up with some options. I am wondering if there is a better use for that space, and maybe we either build a couple of houses close to the lodge, or we get a couple of nice, manufactured homes for us to live in. Plus, we need to think about housing for the kids, too. We'll also need housing for some of the managers we will be hiring, and I think we need better housing for Jeff if he agrees to stay on.. Once we have a plat map, we can identify areas for housing that are close, but not right on top of the lodge. I think I saw two manufactured housing sales lots on the way over here. We may want to check them out over the next couple of days.

"We need to see if we can find an animal shelter around here so we can get a couple of dogs to train as watch dogs. It would be nice to get several puppies so they can all learn together. Since the herding dogs are getting older, we may want a couple of pups to train for that, too. If Mary and Alan agree to come out here, they may bring some dogs with them, but I think we are going to need quite a few for both security and farm work, so it won't hurt to find some here, too.

"Joel, we are going to need a very specific list of repairs for Chase. It would be nice if we could pay him an adequate salary so he and his crew have enough to keep them busy just working for us. That way, we wouldn't have to share his time with any other jobs and stuff would get done faster.

"We need to get commitments from all the kids on when they can be here, so we know how to include them in the plans.

"Some time in the next two weeks, we'll need to go home and arrange for all of our stuff in storage to be shipped here. We'll need to get the transfer of the houses taken care of, too.

"Chris, I am hoping we can start an inventory of critical items this weekend so we can get things ordered. I noticed the mattresses in the guest rooms looked pretty worn, so we may need to replace them. We'll need to see about the linens, and – oh, I just thought of this, we'll need to get busy so we have quilts for all of the guest beds! Good thing we're hitting the quilt store in the morning! If Trina and Mary agree to come, that's one of the first things we can have them work on!

"We'll need to get Scott into the kitchen to see what he needs, too. Once it's clean, we'll need to start packing in groceries. I am thinking that we could take the owners' living area and convert it onto additional kitchen storage and a nice office for Scott. We could use some of the space along with the office behind the reception desk to make a couple of good-sized offices for Gwen and Billy, and still have enough room for storage of materials for the reception area."

Chris and Joel both nodded. "I think that would be a much better use of the owners' living space. We could leave the bathrooms in there, so that the three offices have a private bathroom they can use."

"Great idea. There would also be enough space for a small break area and rest room for the kitchen staff. We'll have to see what Scott thinks.

"Joel, you and Scott will also need to inventory the armory. We need to be sure the door is strong enough for security. I wasn't paying a lot of attention to the door and how the cages were secured because I was too busy looking at all the guns. Also, we might want to think about expanding the reloading station because it is not very big."

"Chris, you and I need to look at the garden and start planning what we want to grow. We'll need to investigate the local agricultural department to find out about soil conditions and what grows well in this area."

Rachel stopped to take a sip of her tea, and Joel jumped in.

"Wow, Rachel, that is some list! I'm sure there is more, but you are overwhelming us. Let's plan out the next couple of days until we get keys. What do you say I wait here in the morning for Scott and Stacey while you two go to the quilt store? While I'm here, I'll borrow a phone book from the camp office, and make a list of addresses for the things here in town like the newspaper and other things. Then, we'll all go to Janet's office and sign the papers. Hopefully, Janet will let us borrow the keys to take Scott and Stacey on a tour afterwards – or maybe she will want to come with us. Thursday, we can do a little grocery shopping. By then, we will hopefully have heard from the kids, and we'll have an idea when to expect them. We can swing by the manufactured home lots to see what they have and how long it takes to get homes set up. Thursday afternoon, we can have an official meeting of the board of directors and review the plans we have so far. After that, we should be able to firm up an offer for both Chase and Jeff. When we get keys, hopefully Friday, we can park the RV in front of the lodge and start inventorying stuff. We'll probably have to stay in the RV for a few days because the lodge is too dirty to sleep in. By Monday, we should have enough of an inventory done that Chris can start ordering supplies and I should have a pretty comprehensive list for Chase."

"That sounds perfect," Rachel said. "You can turn the TV back on if you want. I'm going to sit here and read my latest quilting magazine for a while before bedtime."

~~~

The next morning, Rachel and Chris arrived at the quilt shop just as it was opening. They introduced themselves to the owner, Barbara Blake, and explained their dream of a quilters' retreat.

"That's something we really need around here," Barbara explained. "We usually wind up going into the bigger cities for our retreats, but a lot of the ladies don't like to go that far. Having something this close would be really great."

"Well, Chris and I love to quilt, so you'll probably be seeing a lot of us. We plan to open a small shop in the retreat, not to be competition for you, but as a convenience for the people who might have forgotten something or need something extra. We'd like to set up an appointment with you to see how much of our stock we can get through you," Rachel explained.

Barbara was quite happy, as she would realize a good profit from their transaction. When she asked why they were ordering through her, Rachel answered, "We could order directly from a distributor, but the only ones who would benefit from that would be the distributor. By ordering from you, we are supporting a local business. I also have an ulterior motive. Who better to help us recruit quilters than the owner of the quilt store!"

"Will you have a long-arm?" Barbara asked.

"Most definitely," Chris replied. "We have two friends who we hope will be joining us and both of them know how to use the long-arm."

"What would you think about offering long-arm services to quilters in the area? I have a long-arm, and I do offer services, but I really don't have the staff or time and do it as a convenience for my customers. If you guys offered services, it would be additional profit for you, you'd get to know more of the local quilters, and I would be able to focus on providing the intricate custom quilting that I love to do."

"That sounds like a fabulous idea," Rachel replied. She turned to Chris. "We need to call Mary and Trina tonight and not wait until we are back home."

The two wandered around the shop for a while, picking out fabrics for the first several quilts they planned to make for the lodge. "We need to come up with a special pattern just for the retreat. I wonder if there is a block called 'Serendipity'?" Chris wondered.

"We'll have to check. I've never heard of one, but there are only like thirty thousand different quilt blocks, right?" Rachel answered, laughing.

While they were waiting to have their fabric cut, Barbara came up to them, accompanied by an older red-headed lady. "Girls, I'd like you to meet Eileen McCowen. She is the president of the local Quilt Guild."

After shaking hands, Eileen proceeded to invite Chris and Rachel to the next Guild meeting, to be held the following week. She gave them directions, and both ladies agreed to try to attend.

Two hours later, as they were leaving the shop with several bags of purchases, Chris commented on what a great morning it had been. "We've made friends with the local quilt store, gotten information and an invitation to the local quilt guild, and got recommendations for a doctor, a dentist, and two churches. Plus, it looks like we will also have a new revenue stream with Barbara's blessings."

Rachel laughed, "Don't forget she also gave me the business card for the local long-arm guy, and we've got enough fabric with us now to make quilts for the main lobby and a couple of guest rooms!"

"Maybe now we can do some quilting in the evenings instead of you making us more lists of things to do!" Chris retorted.

"Don't count on it, though, until we can get the main building a lot cleaner than it is now. I think it might be a bit hard to start trying to piece fabrics in an RV that has five people staying in it!" Rachel said, laughing.

Chapter Six

June 15

Friday morning finally arrived, and Joel, Rachel, Chris, Scott, and Stacey met at Janet's office. Although they spent several hours on Wednesday signing papers, there were still a few more documents Janet needed to go over with the group. Finally, she placed the last of the documents in a folder and picked up a ring of keys.

"Which one of you gets the keys?" she asked.

Joel answered, "Give them to Rachel. She is the CEO of this corporation, is the one who actually bought the winning tickets, and the one who had the idea all along for a retreat, so it's fitting for her to have them."

Janet handed Rachel the keys. Rachel didn't say anything, but tears began to pour down her face. Finally, she looked at her husband and friends, and said in a very soft voice, "It's real, isn't it? Nothing seemed real until right this minute. We own a ranch!" Joel and Chris both reached over to hug Rachel and soon, everyone was wrapped up in a group hug.

Finally, they all pulled apart, and Joel announced, "The bus is leaving for Serendipity Ranch in five minutes. All aboard!" Laughing, everyone, including Janet, jumped up into the RV for the short ride to the ranch. Although Scott and Stacey had a brief tour late in the afternoon on Wednesday, it was their first time seeing the ranch in full daylight.

Chris turned to Scott to say something and saw the look of astonishment on his face as they pulled up to the lodge. "Close your mouth, Scott, you'll catch flies!" she laughed.

"I am just amazed. Somehow, it didn't look this grand the other evening."

Janet exited the RV and headed for the door to the lodge. "Your attention, please! Let me be the first to welcome all of you to your new home. Welcome to Serendipity Ranch!" She giggled as Rachel unlocked the door and they all went in.

Once everyone was there, Rachel quickly got their attention. "I know everyone just wants to wander around and look at everything, but

I think we need to get busy in our areas compiling the lists we agreed on. I am going to call the two cleaning services in town and see if we can hire both of them to start cleaning. Let's plan on meeting back at the RV at one for lunch. Chris, as soon as I finish on the phone, I'll catch up with you to help you inventory."

By lunch time, everyone was dusty and hot. Janet fixed everyone sandwiches and iced tea, and they all sat on the porch in the rocking chairs under the ceiling fans to eat.

"So, how has it gone for everyone this morning?" Joel asked.

"I spoke to both cleaning services, and they each will have a crew here Monday morning. They also gave me a recommendation for a landscaping crew, so I called them to come out and clean up the front, the yard, and the area around the cabins. They'll also be here Monday." Rachel consulted her note pad. "I inventoried the linens, blankets, and such. Most of it is in good condition but will need a good washing because it's all really dusty. We are going to need to buy pillows, towels, and new mattresses for both the guest rooms and the cabins. We are also going to need to purchase things like the little bedside coffee pots, hair dryers, and things like that. The rubber bathmats are all pretty gross and will also need to be replaced." She grinned at Chris, "I also got a count, and you won't believe how many quilts we are going to have to make to put one on every bed!"

"Can I help?" Janet asked? "We could use your new quilting room and have a regular quilting party! Do your kids quilt?"

"Marcie does, but the other girls never got into it like we did. Even Noah has tried it. I don't know about his girlfriend, but maybe we can convert her. Back on topic! Chris, what did you discover?"

"I started in the basement storage area." She stopped and shook her head. "It's amazing the things that were down there. I believe Mr. Spencer must have been a prepper, because I found eight brand-new Berkey water filters, the biggest ones, and eight *cases* of spare filters! I also found 23 cases of long-term storage food in #10 cans. Behind the rolling carts, there are 162 buckets of long-term staples – wheat, oats, rice, sugar, salt – amazing! I also found a significant amount of regular food stored. Some of the canned stuff might not be any good – Scott, you'll need to look at that – but I found large industrial tubs of flour, sugar, and salt. I also found several cases of assorted spices, lots of boxed cake mixes, cases of cooking oil, cases of lard, just amazing.

SERENDIPITY RANCH

There were also a number of cases of candles, at least 40 oil lamps, and several cases of lamp oil. One box had 248 packages of replacement oil lamp wicks – yes, I counted them! In the housekeeping storage room, I found enough laundry detergent to last at least 5 years. There was a whole section of cases of little hotel soaps, lotions, and shampoos. There were a lot of other cleaning supplies, too, such as window cleaner, toilet cleaner, and disinfectant spray. I will need to calculate how much is there to see how much more we will need to start."

Scott picked up his note pad to give his report. "First off, the kitchen is amazing. We have enough pots and pans to get started. I think we will need to get new service ware – a few of the dishes are chipped, and I don't think there is enough of anything for what we need. We may want to get dishes and glassware that is personalized with the ranch's logo, once we create one. There are a few other little things we will need, and all of the appliances seem to be working. I think I'd like to get uniforms for all of the kitchen and serving staff. We'll also need quite a few buffet serving pieces, and I've got some ideas for some renovations of the dining room to make service more efficient in there. The hostess station is in poor shape, and we'll need a couple of service stations for the servers. I looked at the owner's living area with Joel, and we think it will convert nicely the way Rachel described. I also looked at the barbecue pit out back, and that needs quite a bit of work if we are going to offer barbecues out there."

Joel patted Scott on the shoulder. "Good work, Scott! I made a list of the major areas needing repair, and I will add in your comments about the dining area, owners' space, and barbecue pit. I talked to Jeff, and he is working on a list of how much tack and equipment we have. He tells me we have three tractors, but they are not enough if we choose to expand the fields and plant more. I asked him to put together a wish list of everything he thinks we need, as well as things he thinks will make us more efficient. I also asked him to let us know how much seed we have, and how much we need. He is going to let us know how much animal feed he thinks we need to carry us for the next year.

"I walked through the barns, and there is a lot of room in the equipment barn for us to build an animal hospital. We'll leave that for last until Noah and his group can get here. I did not see anything major in the barns that needs to be repaired. However, walking through the bunk house, it is in bad shape. It is just open bays like in a barracks with bunk beds and foot lockers. I'll need to talk to Chase to see if it is worth it to fix or if we would be better off pulling it down and building a new one. I expect we will be better off building something we wouldn't feel bad letting our kids live in.

"As for the cabins, I made a list of the things I can see that need to be done. One cabin is in very rough shape. The water lines must have frozen and burst, because there is a high-water mark on the walls, and part of the floor is rotted. Luckily, this is the smallest cabin, but it is going to need major repair. I didn't have time to get to the lodge to see what needs to be done there. I plan to see if Chase has some time available in the next few days to do a walk-through with me."

Janet coughed. "I hope I'm not out of turn telling you this, but Chase is available whenever you need him. He said they didn't have a lot of work due to the poor economy. That was a bit of an understatement – he hasn't had anything to do for the last three weeks except for building a small shed last Tuesday. He and his crew are incredibly excited to be working with you and are ready whenever you want them."

Joel smiled. "Can he come out this afternoon and we can get started?"

"I'll give him a call and get him here! Thank you," Janet replied.

Stacey grinned and waved her hand. "Hey, don't forget about me, I have a report, too!" Once everyone stopped laughing, she continued, "I spent the morning looking at the books and filing system. Mr. Spencer kept good records of his former guests, so we will be able to send them marketing materials and hopefully get some of them to come visit us as paying guests. He also kept a record of all of his accounts – where he bought his bulk linens, light bulbs, animal feed, you name it, he kept a record. That will save us some time when we need to start ordering because we will know who delivers here, and what they carry. There is a whole shelf of catalogs for you all to look at and they appear to be fairly recent. I called the county planning and zoning department, and there is nothing in the current zoning that would prevent us from adding manufactured housing for additional staff residences."

"Oh, good!" Joel exclaimed. "Scott and I visited the two manufactured homes sales lots yesterday, and they have a surprisingly good selection sitting on their lot. Again, with the economic turndown, they've not been selling a lot of homes. They say that once the site is prepared, they can have a home delivered and set up within a week or two. They each have a couple of crews that can prepare the site, so all we need to do is decide where we are going to set them up, how they will be arranged, pick out the homes, and then start on the sites. The homes are actually pretty nice. They even have a couple of triple-wide homes. I picked up a bunch of brochures of the different floor plans, but I left them in the RV. Depending on where we put the homes, we will most likely need to put in a gravel road or two. Speaking of putting in roads, I think we would be wise to consider purchasing a bobcat dozer and maybe an excavator. In the long run, I think it would be more cost efficient for us to own them rather than having to rely on renting them whenever we need them."

Chris looked up from her list. "Just add them to the list of everything else you need. If there are specific brands you want, you need to let me know."

Rachel looked pensive. "You know what else we need to start thinking about? I know it is only the beginning of September, but we need Christmas decorations. Can you imagine how beautiful those curving staircases will be decked in garland and ribbons? And we'll need a big tree, and mantle decorations…"

"Enough," Chris giggled. "Let's worry about having a place for everyone to sleep, first, okay?"

Joel just shook his head. "Rachel, Chris is right – let's get the lodge clean before we start decorating, okay?" He turned to the others. "I also had an idea. I know we decided to make the craft room into the library. I would like to suggest that we partition off an area at the back to make a sort of office / command center for us. We'll need a place where we can watch the monitors for the cameras we will install and where we can keep the main computer equipment and communication gear."

Rachel interrupted him. "I thought we were going to put monitors at the reception desk so the clerk can see them while they're up there working?"

"Well, we are, I think. But redundancy is always good, and if the clerks get really busy, it's nice to have a second area available. Also, if something happens, we can have a second area for security personnel." Joel answered.

"That makes sense," Scott added.

Joel continued, "We'll also need a private place where we can coordinate things in the event something happens. I don't want us to try to use Gwen's or Billy's office, because they won't be big enough in the event something happens. It will also give us a place for the five of us to meet to just go over ranch business, even if nothing happens. The library is pretty big, and even with the big conference table in there, I don't think the office at the back will take away much from the library." He looked around at the others and could see they agreed with him. "All right, I'm adding that to the list for Chase. Anything else?"

Rachel spoke up. "There is a lot of wasted space on the back wall behind the stairs between the conference room and the quilting area . I would like to suggest we close that area off and make it into smaller classrooms for the quilt retreat. That way, we can offer more than one class at a time and that increases the appeal of the retreat. We can use one of the classrooms as a small shop, too. I also would like to suggest that instead of closing off the back of the library, we simply put bookshelves along the walls in the living room area and use the entire library area as our office/ command center."

"I agree," said Chris. "That sounds like a better use of space."

Joel nodded and added it to his list for Chase.

The group spent a little more time discussing other items to put on Chase's list, and then everyone went back to their tasks for the rest of the afternoon.

Chapter Seven

The next two weeks moved at lightening pace. As the kids arrived, they were assigned tasks aligned with their new jobs. One of the first things they did, once the cleaners were in place and Chase and his crew had begun repairs and renovations, was to identify where they would place housing for everyone. After much discussion, the area just past the main parking lot in front of the lodge was selected. Joel drew up a sketch of where each home would go, and then the group had fun naming the various streets that would be built in their new little community. Before Rachel could make a suggestion, Joel laughed and told everyone, "We are not naming the streets after quilting blocks!"

"That's fine," Rachel answered, "but we're not naming them after guns, either!"

After a lot of discussion and much laughter, they finally had names for the nine streets that would make up the residential area. In the end, they compromised. Rachel and Joel found themselves living on Lone Star Court, and Chris and Scott were on Destroyer Alley. The other streets had fun names like LeMoyne Drive, Half-Square Triangle Place, Remington Road, Javalina Trail, Wild Elk Way, Lucky Lane, and Calico Court. Of course, the street names did not really matter, but it did give a sense of community to the little development.

The entire group spent a whole day at both manufactured home lots, and homes were selected for everyone. This made the owners of the manufactured home lots extremely happy. In addition to the homes purchased for the families, ten more homes were purchased, one each for Trina and Mary, four for possible managers yet to be hired, one for Jeff Miller, and three more single-wides to have available for extra housing as needed. The crews were contracted to prepare the sites, and another crew was brought in to create roads to reach the sites. The crews and the manufactured home dealers promised everything would be completed and ready to move in by the first week in November.

Mary and Trina were extremely excited to accept Rachel's offer to work at the ranch, and both arrived in early October, ready to work. Mary and Alan brought three dogs with them, all already trained as guard dogs, and Alan began right away getting the dogs used to guarding the ranch. Trina's husband Chad became the mechanic for the ranch, being responsible for maintaining all of the ranch's vehicles.

Noah, Liz, and Dr. Lydia arrived the end of September with a moving truck full of veterinary supplies. In between working with Chase to get the veterinary hospital established and examining and registering all of the animals on the ranch, the three, along with Alan Garner, went to the animal shelter in town and adopted three litters of puppies. Everyone had fun picking out names for all of the pups. The twelve puppies identified to be herding dogs were all named after disciples or Bible characters. The nine pups who would become guard dogs were named after Greek, Roman, and Norse gods. Alan agreed to train the guard dogs, while Jeff agreed to train all the herding puppies.

Chase's crew made quick work of the repairs to the cabins. By late October, all 18 cabins were ready for occupancy with new furniture, mattresses, and décor. The bunk house proved to be not worth keeping, and so it was taken down and a new, bigger bunk house was built. Not counting the tiny apartment Jeff lived in, the old bunk house slept 12 men in two open bays. Jeff was delighted to move into his brand-new manufactured home, and the new bunkhouse was a major improvement over the old one. It slept 24 people, with all private rooms and several larger rooms for married couples. In addition, it boasted a large common area and a kitchen. Rather than one large bathroom for the entire bunkhouse, the rooms for single people were arranged in pods so each group of three rooms shared a bathroom, and the rooms for married couples had a private bathroom. Instead of bunkbeds, each room had a queen-sized bed. Each bedroom had a small sitting area and a generous closet. Rachel felt if staff were taken care of – especially if they had a nice place to live – it would help encourage staff to be more loyal.

Improvements were made to the shooting range, as well. The original range was just an open area with a couple of tables and a high berm as the shooting backstop. Joel and Scott didn't just want a place to shoot. They wanted their guests to have a great experience shooting. They built individual shooting stands for each lane, and then added a shelter over the shooting stands so that the shooters didn't have to sit in the hot sun to enjoy the range. A small building with rest rooms was constructed. The shooting lanes were improved, with high block walls running down the outside walls on each side of the range. Each lane was marked, and distance markers were placed. Finally, two observation towers were built for the range safety officers and a loudspeaker system was installed.

There were a few changes made in the lodge itself. The library was converted to a chapel, and the craft room became the office/command center. The bar was removed from the game room, and a couple of arcade games were added. The old arcade room became a children's craft and play area. Shelves and tables were placed into the former conference room, and a new quilting area was rapidly taking shape. Mary and Trina were very busy organizing fabric and supplies, as well as helping make quilts for the guest beds. Because there was so much to be done in the quilting area, Rachel appointed Mary to be the Quilt Department manager and Trina to be the Retreat Manager. Mary was responsible for getting the entire quilting area stocked, equipment installed and operational, and the quilt shop ready for business. Trina was responsible for working up plans for several different retreat options, in addition to helping Mary get the area ready. The first week of October was especially exciting when the new deluxe computerized longarm arrived and plans were begun to start offering long-arm services in the community.

Chris was a shopping wizard, stocking the shelves rapidly with everything on everyone's list. In addition, she added greatly to the group's prep supplies. Between Chris and Billy, they were able to implement an inventory system that linked to the accounting system so that they were able to provide a budget report to the group every morning.

In addition to getting the lodge ready, Rachel was busy hiring staff. She and Stacey prepared a staffing plan, approved by the group, and it was decided to allow Rachel final say on who was hired. The first person she hired was a housekeeping supervisor. Edna Galang worked as a housekeeping supervisor for several large hospitals before moving to town four years ago to open her own cleaning business. Her husband died of a heart attack three years ago, and after that, Edna dedicated all of her energy towards making her cleaning business successful. Unfortunately, the economy was poor, and her business was struggling. Her company was one of the original cleaning services Rachel hired to do initial cleaning on the lodge. Rachel was so impressed with Edna's work that she offered her the position and Edna gratefully accepted. Edna's business had three employees – Sally Goins, Charity Hart, and

Stephanie Godwin – and they were hired as Edna's housekeepers. As a manager, Edna was assigned a manufactured home. Instead of placing her employees in the bunkhouse, she requested her girls be allowed to live with her, as they were all pretty close.

The next person hired was Steve Porschenko. Steve was a recent graduate of the University of Texas' Master of Agriculture Science program. At 26 years old and unmarried, he grew up on a farm. His thoughts on farming coincided with those of the group. His official title was Agricultural Manager, and he would be responsible for all of the farming done on the ranch, including cleaning, refurbishing, and managing the greenhouse.

With Dr. Lydia responsible for the health of all the animals and Steve overseeing the farming aspect of the ranch, Jeff Miller agreed to stay on and manage the livestock. He and Lydia were becoming close friends, and so it just made sense for the two of them to work together. They did request a wrangler be hired to work with the horses, especially since the ranch planned to offer horseback riding among its many activities. Jimmy Langston was hired for that role. He'd been a wrangler since he was 16 years old, and Jeff Miller gave him a glowing recommendation. Although he did a year of college studying animal management, he found the classroom was not nearly as appealing as the hands-on working with the horses. He brought his own horse with him, a massive black Percheron named Titan.

By the beginning of November, the ranch was beginning to shape up. The manufactured homes were delivered, and everyone was finally able to move in. Staff were already well-settled into the new bunkhouse, and the animal hospital was open for business, although so far, they had only been treating animal on the ranch.

~~~

On the first Monday in November, Rachel scheduled a formal meeting for all of the leadership at the ranch. It was time to start planning the grand opening. As everyone arrived at the meeting, Rachel passed out packets with a meeting agenda and some information sheets.

"Gee, Rachel, we're getting pretty fancy, aren't we?" kidded Scott.

"Hey, I figured if it was in writing, you might pay attention to it," she answered, laughing.

"Yeah, he would pay attention to it if he could read, but I'm not sure the Navy taught him that skill" exclaimed Joel, laughing.

"Rachel, did you bring the green crayons for Army Joel to take notes?" Scott called out.

"Okay guys, that's enough, you're going to give everyone the wrong impression! It's time to be serious here, okay?" Rachel rolled her eyes, although she was happy to see that the guys we relaxed and kidding. The last few months had been pretty stressful for everyone. She and Chris had been using the quilting area quite a bit and that helped their stress level a lot, but they needed something for everyone else.

"Alright, I am calling this meeting to order. Chris, are you ready to take minutes?"

"Well, of course," Chris answered, shaking her head.

"Okay, the first thing on the agenda is determination of our opening date. I need to know what exactly still needs to be completed before we are ready to open. Let's start with Gwen."

"Thanks, Rachel. I've developed a marketing plan based on all of the information you all have provided for me. This will all need to be finalized and written in stone before our opening date. First, samples of our brochure should be in the package Rachel gave you. Please look at the brochure and think about it from two perspectives. First, as a guest reading it, would you want to come and enjoy our hospitality? Does it show that we offer enough to keep our guests busy and happy, and does it convey the experience we hope our guests will have? Then, review it from your professional perspective. Is it accurate and clear what we are telling the guests? Is there anything missing? Is there anything that could be misinterpreted or could lead the guest to believe something that is not true? Please do not tell me now. I want you to take a couple of hours over the next two days, and I'd like your feedback in writing. I'll need everyone's opinion by Wednesday night. Remember that everything is important, so don't hesitate to mention anything that you may think of.

"The next page in your folder is our tentative fee schedule. Please review the fees I've developed for our various services. We can offer quilting retreats – that is, several days with overnight stays, quilt camps without the overnights, one day quilting seminars, hunting packages by the day or for several days, and family ranch vacations with horseback riding and other ranch activities. All of the hunting and quilting overnight packages can be modified to include bringing family or a

64

spouse. The quilting packages can include supplies, or we can provide a list of supplies the guests will need to bring. For the hunting packages, we are expecting the guests to provide their own guns and ammo, although we could also rent guns and sell ammunition if needed."

Stacey interrupted her. "I'll need to be sure we have all of the appropriate licenses to rent guns and sell ammunition. I will get started on that this week."

"Thanks, Stacey," Gwen continued. "You'll see I listed family vacation packages with all activities included. We also can offer individual vacation packages. I recommend we offer a group discount on the individual rate if a group signs up to do any of the packages except the retreat.

"The next thing on my list is the gift shop. Marcie would like to run the gift shop, and so we will need someone to manage childcare and kids' activities. I am working on identifying stock for the gift shop, but I've got some samples here of various things with our Serendipity Ranch logo." She held up a cup, a polo shirt, a sweatshirt, pens, and several post cards. The logo they finally decided on was a rearing horse with the intricate scrollwork "S" from the main gates in the background. It was a striking logo, and everyone was very pleased with it.

"I'll pass these around for you all to see, and then let me know if you like them so we can get them ordered and stocked.

"Finally, we need to start thinking about hiring three people to man the reception desk. We'll need them to be able to cover 24/7, with Marcie and I covering several hours per week. Thanks, I'm looking forward to your feedback." Gwen nodded at Rachel and sat down.

Rachel looked thoughtful for a moment, and then turned to Gwen. "What do you think about Toby and his wife as part of the reception staff? Do you remember Toby? He's the nice kid I worked with in the deli back home, and I talked to him just a couple of days ago. He'd love to hire on here, and he has great customer service skills. His wife is a sweetheart, too, and she worked as a customer service representative for the electric company back home. She would be good for your staff, too."

"I do remember him. He and his wife would both be great if his health is up to it. How soon can we get them here?"

SERENDIPITY RANCH

"I'll call him as soon as our meeting is over. I expect they can be here within a few weeks. His health is still improving, but I think working the reception position will be a lot easier on his lungs than working in the deli, in and out of the walk-ins. We can put them in one of the single-wides since they have kids. Let's back up, though, and discuss these rates. What does everyone think?"

There was some discussion regarding the rates Gwen quoted, with some people thinking they were a little too low. Eventually they agreed to all of the rates and packages to offer with the understanding that they would revisit the discussion after they were open for six months.

The next person to speak was Scott. "I've gotten the menu plans completed for guests and for staff for the next six months. There's a copy of the plan included in your packet. All equipment has arrived, including our new dishes and glasses with the logo. They look really nice. All staff have been trained and we are in the process of cross-training everyone now. The pantry is stocked, and other than fresh items like veggies, milk and eggs, we could start serving guests in the morning."

Rachel smiled at Scott. "I like your idea of cross training. I think we might want to consider cross-training everyone just in case we ever are short in one area or another. Managers, can you all work together to come up with a reasonable plan for cross-training people to your areas? Thanks, Scott, for a good report!"

Rachel looked down at the pile of papers in front of her. "I am next on the list with human resources. Our benefit plans are in place, and so far, everyone seems pretty happy with the perks of working here. I got a notice from the insurance company that after January first, there will be a 1.2% rate hike for employee insurance plans, but that is still well within the overall amount we budgeted. Billy is doing a great job with tracking all of our accounts, and I have to say that I really appreciate having a report of expenditures in my email inbox every morning. I can't wait until we have some income to report there, too!

"Right now, it sounds like we have four vacant positions- child care and three reception clerks. I will try to get those positions filled in the next couple of weeks, along with any other positions you think we will need. Now, I will hand off to Chris." Rachel smiled at Chris and sat down.

"Thanks, Rachel. First of all, thank you to everyone who has been helping get things logged in and put away on shelves. I believe we are now fully stocked with everything that was on the initial shopping lists. We still need to finish ordering for the gift shop, and we'll need to order brochures and other marketing tools once you all agree on them. All furnishings including beds, mattresses, linens, fixtures, and so on are here. The uniforms for kitchen staff and for housekeeping have arrived. Now that our embroidery machine is up and running in the quilt room, Trina has been frantically working on getting the logo embroidered on the denim shirts and ball caps for farm and animal hands. She thinks she will be done with all of it by the end of next week. We saved a lot of money by being able to do that ourselves. Custom embroidery might be another possible revenue stream for us to consider later on. I have a request from the animal hospital to purchase a heavy-duty washer and dryer, as it is not working out well for them to try to use the housekeeping washers for their laundry. This is a reasonable request, will cost about $3500, and I can have them here and installed by the end of the week if you all approve. There is money in the animal hospital budget to cover this. Can we see a show of hands of all in favor of this purchase?" Everyone raised their hands.

"Chris, does that price include an extended warrantee plan and the cost of installation?" asked Joel.

"It does. They can hook up to the plumbing for the bathroom in the animal hospital, and I figured since you are an electrician, you can do the wiring for the dryer."

Joel raised his eyebrows and looked at Chris. "Oh, good, I was afraid I might run out of things to do! I'll get right on that," he said with a smile.

"Other supplies that have been ordered are the materials for reinforcing the fence. They will be delivered in the next few days, and Chase has a crew lined up to take care of it."

Noah raised his hand. "What are we doing to the fence? Is it something that will affect the animals?"

Chris responded, "No, we are adding electrification that we can control from the lodge. We are also adding surveillance cameras along the entire fence. There are a few places that the fence just isn't strong enough to keep animals in and people out, so those areas will get stronger fencing materials, plus the electric wires ought to help."

"Oh, okay, thanks," Noah answered.

Chris resumed, "Are there any questions?" When no-one responded, she sat down.

"Excellent, Chris! Joel, you're up next."

Joel stood. "I will try to make my report short and sweet. From an animal perspective, we are full up. In addition to what was already here, we've added more goats and sheep, almost doubled the number of hogs, and added some ponies so we can do pony rides for little kids. We also purchased twenty more horses, and eight of them are pregnant. We doubled the size of the chicken coop and we are in the middle of weatherizing it so the birds will be fine all year long. Jimmy has been doing a fabulous job working with the horses and has taught a lot of staff to ride. We got our last shipment of tack in, and again, Jimmy did a great job getting each piece cleaned and ready for use. The tack room looks amazing thanks to his hard work.

"Other than the washer/dryer installation, the animal hospital is open for business. Lydia, you can start seeing clients from the community whenever you are ready. All of the barns have been thoroughly inspected and are in excellent condition with no required repairs. Steve put together a plan for planting come spring, and our new tractors and Bobcats and all of the implements are here and working. All of the farm and animal hands have been trained to use all of them. Steve also finally got the greenhouse overhauled, and they are starting to plant seedlings in it. That's all I've got!"

"Thanks Joel." Rachel looked at her notes. "Alright, Mary, as manager of quilting services, what have you got for us?"

Mary looked around the table nervously. "Trina has six different quilting retreats designed. Two involve paper-piecing, one involves scrap quilting, one is on needle-turned applique, and the last two are pieced quilts. I've got instructors lined up for each class, depending on the dates. I'm pretty excited about the instructor for the applique class. She is from Arizona and said she would be really happy to come teach with us. Plus, her fee is well within the budget. The asking salary for the lady teaching the paper-piecing class is a little more than we were wanting to pay, but she agreed to throw in a couple of short classes for the community at no charge while she's here, so we should be able to recoup the difference in her salary with what we can charge for the community classes. The little quilt shop is now fully stocked, all of the equipment is installed, and we are ready to start services."

"That's awesome, Mary! You and Trina have been doing a fabulous job getting that all set up and ready," Rachel interjected.

"Thank you. Trina and I would like to talk to you about doing a one-day quilt retreat for the guild as a test run. We'd only have 15 quilters and would just charge them a minimal rate to cover supplies and food. We'd teach the class, but it would help us determine if the layout works and would also give us some practice as we've not ever run a retreat before."

"When would you like to do this?" Rachel asked.

"We were thinking in two weeks - Thursday. Eileen from the guild has people lined up and the guild will pay the fee. We know it's short notice, but we think it would be a good idea."

"What does everyone think?" Rachel asked as she looked around the table. "Scott, are you all up to providing meal services that day?"

Scott smiled. "Of course, we're ready. I think it's a great idea, because we've got a few recipes we want to try, and that would be a good opportunity for us."

Seeing everyone nodding agreement, Rachel told Mary to go ahead with the retreat, but to keep everyone informed.

Stacey raised her hand. "I need to check on our insurance liability to be sure it covers injuries to guests from the quilting equipment, but also to be sure the equipment is protected from the guests."

"Thanks, Stacey. I know our liability insurance covers most of the basic activities we are planning on offering, but I really didn't give a lot of thought to liability for quilters – I mean, other than a needle stick or cramps in your fingers from hand-quilting, I didn't think about quilting as particularly risky. You might want to review the policy for any other kind of liability we hadn't thought about." Rachel again consulted her notes and continued. "Let's decide on an official opening date. Gwen and I were talking and thought it would be good to have a soft opening first, where we invited a bunch of friends and family to come spend a few days on the house, so we can all practice, and then have the hard opening date be set for the following week. How does everyone feel about opening on Tuesday, April 4th? We could then do our soft opening on Tuesday, March 21st. That would give us a week after the soft opening to fix anything before the paying guests arrived. Any discussion?"

Gwen looked a bit confused. "That's over four months away. Why are we waiting so long to open?" she asked.

Chris smiled at her daughter. "That's a great question, dear. We still have an awful lot to do. Just because shelves are stocked and furniture is in place, we still have a lot of training to do with staff. We have an entire emergency procedures manual to finish putting together, as well as our routine policies and procedures to finish writing. Stacey is still confirming insurance issues, and even though we have our business license to operate the lodge, there is still paperwork yet to be completed for a lot of the smaller details. It will take a while to get the gift shop stocked and priced, and we have a whole marketing campaign to put in place. Plus, we are thinking that January and February are going to be our slowest months due to the weather, and so we figured we would just wait until March to start gearing up. One last thing-we've all be working like dogs for months trying to get ready. We figured we would need a breather before we actually opened the doors to paying customers!"

Gwen laughed. "Leave it to you, Mom, to give me the Webster's unabridged version of why we're not ready yet. Okay, I think I understand, we've got stuff to do, you need a vacation, and it's going to be cold this winter, right?" Chris just shook her head, grinning.

Rachel looked around. "Any other comments?" she asked. "All in favor, raise your hands." Since everyone raised their hands, Rachel stated those would be the official dates.

"I have one more thing to bring up before we open the floor to questions. In our main lobby, we have two quilts that Chris and I made. One is the Serendipity Ranch quilt. The other is the Ranch Logo quilt with our motto, *Semper Paratus*. I think it is important that we are always ready, not just for our guests that we hope will be coming, but also ready to handle whatever life throws at us. It is no secret that before we opened the ranch, Joel, Scott, Chris, and I were preppers. I want the ranch to have the same readiness for the unknown that we tried to have in our lives before. This just doesn't mean having stuff. It also means skills. I want us to start some required classes for our employees. These classes should include cardiopulmonary resuscitation or CPR, basic first aid, weapon safety, shooting, security procedures, and firefighting.

Everyone should be able to ride a horse, swim, drive a four-wheeler, and help with the harvest. We also need to have a good number of us who are able to can and dehydrate food. I believe staff should be paid to take these classes, and I think we need to start them right away. If you all agree, I will set up competency sheets for everyone so we can track their new skills. This is another reason why I wanted us to hold off opening too soon." Everyone around the table was nodding and began talking at once.

"Does everyone agree?" Rachel asked?

Joel raised his hand. "I think there is one other area we've neglected, and it's a big one. We need to get radios so we can communicate with each other around the farm. The little walkie talkies we've been using are just not adequate. I also think we need to get a good HAM radio set up, with the big antennas and everything. Then, I think everyone will need to be trained on the radios, and a handful of people trained and licensed on the HAM".

Rachel's eyes got wide. "I can't believe we overlooked such a major thing! Chris, we need to get that ordered right away! Joel, can you and Chris take care of finding out what we'll need and get it here and installed? I'll find out about the training. So, adding communication training for everyone, is training plan for employees approved? All in favor?"

All hands were raised, and Rachel noted that the training was approved.

"That does it for our formal agenda. Does anyone have any questions or comments?"

Surprisingly, there were no questions, and so the meeting was adjourned.

~~~

A few nights later, Rachel was sitting at the dining room table in her new home working with Chris on a quilt. Joel was watching TV with Scott. Suddenly, Joel called out, "Rachel, Chris, come watch this."

"What are you watching," Chris asked.

"It's some program by NASA about asteroids. They just said there is an asteroid that will make a pass really close to Earth sometime in early spring." Joel looked upset, so Rachel put her hand on his arm.

"It's okay, dear, that happens all the time."

"No, Rachel, it really doesn't. They said this one may even brush against our outer atmosphere. They are reporting it is a really large asteroid, they think about two and a half miles wide and four miles long. This makes me really nervous."

"Honey, there's not a lot we can do about it," Rachel said, looking at Scott and Chris for reassurance.

"Well, I always thought the economy would be our SHTF event, but I think we need to take this seriously," Scott answered.

Joel agreed. "I think we need to have everything at 100% by the first of February. That means we need at least five years' worth of supplies for about 100 people, and it all needs to be on site by February 1. We also need to think about additional housing possibilities if we happen to have a lot of guests when and if anything happens."

"I agree, Joel, but let's not get too worked up over this one event. We'll follow it closely, be ready if something happens, and go on with life as usual in the meantime," Scott replied.

Rachel nodded. "I agree with Scott. Let's not make a snap judgement that this asteroid is going to cause Armageddon. We can watch it and see if it turns into anything, but, really, guys, let's not freak out over it. I'm still putting my bets on an economic crash or something with China."

Scott smiled. "Yeah, China is talking about 'liberating' Taiwan again, and Taiwan is making noise about independence. That is a lot more worrisome to me right now than a space rock…" Scott saw Joel was about to speak, and continued, "but we'll keep all of our options open and be ready for anything. Who knows, maybe the space rock will hit China and that will be the end of that threat."

Chapter Eight

November 21

The following Thursday, fifteen excited guild members, including Barbara, the shop owner and Eileen, the Guild president, met for the first time in the new quilting area at the ranch. Mary and Trina were nervous, but Rachel and Chris decided to stay out of their way and let them run the show. As their guests unpacked their sewing items, Trina began explaining the day's focus. "Today, we're going to work on the Guild's project of quilts for children in our community. I've got several fun patterns for you to choose from. I know most of you brought fabric, but if you need something extra, there is a bin here of scraps and fat quarters - help yourself to whatever you need."

Rachel and Chris stood outside the door, watching to see how the retreat was going. "Trina is really nervous," Chris observed.

"I can see that," Rachel replied. "She'll be okay once Mary cracks her first joke, though." Sure enough, within a minute or two, Mary had her charges laughing, and Trina was visibly calmer. On and off through the morning as they worked on their other duties, Rachel and Chris popped into the retreat to see how things were going. They were both so impressed to see how well Mary and Trina were working together, and how smoothly the retreat was going. As the day went on, the sounds of happy sewing filled the lodge. By the end of the day, the Guild had seventeen new children's quilts, a number of new friendships were formed, and the Serendipity Quilt Retreat became the Guild's favorite place.

As she was leaving, Eileen stopped to speak with Rachel. "I can't thank you enough for such a wonderful day. We had a fabulous time, and Mary and Trina were both excellent teachers. You have an important resource here for the quilters in our area, and I can't wait for the next retreat!"

Rachel grinned. "I'm so glad you all had a good time today. This has been a dream for a long time, and it is so exciting for me to finally see it come alive. There's nothing like the sound of a houseful of happy quilters!"

Eileen laughed. "Yes, all we could hear all day long was sewing machines and lots of laughter... except for lunch – then, all we heard was chewing! That was an amazing lunch! Your chef needs to publish a cookbook with the recipes – especially that chocolate tart! It's worth another retreat just to come back for lunch!"

Rachel laughed. "Well, we'll have to see if we can top it next time, right?"

"Oh, there will be a next time – lots of next times if I have my way!" Eileen replied. She gathered up her bags as Rachel walked her to the door. "We'll see you ladies at the Guild Christmas party next month, right?"

"Of course! We're looking forward to it!" Rachel answered.

After the last guest left, Rachel and Chris found Mary and Trina tidying up the retreat room.

"Ladies, congratulations!" Chris called out. "You two did a spectacular job. We've heard nothing but praise for your retreat!"

Trina let out a deep sigh. "Thank you. I'm glad the first one is over because I was so nervous at first. I had a great time, though, once I stopped being so worried about making a mistake or forgetting something! And Mary, you were such a great help at keeping me calm and on track."

Mary grinned. "Yeah, I spend my life keeping you on track, I think! Once you got your funny bone engaged, we all relaxed, and then everyone started having a great time. When's the next one?"

Mary looked at Rachel. "Can we do another one?"

"Of course," Rachel answered. "Eileen was just telling me what a wonderful time everyone had and that they want to plan more. When she calls, just go ahead and schedule. No overnight ones until after we open officially in the spring, though."

Mary put her arm around Trina's shoulders. "Looks like we are in business, sis! Let's go finish cleaning up and then see what kind of plans we can make for the next one." The two women headed back to the retreat room, laughing.

Chapter Nine

January 6

The holidays came and went with little fanfare. Many of the staff chose to stay on the ranch for Thanksgiving, and Scott and Rebecca served an amazing Thanksgiving dinner. The one-day practice quilt retreat was so successful, the ranch hosted three more during December. Throughout November and December, almost all of the training was completed, as Rachel set December 31 as the absolute completion date. Reception clerks were hired, and two women, a mother and daughter team, Lillian and Cheri Hines, were hired for the childcare area. Several additional part time hands were hired to help with livestock and farming. All renovations were completed, and the last week of December saw a brand-new quilt on every guest bed in the ranch.

The first week of January, the ranch experienced its first big snowstorm, with over two feet falling in the space of a few hours. Joel and Scott were excited to try out the new Bobcat with its plow attachment to clear the main roads on the ranch. The farm hands were pulled from helping with the animals to help clear walkways. Mid-morning, grid power went out and the ranch automatically switched over to solar and wind. Marcie chose that day to go into labor and after a few hours and a surprisingly easy labor, William Joel Walker was born at six pounds and eight ounces. Mother and son were both fine and discharged from the hospital in town the next day.

A few days later, with heavy clouds and snow continuing to fall intermittently, Scott and Joel were sitting in the dining room enjoying a cup of coffee and chatting. Scott commented that the lights seemed a bit dimmer.

Joel looked around and agreed with him. "I wonder if the batteries are recharging with just the one wind turbine and such heavy clouds. They can't be getting all that much sunlight from the solar to charge the batteries."

"Good point. Do you think we ought to look into getting a diesel generator? After all, if something happened like the Yellowstone caldera exploding or a nuclear exchange, we could experience a long period without enough sunlight to fully charge the batteries. I'm not sure we want to have a house full of guests and not enough power for things to work."

Joel nodded. "Yes, I think a generator is a good idea – a commercial one like we used in the army to power tent cities. We'll also need to get a pretty big storage tank for the diesel. Right now, the farm tank only holds a thousand gallons, and I'd bet we need five times that much to run a big generator for any length of time. I think while we're at it, we might also want to get some replacement solar panels and a couple more of those wind turbines. Let's talk to the girls and see what they think. I'm sure they'll agree, especially if we remind them we need power for their sewing machines!"

Scott laughed. "Well, technically that's not true. Don't you remember a few weeks ago the girls bought several of those foot-powered machines? Treadle machines, I think they're called."

Joel rolled his eyes. "Well, then tell them we need the extra power to keep the chocolate ice cream cold!"

"That's more like it."

~~~

That evening, while Chris and Rachel scoured the internet trying to find the best deal on a generator, Scott and Joel were watching the news, when a story came on about the asteroid.

The International Astronomical Union today announced the name for the newly observed asteroid. According to Dr. Timothy Waldstrom, PhD, the asteroid will be known as Higgens-Moss, named after the two astronomers who discovered it. Scientists have plotted its orbit, and are still assuring everyone that, while the asteroid will be close, it will not actually enter Earth's atmosphere. The new window for the projected date of arrival is between the 22nd and the 25th of March. NASA is planning to send up a crew at that time to study the asteroid as it makes its closest pass to Earth. According to NASA, it will be visible to most of the northern hemisphere for about three days as it makes its approach, and then heads off into outer space. It won't be back near Earth for at least 1800 plus years, so you might want to plan on checking it out while it's here.

In other news, North Korea launched yet another intercontinental ballistic missile, this one landing just outside US territorial waters. Let's go now to our network correspondent in Washington, DC.........

Joel turned the TV off. "Guys, I am starting to have a really bad feeling about this asteroid. Chris, how close are we to having those five years of supplies for 100 people?"

"Let me think. I have one more shipment coming this week, and two next week, and that should do it. I also have a shipment of medical supplies coming that I found online."

"I think we ought to get more. I think we should go ahead and increase it to seven years' worth." Joel said. Scott slowly nodded his agreement.

"This asteroid really has you spooked, Joel. Is there something you're not sharing?"

"I dunno, Scott. It does have me spooked. There's a little voice in the back of my head telling me to take it seriously because this could be it, you know? I don't mean to sound paranoid or anything, but it's just a feeling. I think we need to be ready for it."

"Well, Joel, it's okay for you to be spooked, but just make sure we order a lot more toilet paper," called Rachel, giggling. "You might want to get a ton more coffee, too, since I do not want to go through the apocalypse without coffee!"

Chris laughed, "Yes, and I think we might need another fabric order, too, just in case!"

Joel looked serious. "You guys might think it's funny, but mark my words, they are holding back from us. If that asteroid even touches our atmosphere, it will be drawn in and will impact earth. God only knows what will happen then."

The other three stopped laughing and were silent for a minute or two. Rachel was the first to find her voice. "We need to think about our soft opening and be sure that we invite everyone who is important to us. After all, if we have them here for the opening and something happens, they will hopefully be far better off than if they were anywhere else. We could even put an asteroid-watching party as one of the activities in our invitation." Rachel took a deep breath. "We need to think of everyone we want to have here, but also everyone we NEED to have here if something happens. We could use a doctor and a few nurses, a teacher or two, some law enforcement or military folks, what other roles?"

"Some clergy would be helpful, along with anyone who knows about carpentry, blacksmithing, and, well, I'm not sure. Maybe a couple of gunsmiths, pharmacist…" Chris' voice faded away as she looked off into space, imagining the horror of an asteroid impacting Earth.

Scott, trying to reassure everyone, added, "Look guys, it probably won't happen, but probably is not good enough for us. We are way better off and much more ready than most people if this thing really does impact. I suggest we listen to Joel's little voice and assume that it IS going to impact and operate with that in mind. I also suggest we do not discuss it with anyone else except maybe Stacey until we are much closer to the event. Here's a thought. When we get closer and it looks like it may happen, do we want to allow staff members to invite their families to be here for the 'viewing party'? It will make it a lot easier for all of us if we don't wind up losing staff who need to go find their families, and especially easier if we don't have to be the ones going to find families."

The others agreed with Scott and decided to keep a cautiously optimistic view publicly, while behind the scenes, they would brainstorm what else might be needed.

Later that evening, long after Chris and Scott returned to their own home, Rachel couldn't find Joel. After searching the house, she found him out on the back patio with his telescope, searching the night skies.

"Honey, don't you think it's a little early to be seeing the asteroid?" Rachel asked, putting her arm around her husband. She was startled by the sad look on Joel's face. "Honey, you are getting way too wrapped up in this asteroid. If it hits, it hits. There is not one single thing we can do to prevent it or change what will happen. The only thing we can do is make sure we are ready for it so that we and our friends and family have a better chance of making it in the new world in which we'll find ourselves." Rachel looked resolute. "We have to rely on our faith. I do believe that God helps those who help themselves. The more ready we are, the more protection God will give us."

Joel turned and put his arms around Rachel. "As usual, you are right, dear. I am just so worried that we are missing something, and that because of that we won't be ready. It makes me incredibly sad, knowing that if Higgens-Moss hits anywhere in the world, many thousands, millions even, might die, and life will be forever changed for the rest of us. I'm sad that our grandchildren may never know all of the wonderful things we have nowadays, and I am especially saddened to know that we are more than likely going to have to fight to protect what we have.

It is such a heavy burden on my heart, and I can't help but think about it constantly."

"Joel, my dearest, you have to let some of that go and have faith. You also have to admit there is still a chance it won't hit. Let me share some of that burden with you. It's not right that you carry it alone. Why don't we spend some time tomorrow looking at all of the worst-case scenarios to be sure we're ready for all of them."

Joel looked at Rachel lovingly. "I sure picked right when I married you. Let's do that right after breakfast. I want to get others involved, too. We can't hide the inevitable, but we can start working on putting a positive spin on things, I guess… and you're right about faith. I know that He is watching out for us, but I guess I forget that sometimes. Thank you for reminding me."

Rachel hugged Joel tighter and kissed his cheek. "Come on, honey, let's go to bed and get some rest. We can tackle this in the morning."

The next day, Joel assembled a group of people to brainstorm. He included not only Scott, Chris, and Stacey, but also Gwen, Rebecca, Jimmy, Steve, Lydia, Noah, Liz, Marcie, Billy, Jeff, Edna, Mary, Trina, and Chase.

"Okay, folks, I'm sorry to pull you away from your work when we have so much to do, but I think this is important. I have been worried sick about the possibility of this asteroid hitting. The government is downplaying it and making it sound like it will just be a fun science exhibition, but I don't trust the government to tell us the complete truth. I am hearing a lot more dire warnings from some of the scientists on the HAM radio. So, in order to help me sleep better and keep my dear wife from worrying about my mental health," Joel said, winking at Rachel, "what I want us to do this morning is to think of all of the worst-case scenarios and then discuss what we could do to mitigate each of those scenarios. I'm not doing this to make any of you more worried than you may already be- in fact, I am hoping that we will find out just how ready we are." He looked at all of the faces around the table and saw a combination of expressions ranging from fear to surprise to a firm resolve.

"The scientists are saying this asteroid is approximately two and a half miles across. I've done some research and learned that it will travel somewhere between 18 and 50 kilometers per second once it hits our atmosphere. We are not going to consider what will happen if the intact asteroid strikes the lower 48 states. Unless it hits in Maine or somewhere along the Canadian border, we would be buried in over a meter of ejecta, and the resulting air blast and fireball would probably kill us all anyway." Joel noticed Marcie had her hand up. "Marcie, do you have a question?"

"Yes, Dad, I don't mean to sound ignorant, but what do you mean by ejecta, airblast, and fireballs?"

"Oh, I'm sorry, I forgot not everyone has been obsessed with this. Ejecta is the debris that the asteroid will throw out when it hits. It is a combination of particles of the asteroid itself, as well as material from where the asteroid landed. It's like the ash that is thrown out when a volcano erupts. When the asteroid hits, it creates a huge ball of fire that rapidly spreads outward. This can be hot enough to burn you many miles – even hundreds of miles! – away from the impact site. The airblast is a really strong wind that is created as air rushes out from the explosion. Does that help?" Marcie nodded. "So, who wants to think of the first scenario?"

"I will," said Scott. "But first make a note that if we get any kind of ash, we need to be able to remove it from all of the building roofs, because that stuff is really heavy. We'll need to come up with the tools and a plan." Joel jotted notes as Scott spoke.

"Good observation. They make special brooms or shovels for clearing snow load from the roof – I'll look into that first before we start getting too creative." Joel finished his note and turned back to Scott. "Okay, first scenario?"

Scott continued. "What if it hits out in the middle of the Pacific Ocean somewhere?"

Joel smiled at his friend. "That's a good one. Depending on where it hits, we could expect earthquakes, although probably not much worse than some heavy shaking and some glass breaking. Probably no ejecta, no fireball, and no air blast. We could see tsunami waves on the west coast, again, depending on where in the Pacific. We would lose Hawaii and would probably see a lot of damage on the west coast, potentially triggering the San Andreas or the Cascadian faults. That would affect us by a potential collapse of infrastructure and the economy and an influx of refugees moving our way. Collapse of the economy would mean that anything we had could not be replaced unless we had the means to produce it here. Refugees could mean security issues for us;

it could also mean adding to our numbers. And, if we add to our numbers, we will have to have a place to put people. So, I see potential mitigation here as making sure we have back-ups for our back-ups – and maybe even back-ups to the back-ups for our back-ups!"

"What about if it hit somewhere in the Atlantic Ocean?" asked Rebecca.

"Well, depending on how close it is to the mainland United States, we would probably see anywhere from 10 centimeters to a meter of ejecta, the air blast would still be enough to blow down poorly-built structures, and the earthquakes would be strong enough to rattle things good and maybe break glass," Joel responded.

"The ejecta can't be good for crops, and especially for animals or humans to breathe. Do we have any way we can protect the grazing areas? And what about respirators for both humans and animals?" asked Jeff.

Edna added, "And how can we keep all of that ejecta dust from seeping into the house?"

Chris said, "We already have several thousand N-95 particulate face masks that we got in case Covid started up again. Joel, do you think those would work against ejecta?"

Rachel jumped in. "I still have yards of the face mask filter material I bought when we were making face masks during the pandemic. I'll bet we could use some of that to make masks for the animals, especially the dogs and horses."

Marcie chimed in. "I'll bet we could use some of that filter material to make a cover for William's baby carriage, too."

Rachel smiled at her daughter. "We'll order a few more bolts of the filter material."

Liz Torres shyly raised her hand. "Noah and I can work on developing masks and eye protection for the animals if you'd like."

Rachel smiled at her son's girlfriend. "That would be wonderful! Thanks, Liz!" Liz beamed and Noah squeezed her hand under the table.

"I'll have to work on training the horses to wear the masks. Don't forget we'll need some kind of eye protection for them, too," Jimmy added.

Joel smiled at the enthusiasm he saw around the table. He was glad everyone was on board to help with preparing for this possible disaster. "N-95 masks should work fine. Homemade masks will work with filter material if they fit tightly around the face without gaps to let in ash. We'll have to figure out what to use for animal eye protection. Noah and Liz, I'll leave that to the two of you."

Scott added, "We've got a little bit of plastic sheeting we used while we were renovating the cabins. We probably need to get a lot more. We could use that to help seal the buildings against seepage." Chris made notes on her ever-present pad.

Steve, who was usually very quiet, surprised everyone by adding, "I think we can get a number of large tarps and fix them so they will cover large areas of the pastures. I know they make 100' x 100' tarps because my parents in Mississippi needed several of them after Hurricane Katrina blew the roof off of their house and a couple of barns. We could probably cover a few acres of grazing land with tarps the night before the event is supposed to take place, and then if it does, we at least will have a little land available right away – well, as soon as the ejecta stops falling - for the cattle. We only need to cover a couple of acres, though. The ash, as long as there's not too much of it, is actually good for the soil and adds nutrients. Once the ash stops falling, we can just plow it all under and mix it well with the soil. Too much ash, though, can cause a lot of problems with the soil. We need to consider the trees – ash can be very detrimental to young trees. We might want to investigate some kind of cover for the young fruit orchard. We could also set up a couple more greenhouses between now and then, including maybe setting up a large one over the fruit trees. As long as we can protect the greenhouses from falling debris, we should be able to use them to grow more food for both the livestock and for us. Lastly, we need to consider the equipment we use for plowing and grading. We'll need to figure out some kind of pre-filter for them so the air filters don't get too clogged up and have a lot of spare parts, as the ash can be pretty rough on metal parts." Steve sat back and folded his hands.

"Wow, Steve, that's great thinking." Joel cleared his throat. "As you were all talking, I started to think, maybe we are going about this wrong. Instead of thinking of individual scenarios, maybe we should be addressing all of the possible consequences. If it hits and triggers earthquakes, that might also trigger volcanoes, in which case we will have even more ejecta to deal with. Building on what Steve said, what else do we need to consider regarding the ejecta?"

Scott scratched his head. "We will need a way to get people from one building to another without having to go through a million masks. We ought to consider some covered walkways between the cabins, barns, and lodge. At least, we could use plastic sheeting on the sides of the walkways to prevent the ash or dust or whatever from getting in. We also will need some kind of cover for chimneys to avoid letting a lot of ash in, but still let us use the chimneys for heat as we need them."

Joel looked thoughtful. "Covered walkways would be good, but we would probably need too many of them. We might do better thinking of some way to transport things – meals, supplies, things like that – from one place to another while protected from ash or ejecta."

Jeff raised his hand. "What about something like one of the four wheelers with some kind of plastic tent over it? The driver and any passengers would still need to wear protection getting in and out, but we could hook up a covered trailer to the four-wheeler to use to move things from one place to another."

Scott nodded. "That could work. We could also make some kind of tent-like cover for the buggy and hook it up to a four-wheeler to transport people from one place to another. If we made sure each cabin or house had an overhang of some sort that would protect people, we could pull the buggy right up under the overhang for people to get in."

"I'll start working on plans for building something for a couple of the four wheelers and the buggy," Jeff volunteered.

"Thanks," Joel said. "Scott, you may want to think about limiting the number of meals served in the dining room while the ejecta is falling, and maybe send boxed meals out for breakfast and lunch. That would cut the risk by two thirds of people having to leave the cabins for meals. We could still have dinner in the dining room, so people have a chance to get out of the cabins and interact with each other. We don't want people to feel like they are in another covid lockdown. We could also plan entertainment for everyone either before or after dinner – or both!" Seeing everyone nodding their agreement, Joel turned to Chris. "Could you be sure we have plenty of things like board games, cards, and maybe movies that we could play on the big flat screen in the main lodge living room? And plenty of supplies for packing box lunches?"

"Certainly," answered Chris, making a note on her pad.

"Won't a lot of particulate matter floating in the atmosphere cause a drop in ambient temperature and a possible prolonged winter?" asked

83

Lydia. "People will be coming here the end of March, and may bring winter coats, but probably won't unless we tell them to do so. If we don't, we'll need to have winter wear available for ourselves and guests. I suspect it might get a lot colder here than we are used to or that's normal for Texas that time of year. Also, anyone with respiratory problems may be affected more by even minimal exposure to ash. I recommend we have a few oxygen concentrators available, just in case. Also, we will have to keep the animals, especially the sheep, inside the barns while ash is falling, as the ash is very heavy when it gets lodged in their coats. In the case of sheep, it can make their coats so heavy they can lose the ability to walk, especially if the ash gets wet."

Jeff spoke out. "That reminds me of something else. If we get too much ash in the lake, it will kill off the fish, and we may not have any way to restock, even if we are able to get the lake dredged out. We probably ought to save some of the fish from the lake in an aquarium or an indoor pool so we will continue to have fish."

Steve responded, "If we do that, we ought to put fish in one greenhouse and set up some hydroponics. That would save the fish and also contribute to growing more things."

Chris was trying to capture all of the ideas being thrown out, rapidly filling several pages of her pad. Finally, she stopped writing and looked up. "I am thinking that even if we wrap all of our buildings in plastic, we will need to construct something like an air lock to keep the dust out. Otherwise, it will make cleaning up pretty hard. I remember reading that after Mount St. Helen's erupted, the ash from that was really hard to clean from surfaces. I also remember hearing that ash can cause problems with wind turbines, cooling fans, and other stuff. It's also really heavy when it gets wet. It can short circuit transformers and other electrical items, too."

Joel nodded. "All right, that makes me think of two other problems. First of all is our solar set up. We'll probably need to take down or cover most of the panels before-hand. They won't get a lot of sun anyway, and so it's better to shut them down than risk damage. We also will need to have plenty more replacement panels, probably at least double the number we have now. We also ought to have spare inverters and batteries as well." Joel stopped and looked thoughtful for a moment. " There's not much we can do about the two giant wind turbines, but we can investigate some of the small household sized turbines and just have them ready to set up afterwards. I'm surprised we didn't think of that even before all this," he mused.

"Geeze, Dad, you can't think of everything," laughed Rebecca. "The talk of ejecta is scary enough, but I can't help but think of earthquakes. I remember the little earthquake we felt when we went to San Francisco, but I'll bet these will be a lot more than that, especially if the San Andreas and or Cascadian faults are triggered. Are our buildings strong enough? Do we have replacement windows if some of ours get broken?"

Joel smiled at his daughter. "More good ideas for us to investigate and do something about while there's time."

Chase raised his hand. "If we are going to have the possibility of damages from earthquakes and air blasts, then it might be a good idea to have a lot of lumber and building materials on hand. This may sound crazy, but I think it would be a good idea to buy up one of the local lumberyards. If you need to rebuild barns or cabins, that will take a lot of lumber. If you have a lot of additional people come in, they can't live in tents forever, and so you'll need lumber to build places for them to live. I'm not talking just wood. You'll need nails and screws, shingles, wire, plumbing, everything that goes into building a house or barn. I can't even begin to estimate the cost, but I think it would be a very prudent thing to do."

Joel looked thoughtful. "I don't want to strip one place of all of its stock. We can make large purchases at a number of different places. The cover story is that we are expanding our cabins and building some additional storage buildings. That would actually be true, I suppose. Chase, would you get with Chris and make arrangements with her to get what you think we need?" Chase nodded, a shocked look on his face.

Scott took a deep breath, and then spoke. "I am most worried about our security. We need to consider that not everyone coming to our gate will be a refugee in need of help. If we have any kind of failure of infrastructure as a result of this event, there are going to be evil people who will take advantage of the situation. They will want what we have and won't be nice about it. How will we protect the ranch, and more importantly, the people on it? Even if every staff member here was available to stand watch on the fence, we couldn't see everything all the time. That is really worrisome to me. We need some kind of force-multipliers to help us stay safe. Before anyone asks, a force-multiplier is something that will increase the effectiveness of a force. For example, the camera at the gate is a force multiplier because it means we can see what's out there without actually having someone standing at the gate. I know we've electrified the fence and put up cameras, but I'm afraid that might not be enough in the face of a determined enemy."

There were a few seconds of silence after Scott spoke, and then everyone began talking at once. The discussion went on for another thirty minutes, with many good ideas being voiced. Chris filled up fourteen more pages with the ideas being expressed and with the lists of things they needed to purchase, adapt, or build.

~~~

Throughout the rest of January, Chris got busy ordering more supplies as a result of that meeting. She quietly ordered several extra-large military tents, heaters for each tent, and eighty folding cots with mattresses. The bunk beds from the old bunk house were refurbished and placed into one of the storage barns. An additional metal pole barn was set up to hold all of the supplies ordered just in case. She found a supplier and was able to order twenty 100' x 100' blue tarps. Another supplier was able to provide 50 industrial-sized rolls of plastic sheeting. The last week of January, five new greenhouses were delivered and installed. They were unable to find one big enough to fit over the orchard, so Steve ordered a number of additional fruit and nut trees and planted them inside the largest greenhouse. One greenhouse was set up for hydroponics, and one cold day in early February, Steve, Jeff, Joel, and Scott went out to the lake to catch enough fish to stock the hydroponic tanks. Additional winter gear was ordered in a variety of sizes. Chase and his crew went to every lumber yard within a hundred miles of the ranch and bought many truckloads of supplies, all stored in a second metal pole barn set up next to the first. By the time they were finished, they had enough supplies to build a small development.

The new generator arrived the second week of February. It was a lot bigger than Joel expected, so he and Chase build a concrete-reinforced cinder block building to hold the generator. They installed a triple-filtered exhaust and vent system to keep any potential ash from reaching the generator. A separate section of the building held the three new diesel fuel tanks purchased at the same time. Joel arranged for the tanks to be filled the first week of March.

The media continued to provide news stories about the impending arrival of Higgens-Moss, emphasizing with each story that there was absolutely no danger of the asteroid hitting the Earth. It didn't matter to Joel, though, because he was absolutely certain the asteroid would hit, but he felt so much better that his group would be prepared if it did.

Gwen created invitations offering a complementary five-day vacation at Serendipity Ranch to celebrate the grand opening, including a gala Asteroid Watching party on the night the asteroid was supposed to be most visible. Of the thirty-seven families invited, all but two accepted.

Chapter Ten

March 20

The ranch was crazy with activities the night of March 20th. Guests were scheduled to start arriving in the morning, and all hands were on deck getting ready. Welcome baskets had been prepared for each arriving family, and the ranch was sparkling clean. Fresh flowers, grown in the greenhouse for the occasion, graced all of the tables. Finally, around eleven o'clock that night, Joel, Rachel, Chris, Scott, and Stacey sat down in the sitting area in front of the massive fireplace.

"I am exhausted!" Chris exclaimed. "But… we are as ready as we are going to get. I can't believe how much we've gotten done in such a short time."

"You four really know how to work together," Stacey remarked. "I have never seen such great teamwork among people. I can't believe I've only seen one argument in all this time, and even that was pretty minor. I wasn't sure with all that needed to be done that we would be able to open tomorrow but look around – we're ready!"

Joel answered, "We are ready – for our guests tomorrow and for whatever happens Thursday with the asteroid. The staff took our announcement last week about the possibility of an asteroid strike and inviting families to the ranch for the asteroid watching party just in case really well. I've not seen any panic, although I've noticed a few worried expressions over the last couple of days. Not counting staff families, we have 35 guest families coming. Of that, several are just couples, and we are grouping them up in a few of the larger cabins. I believe we will have at least 87 guests. That's a bit more than we wanted, but considering the circumstances, I can't imagine leaving anyone off the guest list."

"That's not counting Janet and Chase and their son, who will be staying with us," Rachel said. "and I think the son is bringing his girlfriend and her parents. No matter, we have the room, and since their son is a pharmacy technician, he will be good to have on board. I'm not sure what the girlfriend does, but I think she's either a nurse or med tech. I have no idea about her parents, though."

"That's not counting Reverend Arnold either." Chris added. Reverend Charles Arnold was the former pastor at the Methodist Church the group used to attend in North Carolina who had retired several months before Rachel bought her lottery tickets. He was living in a senior retirement community and the group had maintained contact with him. "I'm really happy he agreed to come out and that he was willing to stay with us. You know, he has had such tragedy in his life. Two of his kids were killed in a car wreck five years ago. His daughter is in the Army and is stationed in Germany, so he doesn't get to see her very often. Then, his wife got sick. He took care of her for 18 months until she died from breast cancer two years ago. Yet, he's such a cheerful and caring person."

Stacey added, "I agree. I enjoyed listening to him preach every Sunday. He was always so uplifting. My brother and sister-in-law and their kids will be staying with me. He's on leave from the army right now, so that will be a big help if the SHTF. Oh, and last night, he called to tell me he was bringing his best friend, Tom, Tom's wife and their two kids. Luckily, I've got the room, so they'll be able to stay with me, too."

"It's a good thing we got the tents and cots, since I expect if the asteroid hits, we'll have an extra thirty or forty staff family members staying here, too," Scott added with a smile. "The more, the merrier, and the better it will be to try to survive whatever happens. We just need to be prepared, if it does happen, to get everyone on the same page at once. We also have to be firm that anyone who doesn't want to play by the rules gets to leave."

Scott laughed. "I guess it's a good thing we've got the Chief of Police and his family coming as guests, then. Just so you all know, Joel and I plan to meet with him tomorrow to go over security in the event the asteroid strikes. He knows that his staff and their families are welcome here in exchange for helping with security. I also talked to Dr. Cliburn in town. He and his family can't make the watch party, but they'll be here tomorrow night for the welcome festivities. They know they have a place here if something happens, although he prefers to stay in town so the townspeople have access to medical care."

"That's too bad. Hopefully, he'll change his mind. It might get pretty rough in town if something happens." Joel frowned. "Speaking of getting rough, I'm glad my Aunt Betty is coming, but I wish she wasn't bringing her husband."

Rachel laughed. "Why, dear? Just because he is about the laziest, most argumentative person we've ever met? I called Betty yesterday and told her she was going to have to keep Ralph under control or – family or not – he would be out of here. She said he promised to behave, but we need to keep an eye on him. Of all of our invited guests, he is the only one I would expect to cause trouble."

"We need to be sure when we talk to the Chief tomorrow that we have a very specific plan for troublemakers, regardless of whether or not the asteroid strikes. I'm glad we decided to not serve any alcohol during this event, although I'm sure people will bring it in with them. The last thing we need in a crisis is a bunch of people getting drunk. I mean, it would be nice to serve wine with dinner, but I think we'll be fine with the non-alcoholic stuff. I did lock up all of the beer, wine, and alcohol we had in the closet in my office. Don't need to have it around to tempt anyone," Scott said.

"Yeah, especially your Uncle Ralph!" snickered Chris. "Remember the time he came to the barbecue at your house and got drunk as a skunk and was sure the satellite disk on the garage was a ray gun set to kill him? When he started throwing things at the disk, I thought Joel was going to stroke out. It's a good thing you guys tackled him before he did anything too destructive."

Rachel giggled. "Yeah, I was almost hoping the disk would come alive and zap him to get him to stop causing such a ruckus!"

Joel yawned. "Guys, we are going to have to be up really early tomorrow, so we probably ought to get home and get to bed. I'll see you all around six tomorrow morning." He stood up and helped Rachel up as Scott and Chris also got to their feet.

As they were walking back to their house from the lodge, Joel scanned the skies above. The sky was clear, and a million stars could be seen, with no trace of the asteroid visible with the naked eye. Joel prayed that it would stay that way, but in his heart, he knew that come Thursday, the asteroid would arrive, and everything would change for all of them.

Chapter Eleven

March 21

Finally, the big morning arrived and everyone on the ranch was in a state of excitement waiting for the first guests to arrive. In order to eliminate traffic jams at the main entry, Joel stationed two ranch hands at the main gate, and there were signs and balloons leading the way to the main parking lot. Four of the hands were driving the ranch's two horse-drawn buggies to carry people and luggage from the parking lot to the main entry. There were also a number of staff members at the main reception desk waiting to carry luggage for the guests. Gwen and her staff were eagerly awaiting arrival of guests to try out the routines they had been practicing for weeks. Gift baskets for each guest family were neatly stacked behind the counter waiting to be distributed. The staff members were nervously whispering to each other. Suddenly, Gwen's radio buzzed as the staff at the gate called to say the first guests had arrived. Gwen flipped the switch and suddenly music began to play from the many loudspeakers set up for the occasion.

Rachel, Chris, and Stacey were on duty on the front porch to welcome guests as they arrived at the ranch. "This is it," Rachel called out. "This is what we've been waiting for!"

Chris hugged Rachel, and then Stacey. "I'm so excited. Who would have ever thought a lottery ticket would lead to all of this!"

"I'm just so happy you both allowed me to be a part of this!" Stacey exclaimed.

"We wouldn't have it any other way! You're a part of the family now," Chris answered.

As the three stood nervously on the porch, they heard the tinkling of the bells on the horses pulling the first wagon. As the wagon stopped, four of Rachel and Chris' quilting buddies from North Carolina hopped out of the wagon. Amidst squeals and hugs, Rachel and Chris introduced their friends to Stacey. "This first crazy woman is Kathy Harrison and her husband Hank. We've been in lots of classes together, and she always cuts up and makes them fun." As Stacey shook hands with the Harrisons, Rachel introduced the next couple. "Next is Marie

Jarrett and her husband Stan. Marie heads up one of the charity quilt groups for the guild in North Carolina."

"That must be really hard, to spend time making beautiful quilts and then giving them away," Stacey observed.

"Not really," Marie answered. "We put lots of love into those quilts, and then we give them to people who really need to be surrounded with that love. We still make quilts for ourselves to keep, but there is something very special about seeing the reaction of people when they are given a quilt made especially for them."

"I hope we get time to chat, because I'd really like to learn more about what you do," Stacey replied.

"Hey, you're holding up progress here! Next, I want you to meet Francine and her husband Raymond. "Francie and Ray are both quilters, that is, when Ray is not busy being a pilot for a local puddle-jumper company!"

"Wow, I wanted to be a pilot when I was younger, but law school won out," laughed Stacey.

Ray smiled. "You never know… maybe you will still get to be a pilot someday."

Stacey grinned at him and nodded, as Rachel introduced the last couple. "Last, but certainly not least is Aimee Carter and her husband Sam. Aimee is our applique queen. She does the best hand stitching of anyone I know!"

Aimee blushed, as Stacey told her she hoped to be able to see some of Aimee's work while she was there. Finally, Chris, who had been quiet all this time, interrupted. "Guys, we have all week to visit, but there are more people coming. Let me show you where to register and get your room keys."

As the group passed by to go register, Rachel looked at Marie with a grin and asked, "Why am I not surprised that you four are the first ones here?"

Marie giggled. "We actually got here last night and stayed in town. We were all up at five this morning, too excited to wait any longer! We can't wait till you have time to visit with us, and we all brought lots of fabric to try out your new quilting room! We can't wait to see Trina and Mary, too!"

"They'll be glad to see you, too! Oh, and I'm looking forward to introducing all of you to Barbara, who is our local quilt store owner, and to Eileen, the president of our Guild here," said Rachel. She assured the four friends that they would definitely have time to do some quilting and that after they got settled in their cabin, they should come back to the main area for a tour of the ranch.

"We're putting the eight of you into the biggest cabin. It has four bedrooms, so you should have enough room. The guys inside will bring your luggage for you, and all you need to do is go see Gwen at the desk," Chris explained.

After showing their friends to the registration area, Chris returned to the porch to get ready to greet the next group. A few minutes later, Kathy came running back out the front door. "Okay, which one of you made the two quilts hanging in the lobby?" she asked.

Chris looked at her, puzzled. "Rachel made the Semper Paratus quilt and we both made the Serendipity Ranch one. Why?"

Kathy smiled. "Those two quilts are absolutely stunning! I want to learn how to make the Serendipity Ranch one."

"Thank you!" Rachel said. "We'll teach you and anyone else who wants to learn tomorrow."

"Wonderful, I'll look forward to it!" Kathy answered, as she went back to the registration area and her waiting husband.

Soon, the next wagon arrived with another family, and so it began. People were arriving regularly, and occasionally, the wagons were full of people and a four-wheeler accompanied the wagon with a trailer full of luggage. By noon, all of the guests had arrived. Scott and his staff set up a buffet lunch and it was so exciting to see the dining area filled with happy people eating lunch and getting to know their fellow guests. At check-in, each person was given a name tag and asked to wear it, at least for the first day so people could get to know each other. When everyone was seated with food in front of them, Joel, Rachel, Scott, and Chris stood up at a podium placed in the dining area for this purpose.

"Welcome everyone," Joel began. "Welcome to Serendipity Ranch. We are so excited you are here! We've planned a busy five days for all of you! This afternoon, we will be giving tours of the ranch. I know that might not interest the younger kids, and so Lillian and Cheri will be providing activities for the little ones here in the main sitting area. After the tours, we'll give you some time to wander around and take in some of the different activities available here. At five, we ask all of you to assemble in the picnic area outside near the barbecue pit, as we'll be having a Texas-style barbecue. After dinner, we have a surprise for you. Tomorrow, you'll have the choice of horseback riding, a trip to our shooting range, or several other activities listed in the handouts you got at check-in, and a real live rodeo tomorrow evening after dinner. Thursday evening, we will be having an asteroid-watching party out in the field, and we have a number of telescopes for you to use. I'm going to turn things over to Scott, who will tell you about meals."

Scott stood up to the microphone. "I echo Joel when I say how happy we are to see all of you. Meal service will be here in the dining room every day. Breakfast will start each morning at seven and will be buffet style. Lunch will start at 11:30 and will also be buffet. Dinner will be served each evening at five. Tonight, we are hosting the Cowboy Barbecue outside, but the rest of the week, dinner will be served in the dining room. I'll have snacks and drinks out each afternoon and evening for you to help yourselves. If there is anything special you'd like, please let me know and we'll try to accommodate you. Rachel now wants to go over some safety information with you."

"Thanks Scott," said Rachel as she stepped up to the microphone. "We want you to have a fabulous time here, but we also want everyone to be safe. For that reason, the range will remain locked unless there is a Range Safety Officer or RSO available on site. If you want to do some shooting, please let one of us know and we will arrange for the range to be opened for you. Likewise, the pool area is fenced, and the pool is covered for the season. With the March weather we are having, it's probably too cold for swimming, but the hot tub is available. We're happy to remove the pool cover, though, if any of you want to brave the temperatures and swim – keep in mind the pool is not heated! We will not allow any kids under twelve in the area without a parent. We have a couple of lifeguards available, but if they are not present at the pool, you swim at your own risk!

"Next, this is a working ranch, and we have a lot of animals. We want you to be able to see and enjoy our livestock, but please do not go into the barns or corrals without someone to guide you. We will have a petting zoo for the kids (and for the grown-ups too if they want!) so they can see and enjoy some of the baby animals. We have maps and equipment available if you want to go hiking. There's fishing in the lake, and we have a few rowboats available if you don't want to stay on the shore. If you do decide to go hiking or fishing, please let someone know, so we know where to look for you if you're not back in time for a meal. The ranch is huge, and we don't want anyone to have their fun spoiled by getting lost.

"If anyone has any medical issues, please pick up any phone and dial zero. The operator will take your information and get the appropriate help. There are small refrigerators available in each guest room if you have medications that need to be kept cold. All staff here are trained in first aid and first aid kits are available in all activity areas. Last but certainly not least, Chris is going to tell you about services available here."

"You guys are being way too quiet! We want to be sure you are having a good time!" Chris called out.

One of the men yelled back, "We've got our mouths full of Scott's great lunch, but we can get rowdy if you want us too!"

Chris laughed. "Nah, don't get rowdy until I'm done, okay? I want to let you know about services here. We have a full housekeeping staff. If you are comfortable in your room and don't need anything tidied up, just put the *do not disturb* sign on the outside doorknob and housekeeping won't bother you. Otherwise, they will come through daily to freshen and restock your room. If you do choose to swim, there is a cabinet next to the pool with swim towels. Leave these in the hamper in your bathroom and housekeeping will take care of collecting them. The game room, living room, and chapel are available for use twenty-four hours a day. The kids craft area is open and attended from eight in the morning until six at night. Other childcare services can be arranged through the reception staff. The quilting room is open on request. If you need to buy souvenirs to bring home, the gift shop is open daily from eight in the morning until six in the evening.

"As Scott mentioned, the kitchen staff is happy to help you with special requests when possible. We have equipment available for sports such as softball and volleyball. Sorry, but we don't have tennis courts or golfing available. We have a number of bicycles if you want to just ride. If you have need of laundry services, call housekeeping and they will be happy to help you." Chris turned to Rachel. "Rach, am I forgetting anything?"

As Rachel shook her head, Joel's Uncle Ralph called out, "Where's the bar and when does it open?"

Joel stepped up to the microphone. "There is no bar. We decided that for this first test run, we would not offer any alcohol. We believe we can all have fun without the need for booze, and we have plenty of other beverage choices for everyone to enjoy their meals. I hope this is not too upsetting for anyone, but that's just the way it is."

Ralph stood up. "That sucks. I guess I'll just have to go into town and get a couple of bottles."

Joel looked directly at Ralph. "If you do, that's your choice, but you'll need to stay in town if you do. We will not tolerate any disruptive behaviors from anyone, family or not. If anyone acts out in a violent or disruptive manner, they will be escorted off the property. There are kids and families here and we want everyone to have a great time, and not feel threatened by anyone. Do I need to say any more on this?"

Betty grabbed Ralph by the arm and pulled him to his chair. "You don't need to worry, Joel, I'll make him behave!" she called out.

"Thanks, Betty. I'm sorry to have to sound so stern, but we do want everyone to feel safe. Now, with that out of the way, are there any questions?"

There were a few hands raised, so Joel called on his old Army buddy, Frank Willis, first. "Joel, first let me tell you my wife and I are just tickled you invited us, and we want to thank you for that! My question is a serious one. The news is telling us the asteroid isn't going to hit, but Maisie and I are worried that it might. If it does hit, what will happen to all of us who are so far away from home?"

There was a sudden loud murmuring in the crowd, and Joel could tell the crowd's anxiety level ratcheted up by quite a few notches. He tapped on the microphone several times to get everyone's attention. "Frank, you and Maisie are right to be worried. I am worried, too. The news keeps reassuring us that it will be close, but not close enough to do any damage. We are watching the news reports, as well as getting reports from several scientific outlets via the HAM radio. In the event the asteroid hits, assuming it doesn't hit Serendipity Ranch, you are all welcome to stay here until such time as you decide you want to try to get home. If you want to leave right away, we will do what we can to help you. If you choose to stay, that's fine, too. I would ask that we all pray it is just a near miss, but if it is not, we will deal with it. We will talk more about this Thursday, and if anything changes between now and then with the asteroid, we will let you know. Now, please don't spend time worrying about that when we have so many fun activities planned for all of you!"

Joel took a few more questions, mostly about locations and availability of activities, and then said, "We'll give you another 30 minutes to finish lunch, and then we'll begin our tours. If you look on your name tag, you'll see a colored dot. We'll have various colored flags outside the back doors. Please stand near the flag that matches the dot on your name tag, and your tour guide will then take your group."

~~~

By five, all of the tours had returned to the lodge, and the smell of meat being grilled was driving everyone crazy. As the crowd assembled in the picnic area, they could see serving tables laden with vats of baked beans, several kinds of potato and macaroni salads, corn on the cob, trays of deviled eggs, a large raw vegetable tray, and fresh-baked rolls and corn bread. A separate table held an assortment of cakes, cookies, and pastries. Scott walked away from the barbecue pit and rang the large bell, getting everyone's attention.

"We're just about ready to eat. Reverend Arnold, can I ask you to say a blessing before we start?"

"Most certainly, Scott." He folded his hands and bowed his head. "Let us pray. Merciful Father, we thank you for our wonderful hosts and this opportunity to have fun and fellowship with each other. Bless us, O Lord, with your divine grace. Bless these Thy gifts, which we are about to receive from Thy bounty, through Christ our Lord, making us ever mindful of and responsive to the needs of others. In your name, we pray, Amen."

The crowd answered with a loud Amen, and people began to line up for their food. Within a half an hour, everyone was seated in the picnic area with a heaping plate in front of them. When dinner was almost over, Joel stood and introduced a local group of musicians. Dressed in traditional cowboy attire, the group began to play old country western songs, including 'Deep in the Heart of Texas', 'Bury Me Not on the Old Prairie', "Red River Valley', and "The Lone Star Trail". They played for over an hour, and finally finished with a haunting version of Dolly Parton's "I Will Always Love You". They were met with thunderous applause, and since everyone was having such a great time and with permission from Joel, the group kept on playing. Finally, after the last notes of Johnny Cash's 'Ring of Fire' faded away, the band packed up and left. By now, it was dark, and torches had been lit around the picnic area. Some of the families with younger children were rounding the kids up from the playground to head off to bed. Other groups were sitting around the picnic area, chatting with new and old friends while enjoying the glow of the fire in the barbecue pit. After visiting with as many of their friends and family as they could, Joel, Rachel, Scott, and Chris bade everyone a good night and headed into the lodge.

"Wow, for day one, that was pretty spectacular!" Chris said.

"I agree, and it sure is great to see everyone. We're off to an awesome start," Rachel agreed. "I promised our quilting buddies to turn them loose in the quilting room tomorrow, along with several other ladies who also wanted to spend some time playing with fabric. Do you want to quilt with us, or do you have other plans?"

"As much as I would love to spend the day sewing, I promised to spend some time with Scott's niece Katie and her new husband. Since Scott is conveniently tied up in the kitchen, I'll be taking them for a short horseback ride out past the lake. Jimmy Langston is taking a group on a longer horseback ride up into the hills, but I don't want to go that far, and Katie says she is not up to a long ride. Not to change the subject, but I am really proud of how everyone did today. Gwen said registration for everyone went so well, there wasn't a single glitch. Everyone seemed to be happy with their rooms, they loved the little welcome baskets, and all of the luggage showed up in the correct places. Scott, the little bags of cookies you put together for all the kids went over really well, too!"

Scott grinned. "I'd like to take credit for that, but those were Rebecca's doing, not mine. Did you see the cookies? She made little horses and cowboy hats and stagecoaches… really creative and the kids loved them. As a matter of fact, if there are any left, she is putting them out for tonight's bedtime snack." Scott noticed Joel staring at his phone with a worried look on his face. "Earth to Joel, are you okay, buddy?"

Joel's attention snapped back to Scott. "I'm sorry, I was just looking at a news report on my phone. We've gone from a one in 45 million chance of the asteroid hitting to a one in 300 thousand chance. I don't like the odds narrowing so much, even though numbers really don't mean anything at this point. Guys, I know I am being really paranoid about this, but can we four get together tomorrow night after the rodeo to be sure we are all on the same page? I'd like to include the Chief and my friend Frank Willis. Frank makes his living as a security consultant, and I think he can offer up some good ideas on what we will need to do if the asteroid strikes."

The rest of the group thought that was a good idea and agreed to meet in the command center. Scott volunteered to talk to the chief, and Joel promised to have a quiet visit with Frank to bring him up to speed. After spending a few more minutes talking about the day, the two couples went home to get some rest.

Chapter Twelve

Day two started out with a bang, literally, as thunder and lightning raged and the clouds opened up, dumping rain. Luckily, the rain stopped in time for everyone to make it to the lodge for breakfast, but the morning skies remained cloudy. After breakfast, Rachel rounded up her group of quilters. Because of the weather, she had several other people ask to join their group instead of outdoor activities. Still, Joel took a large group to the range and Jimmy had plenty of people to join his horseback-riding group. Liz worked with the childcare group to hold a petting zoo, and the kids loved being able to hold and pet some of the smaller animals.

In the quilting room, Rachel was surprised to see all twenty sewing tables were occupied with two other ladies standing off to the sides. Rachel offered them the use of the treadle machines, but both ladies said they would just help with pressing and cutting if that was okay. Rachel got a couple of folding chairs for them, and soon everyone was busy working together in various projects. Mary and Trina buzzed around the room, offering help, getting supplies and keeping everyone engaged in their projects. Rachel promised to teach her four quilting friends how to make the Lodge's Serendipity quilt block, but as soon as she started, so many others asked to learn, so she finally just gathered everyone around to show them.

"When I first went looking for a block for us to use, I found a lot of quilts named 'Serendipity', all of them different. I didn't find one particular block identified as a Serendipity block, so Chris and I decided to make our own. We both love the woven star pattern, so we put that in the center. We surrounded that with four friendship stars. Our big hope is that our retreat center will lead to us making lots of new quilting friends. Then, we surrounded all of that with a cross to remind us of the way we wanted to live our lives and run our retreat. It may look pretty complicated," she said, holding up the block, "but there are a couple of different ways you can make it depending on how big you want it to be. The first time we made it, we used all half-square triangles and solid squares. We started with a two-inch finished square and it came out to a 24" square block! The second time we tried it, we did a lot of snowballing – have y'all ever snowballed a half-square triangle? – and flying geese, and it still came out pretty big. We decided the half-square triangles gave us a better, flatter block and be much easier to assemble, so that's what we used for the quilt hanging in the lobby. You can control the size of the quilt by the size of the block. The one in the lobby uses a four-inch half-square triangle and we just bordered that and added some flying geese for fun, and that became our Serendipity Ranch quilt!" She quickly passed out a handout with cutting and stitching directions.

As everyone looked at their handouts, Rachel continued, "We made the one you see in the lobby with blue, green, gold, and purple batik, but you can use whatever colorways and fabric you'd like. If you look over the longarm, you'll see the first block we made with just fabrics we had on hand using two-inch finished squares. We didn't put any borders on it, so if anyone wants us to take it down for you to look at while you make your own, we're happy to do that. For those of you who didn't bring fabric or don't want to use what you brought, we've cut a number of fat quarters for you to use. Please help yourselves."

One of the quilting guests raised her hand. "I'm a little new at this. How do I know how big to cut my half-square triangle pieces?"

"That's a great question!" Rachel answered. "Once you decide what size you want them to be finished, you can do one of several things. I have these rolls of half-square triangle pattern paper that you can stitch the fabric to the paper and then when you cut the squares out, they will be the size listed on the roll. Or you can do a quick calculation. Generally, the rule of thumb is to cut your squares for half-square triangles 7/8" larger than the unfinished size. I hate dealing with such small measurements, though, so when I do it, I just cut it an inch larger and then trim my squares. So, if I wanted a half-square triangle to be 4 ½" unfinished, I would cut my fabric squares 5 ½" and once they were done, I'd trim them to 4 ½"."

"But doesn't that waste a lot of fabric?" someone else asked.

"Not really," Rachel responded. We're talking about adding an extra eighth of an inch, so there's not a lot of waste. We do save all of those little snippets, though. Even though they're really tiny, we use them to stuff dog beds."

The room settled down into a warm buzz as fabrics were pressed, cut and people began to sew. Once people got settled at their machines, they began to chat with people at neighboring machines. After a while, what started out as a bunch of strangers morphed into a group of friends.

More experienced quilters were helping newer quilters when they ran into problems. Mary, as usual, kept up a running banter that had everyone entertained and laughing. Everyone was quite startled when Rebecca stuck her head in the door to announce lunch was ready. Not surprisingly, after lunch the group chose to continue working on their quilts rather than participate in outdoor activities, even though the sun was now shining through cloudy skies. Chris returned from her ride with Katie and joined the quilters in the afternoon. By dinnertime, several of the ladies had completed their quilt tops, and asked if they could use the longarm the next day to finish their Serendipity Ranch quilts.

After dinner, the guests all assembled on the bleachers next to one of the horse corrals. They were treated for over an hour to a demonstration of cowboy skills. Jeff rode his Appaloosa and Jimmy rode his Percheron, and both were able to get their horses to do amazing stunts. Some of the ranch hands demonstrated how to rope a calf. The pups being trained as herding dogs demonstrated herding a small group of sheep (with only a couple of cute mistakes!). The final demonstration was a bull-riding exhibition by Jimmy. Many people were quite nervous watching Jimmy on the bull, but the ranch hands dressed as rodeo clowns kept everyone laughing. Finally, when the last of the animals left the rodeo and were safely in their barns, Joel announced a firework show. For the next 40 minutes, the guests were entranced to see the beautiful fireworks set to patriotic music. After the last boom, as the final embers faded away, the crowd broke up to go back to their rooms for the evening. Even though it was late, the two couples, along with the Chief and Frank made their way to the conference table in the command center for a discussion.

Joel started the conversation. "We are here this evening to discuss our security needs in the event the asteroid hits. I don't think there will be problems inside our fences, but I am worried about problems coming from outside. Chief, we asked you and Frank here to see if you could help us devise a plan for security in the event things get dicey. We've already done a few things. We have good communications available with radios, although I expect they won't work well if there's a lot of ash in the air. We have remote-controlled cameras every 25 feet along the entire perimeter of the ranch, with additional cameras around the lodge, cabins, and barns. Each camera position also has a motion-sensor light, but power has not been turned on to the lights yet. That is just a quick connection of the wires here at the lodge.

"All staff have been trained to be competent with both handguns and rifles. Almost all staff are proficient with horseback riding. We also have a fleet of four-wheelers that can be used to patrol. The property is surrounded by an eight-foot game fence which has been reinforced with small diameter chain link in some of the areas we thought it would be easy to breech the game fence. We've cut back foliage to ten feet on both sides of the fence, and the entire fence has been wired to be electrified. We can control the electrification remotely from the lodge. We also cut down any trees outside the fence that were overhanging. Our plan was to have our staff ride in small groups to patrol the fence and watch for problems, but that doesn't seem like it's enough."

"I ran about 40 people through the range today and learned we have a number of excellent shooters. In addition, out of that 40, five have law enforcement experience and sixteen have military experience. We also have a retired Texas ranger in our group. One of our military personnel – Stacey's brother William - is actually a sniper. It was amazing to see him pick off the targets at the 100- and 200-yard lines, and his buddy Tom is almost as good as he is!

Chris interjected, "Where is Stacey? Did anyone invite her?"

Rachel answered, "I talked to her, but she felt it would be better for her to be with her guests this evening. I think she wants to give Will and Tom a heads up on our planning so far."

Joel cut in. "Yes, she talked to me, and we decided without giving away all the details, we would let the guys in on some of the security decisions we've made so far and see how they may be able to help. We didn't want to bring them here since we don't know what their skills are – other than sniping! – and we didn't want this meeting to get too big. So Chief, what do you think so far?"

"Well, y'all have made a good start, I suppose," answered the Chief. "If this hits, I am obligated to get to the town to oversee safety there, but I'd like to leave my family here, if that is alright with all of you."

Rachel interrupted, "Of course it's okay. Plus, if any of your officers want to bring their families here, they are welcome to do so."

The Chief looked surprised. "That would sure take a lot of worries off my officers. In any case, getting back to your security, let's be sure we all have each other's radio frequencies. We can set that up in the morning. We will be patrolling the town to watch for problems, and if you all are threatened by anything you can't handle, call us and we'll respond. How are you set for weapons?"

Scott snickered when Joel answered, "we have plenty of weapons. Between what we had and what we've purchased, we're good. Plus, we've got a good stock of rifle and handgun ammo. and Scott and I both reload, so we're good there. When we knew we were going to run a range, Scott and I both got our Federal Firearms license so we could purchase what we needed. We also bought some non-lethal tear gas grenades and flash-bangs, although we don't have real grenades. We have two Barrett .50s and our sniper brought his own weapon – would you believe a CheyTac M200 Intervention rifle? I'd never seen one before, but he tells me it is accurate out to almost 6000 yards! Anyway, that is about all we have. Oh, and we also have a lot of fireworks left over from tonight's show."

"Wow! I hope this asteroid misses us because I'd sure like to come fire that CheyTac if he'll let me!" laughed the chief. "I can get you all some grenades tomorrow. I doubt I can spare more than a case, though. How are you set for ballistic protection?"

Joel answered, "We purchased 20 male modular vests and 10 female ones. They are all equipped with armor, stomach, and low back protection. We also bought 30 kevlar helmets, eye protection and gloves. Each staff member has custom fitted combat boots and an armored combat shirt. I've got six sets of night vision glasses and two pair of night vision binoculars. Plus, we've trained all of the staff on how to use the protection."

"Damn, you're better equipped than most of my staff, I think! Now, tomorrow night, I'll be there for the party, and I'm bringing a couple of my officers with me. That's a good chance for their families to slip in relatively unnoticed. If anyone gets out of hand, we'll arrest them on the spot. If the asteroid does hit, and I honestly believe it will, my officers and I will have to leave right away to get back to town."

Scott spoke up again. "Chief, I can't help but wonder about all the people in town. Has anyone done anything to prepare them?"

The chief nodded. "Yes, a couple of the churches have been passing out information on how to prepare, but the mayor has been pretty vocal about not 'scaring' the population. He thinks all the talk about the asteroid hitting is conspiracy theory from the extreme right-wing lunatics. Guess he doesn't realize his police department must be right-wing lunatics, because we are all pretty convinced. The mayor won't be in town for the event, though, as he and a couple of the other mayors in this area are headed to Austin in the morning for the big asteroid watching party being put on by the Texas Democratic party.

"I think most of the ranches and farms around here are prepared, although not to the extent y'all are. I've heard that quite a few people are planning to go up north towards Oklahoma or over to Austin to get a better view of the asteroid – in fact, they've got a couple of busses rented to get them there. Guess they aren't thinking much of how they'll get home in the event it hits, and quite frankly, if they are so stupid as to go, they really don't need to come back. I know that the city got a stock of emergency supplies a few weeks ago from Homeland Security, and I used a good chunk of my budget to order in extra rations for my officers.

"My biggest worry is that the town is overrun. If that happens, my plan would be to fall back to here and supplement your security with my officers. I expect if there is much in the way of ash falling, we will lose citizens with lung problems or who don't wear a mask to go out. I also expect that if power fails, we'll lose a few as well. I pray that things will stay calm in town, but I don't expect it. Even though we only have a few thousand residents, we have enough troublemakers that I expect will stir up problems. That reminds me, I'll bring you a box of zip ties in case you have to detain anyone."

Rachel laughed. "Good, we can zip tie your Uncle Ralph to the barn if he misbehaves!"

Everyone laughed, and Joel explained Rachel's comments to the chief. The chief laughed but advised them seriously not to let anyone get away with bad behavior. He explained that people may do stupid things when they are scared, but that the group would need to put a stop to anything stupid or malicious before people got hurt.

"Look," said Joel, "if things start to break down in town and you come across good people who need a safe place to stay, especially kids, please contact me and we'll see about taking them in. We can't take the whole town, but we will do what we can."

"I appreciate that, my friend. Meanwhile, say your prayers that this is all just a drill, and the asteroid passes us by."

"We have been praying fervently for that. Now, Frank, you've been awfully quiet while the Chief was talking, but I am sure you've got some stuff to tell us."

Frank grinned. "Well, let me preface what I am about to say by assuring the Chief that as long as society exists, we won't be breaking any laws. If the asteroid hits, though, all bets are off. I am going to speak hypothetically for now, mostly so I don't get arrested!"

The chief laughed. "I promise, we are only talking, and I won't arrest you for anything you say *hypothetically*."

"Oh, good. The first thing I would recommend is setting this office up as a real command center. In the military, commanders have a staff to help the commander run their units to stay organized. We need to set a similar system up here, and I would suggest we implement that right away."

Joel looked at Frank questioning, "Are you talking about the S1 and S2 and all that?"

Frank smiled. "That is exactly what I mean. I know you two knuckleheads were in the military, but I doubt either of you ever served on a command staff, so I'll talk you all though it. We won't be as formal as the military, but it will help you all stay organized. I am going to modify a few of the roles to fit our situation here if you all don't mind. Rachel, do you have any heavy paper or card stock?"

Rachel got up and went over to a file cabinet. She pulled out a stack of card stock and a couple of markers and handed them to Frank.

"This is perfect," Frank said, as he began to fold the card stock making table tent cards. He then began to label the cards. "Let's see, Rachel, you are going to be the Commanding General." He put a labeled tent in front of her. "That means everyone reports to you, and your job is to make sure everyone else is doing their job."

Frank placed a tent card in front of Scott. "The first area is called G1 and relates to personnel. Scott, this will be your area. That means you'll oversee meals, housing, sanitation, and other human needs. You'll also oversee medical needs. If I remember correctly, you have a few medical people here, so you'll want to find the most qualified and make that person your chief medical officer. You'll also need to appoint someone to watch out for environmental sanitation- making sure things stay clean, safe, and healthy. This includes garbage disposal, bug issues, latrines if needed, and things like that." Scott took a deep breath and began jotting down notes.

Frank put another table card down on the table. "The second area is G2, and this is your intelligence section. Stacey isn't here, but I think this will be her section. Her brother and his friend would both be very helpful to us in gathering important information, as will Stacey."

Rachel raised her hand. "What kind of intelligence are we talking about?"

Frank smiled at her. "Everything from gathering weather reports to what is happening in the community, to what is happening in the world. The reason I suggested William and Tom is that both are experienced in covert operations, meaning they are both sneaky fellas, and can go places to get information the rest of us probably can't."

Rachel nodded, and thanked Frank. He went on, "Third is G3, operations. Joel, you will be responsible for this area. You will oversee the physical plant, maintenance of all buildings on site, oversee the management and health of the livestock, and ensure daily operations are carried out. In other words, you will make sure this ranch continues to function in the best possible way."

Joel took the tent card with his name on it and set it in front of him.

Frank continued, "The next area is G4, logistics. Chris, this is yours. You are going to be responsible for several things. I know you've already been managing the supplies for the ranch, but you'll have other things to oversee as well. You'll need to appoint someone to take care of tracking all supplies. That includes what you have now, what guests may have that will be needed, and supplies you don't have that will need to be found or salvaged later on. Once things settle down, you will probably need to coordinate with your team for salvage teams to go out into the community to obtain things that the ranch needs. I'm not talking about taking things from people," he continued, noting Chris' shocked look, "but finding things that have been abandoned. You will also oversee transportation, including vehicle maintenance and procurement. Again, appoint someone."

"The next section is G5, which is officially called civil-military operations. I will take this area and will change it to mean internal and external security. I will coordinate with the chief and his officers and will oversee all security measures to keep the ranch and its occupants safe. I will also oversee training people to participate in the defense of the ranch."

Joel cut in, "We've already started some of that training with staff. They all know how to shoot and a few other things."

"That's great," Frank answered. "We're going to kick it up a few notches, though, so we can be sure we are really keeping everyone safe. The last area is G6, our communications section. This person will be responsible for communications coming into and leaving command. I would like to recommend Gwen for this role, as she communicates very clearly. Part of her role would be acting as a public information officer – in other words, keeping people informed and squelching rumors that could lead to panic. She would also oversee the communications systems here on the ranch, monitoring the HAM, and establishing ways to communicate information with everyone rapidly. I expect cell phones and land lines will go pretty quickly after the event, and I don't know how well supplied you all are with walkie talkies or radios and such, and we don't have time now to go through that.

Frank looked around to see a mix of expressions on everyone's faces. "Does this system make sense to everyone and is everyone okay with the way I've broken out assignments?"

Rachel was the first to speak. "Yes, it does make sense. As the commanding general, though it doesn't seem like I have much to do."

Frank laughed. "Ah, Rachel, you'll be the busiest one of all, because you will be making sure you know exactly what the rest of us are doing all the time. We will come to you whenever we run into problems, and you will give final approval to anything we do outside of routine things. So, when Chris has a team going out for salvage, she will need to run it by you for permission. When Scott wants Joel to build another bunkhouse for more housing, they will both need to run it by you. You are the checks and balances. We will meet at least daily as a team to give brief reports, let me emphasize BRIEF, on what we're doing and to address any issues going on. This is where we will all work as a team to combine each of our areas into a smooth operation."

Frank was happy to see everyone nodding and agreeing. "Okay, then. Now that we have that taken care of, I have some immediate security concerns that I'd like to present. First of all, I would recommend we make some defensive weapons to use on our perimeters in the event an attack seems likely. I doubt it would happen for a couple of weeks, as long as there are groceries to be had in town and the ash is falling. We can make cannons, claymores, and a few other exploding devices to start with- I've been poking around the barns and you've got most of the supplies we would need. What I didn't see, I suspect you have locked up somewhere, knowing you, Joel!" He and Joel laughed and bumped fists.

"I also recommend we prepare some better lighting for the front fences, especially for the area on either side of the gate, that we can turn on if we need it. Bright lights on a dark night can blind attackers and throw them off. I would also suggest that we get that excavator busy and dig some fox holes for our guards. A few fortified areas along the fence would be good, too, maybe earthen berms big enough to protect the horses as well as the guards. First thing in the morning, Joel, you and I need to take a ride along the fence to see where we need to place those areas. I saw that you had a lot of barbed wire in the storage barn. We might want to string that around the living areas of the ranch, just in case someone gets through the fence, it will slow them down some."

The group spent a few more minutes discussing the organization of the command staff, training staff already had, additional training that may be needed, and how they would handle discussing all of this with their guests the following day. Joel closed the meeting reminding everyone that tomorrow may be the day that changed their lives forever, and they had best get some rest now because who knew when they might be able to get a full night's sleep after tomorrow. He suggested the full command team get together tomorrow after lunch so they could begin to make job assignments for each of their areas. "I think we are going to be really busy in the morning getting ready for the asteroid to hit, but by lunch time, we should have teams doing the major things and we should be able to break away to meet." Joel explained.

~~~

Early the next morning, Joel and Rachel were awakened by Joel's cell phone ringing. He shook his head and looked at the clock, seeing it was only 4:00 AM, but when he saw it was a call from the chief he answered right away.

"I'm sorry to call you so early, but I was just checking my email. I got a priority encrypted notice from the state putting us all on alert. Apparently, the scientists have narrowed the odds of the asteroid hitting us as 'highly probable.' They don't give any numbers but recommended that we be prepared for the asteroid to strike sometime this evening. The email also went on to say that at this point, the government will not alert the public to prevent panic." He mumbled a few swear words to describe his opinion of the government, and continued, "I've already called my officers and except for the ones on routine patrol, they will all be coming here in the morning to meet with us. They are rounding up all of the officers' families and will be transporting them here in the morning. I wish I could get you numbers, but other than telling you I have sixteen officers, I honestly don't know how many family members will show up."

"That's fine, Chief. Tell them to be sure they bring clothes, whatever food they may have, and especially winter clothes, blankets, and pillows. If they have small children, they should bring things like play pens and strollers, too. We have some cribs, but if they can bring any, we'd appreciate it. Oh, and bring toys to keep the kids entertained, too. I will change today's activities and we will address the group right after breakfast."

"Thanks Joel. I am headed to town in a few minutes to coordinate all of this, but I will be back to meet with my offers and you all around 10 if that's okay."

"That works, Chief, thanks for the warning, and you stay safe."

"You, too, Joel."

Rachel, who had overheard the entire conversation, began to cry. Joel held her for a minute, tears pouring down his own face as well. Finally, they pulled apart. "Come on, Honey, we've got to get dressed and let Scott, Chris and Stacey know. Then, we'll need to plan what to say to everyone at breakfast. I think it would be best if we cancelled most of the activities we had planned for today to get organized."

Rachel nodded and wiped her eyes. They both dressed quickly and headed next door to wake Chris and Scott. As Scott and Joel headed for the lodge, Rachel and Chris went to get Stacey. A few minutes later, the three women were in the dining area drinking large cups of coffee.

Several staff members were already in the dining room, and a few more drifted in as Joel and Scott began to let them know what was happening. Joel pulled the large whiteboard out of the library and was making lists.

"We'll need a group to get out to the solar farm and take down the panels. There is room to store them in the pole barn. Steve is already planning to cover the pastures closest to the barns with tarps. We'll need him to do that sooner rather than later. Once the sun is up, someone needs to call Dr. Cliburn and see if they can convince him to come out here for the duration. Scott, we need to start the rationing plan you developed, so don't let your staff cook too much, and let's save all the frills. We need to get the military tents set up and the cots assembled, because with the police families and staff families, we're going to have a lot of extra people. Once we figure out who's staying and who decides to leave, we may need to rearrange room assignments. After we talk to the staff, we'll need to get a couple of people guarding the front gate and start patrolling the fence. I don't expect any trouble today, but it doesn't hurt to start right away. I'll get the motion lights hooked up today. We'll also need to get busy on the fortifications and fox holes. I'll see if Frank would just take responsibility for getting that done. Stacey, will your brother and Tom stay here, or will they try to get back to their units?"

"Well, since Will is stationed in Japan, and Tom is stationed in Alaska, they both feel like this is not going to be an opportune time to travel, and so both of them are available to you for whatever you need them to do."

"Excellent," Joel continued. "When the asteroid strikes, we won't get ejecta right away unless it is relatively close. I am guessing we will have at least 24 hours before we start to see any kind of ash fall. Still, we need to get a team wrapping all of our buildings and the covered walkways with plastic. We need to get the extra filters attached to all of the equipment today. We'll need to get the shutters on the windows for the chicken coop before they wrap it." Joel paused. "There are so many things to do, I'm so glad now that we planned for all of this because could you imagine starting from scratch right now?"

~~~

Joel sent out staff to wake up the rest of the employees and all the guests and have them assemble in the dining room at 7:00. Scott had a hearty breakfast ready, and people were filling plates as they arrived. At 7:15, the room was full of anxious people. Joel stood at the podium and addressed the crowd.

"I am sorry to get all of you up so early on what should have been a vacation day in paradise. However, very early this morning, I was informed that NASA determined there is a very high probability that the asteroid is going to hit this evening." Joel paused as the air seemed to leave the room. All across the room, there were shocked faces, and more than one person began to cry. "As I told you Tuesday, we suspected this might happen and we made plans for ways we could survive. As I said on Tuesday, every one of you is welcome to stay here where we can assure you you'll be reasonably safe. If you feel you need to leave, please let us know before you go, and we will be sure you have food and water for your journey. We hope nobody will leave, but we trust you know what is best for you and your family. No one is a prisoner here, and we won't stop anyone from leaving, but we highly discourage it. If you choose to stay, once the asteroid hits, we will all need to work together to make sure we give ourselves the best chance possible to not only survive the catastrophe, but to thrive in spite of it. This morning, we will be getting a few more guests – the families of the police officers in town will be staying with us, along with family members of our resident staff. Because we need to get ready, we are cancelling the planned activities for this morning. As you can see on the whiteboard behind me, there are a number of things that we need to get done for everyone's protection. If you are able to help with any of those items, we would certainly appreciate it. Over the course of this morning, we will be speaking with each of you individually to assess skills and determine how we can best use your skills to help us survive. For now, let me have a show of hands. How many of you are healthcare personnel?"

Eight hands were raised. One older gentleman stood up. "My name is Dr. Richard Hawthorne, and I am a retired family practice physician. I would be happy to assist with providing medical services."

Another man waved his hand. "I'm a dentist," he called out. The other six included a pharmacy tech, four nurses and a physical therapist.

"Thank you," Joel said. "How many people do we have with any form of law enforcement, military, or security experience?" Eighteen hands were raised. He continued to call out other professions that the group determined would be necessary.

"As I said, we'll be talking to you further to identify other skills you may have. Even things you do for hobbies might be a needed skill. We are all in this together, and we WILL survive! This morning is going to be very busy. I would suggest that the little kids be allowed to continue with their activities, and if there are a couple of parents who might want to stick around and help keep the kids calm, we would appreciate it. I'd like to open the floor up to questions, but we need to keep our time here short as there is so much that needs to be done before tonight. And yes, we will still have the telescopes out in the field, and we will still have an asteroid-watching party tonight. I'm just not sure how much of a party it might be, but we will see. Questions?"

One of the ladies who had been quilting yesterday raised her hand. "I read that if the asteroid hits land anywhere there would probably be a lot of dust that stayed in the atmosphere, causing something like a nuclear winter and making the temperatures drop. We brought jackets with us, but we don't have anything like winter coats. Is there a way we can buy coats and warmer clothes?"

Joel asked, "How many people here would need warmer clothes if that happened?" About 40 people raised their hands. He turned back to the lady who asked the question. "We have a stock of winter gear, and I believe there should be enough for everyone who will need it to work outside. Next?" Several other hands went up, and he called on a young man sitting near the front.

"I see on your list that you are taking down the solar panels. What will we do for electricity if that happens?"

"I'm really glad you asked that. Right now, we are on grid power. I don't know how long that will last, but we have many back-ups including a huge battery bank that is at full power this morning and a commercial generator like the kind the army uses to power its tent cities. We also have two wind turbines. If something happens to keep them from working, we also have a number of smaller wind turbines that we can set up and use. I would ask, though, that when we lose grid power, we would appreciate it if everyone would be very mindful of using electricity. Don't leave lights on if you're not using them, and please avoid using the microwaves in your rooms if you can. We'll also limit how much we use the commercial dryers, as they take a lot of power. We'll hang clotheslines outside as soon as any ashfall stops."

"What will we do if there is ash fall? We can't breathe that stuff. How will we get from our rooms to the lodge or wherever we need to be?"

"Another great question. Once the ash starts, you can't go outside without protection. We will provide you with masks and eye protection. Our quilting group started making masks with filters in them yesterday,

113

and they will continue working on that this morning. We bought plenty of the filter material to go inside the masks, so everyone will be protected. We also have hoods for our animals that need to be outside such as horses and our security dogs. We will try to keep most of our activities indoors, but for those who have to be outside, please don't worry, we'll make sure you'll be protected. We'll be delivering breakfast and lunch to your cabins, but we will still have dinner here in the dining room. We've engineered transportation to pick you up from your cabins and deliver you safely here to the lodge. We'll let you know what time to be ready. We'll also be planning on entertainment for you either before dinner, after dinner, or both. Also, we have a large stock of games, cards, puzzles and other things to help you pass time during the day while you are in your cabins. Please be sure you take a couple of them with you tonight. Bring them back with dinner each day and trade for something for the next day. Of course, some of you we hope will not be in cabins but will be helping us with various things, and we don't expect the fall of ejecta to last longer than a week or so.

"We are also wrapping all buildings with plastic this morning to try to keep the ash out of our buildings. Please do not cut or disturb the plastic in any way. While we're on the topic of ash fall and other things the asteroid might cause, we do expect some earthquakes, although we expect them to be mild. If you've never been in an earthquake before, it can be a little unsettling. If you are outside, you may want to sit down on the ground in an open area away from trees and buildings. If you are indoors, stay away from outer walls and windows. Also, stay away from fireplaces and large pieces of furniture like bookshelves. Try to stay near inside walls. You may want to crawl under a desk or sturdy table. If you are in bed and can't get up, cover yourself with blankets and pillows. Make sure you have shoes handy, and don't try to walk anywhere without shoes, as there may be debris. One of the things on the list today is to tape all of the windows. We'll also be moving fragile items such as our oil lamps to a safer place. You can help by looking at things in your rooms to ensure there are not any dangerous items that could fall and hurt you. You don't need to worry about art on the walls-those are all securely fastened to the wall and have plexiglass, not glass fronts. I expect we will feel earthquakes almost right away after the strike, and then may feel some aftershocks, especially if the strike triggers any of the major fault lines. You'll be happy to know that there are no major fault lines in Texas."

The room got very quiet, and there were no further hands raised. Joel asked Reverend Arnold to say a prayer for their protection and comfort. Reverend Arnold stood and prayed for about five minutes. When he was finished, there were a few murmured Amens, but the crowd remained very quiet. Joel told everyone to finish breakfast, and that he would address everyone again at lunch with any new information. He also reminded them that people would be coming around to get information, and that if anyone was willing to help with the various projects, he would appreciate it. He also reminded everyone to go check their rooms and make sure anything loose was either put in a dresser or closet or put on the floor.

Gwen, her receptionists, and Marcie were given the task of interviewing all guests and staff to find out occupations, skills, and useful hobbies. Using an index card for each person, they split up and began interviews. Meanwhile, Joel organized groups of staff and volunteers to begin to tackle some of the larger jobs on the list. Scott's crew put together a simple buffet lunch of soup and sandwiches, and then prepared the same for the evening meal. Scott wanted them to be finished with all cooking by late afternoon so the gas in the kitchen could be turned off and the kitchen made safe from any earthquake activity that might occur.

At ten, the police chief and his officers arrived, along with three school buses of family and supplies. The buses were parked near the military tents that were being assembled, and the family members went to help get cots set up inside the tents. The chief found Joel and pulled him aside.

"I got word from Homeland that they expect the asteroid will strike this evening sometime around 7:30 our time. They are projecting a hit into the Pacific Ocean but can't be specific about where in the Pacific. I brought you the case of grenades I promised. I also have a case of smoke grenades and a box of zip ties. Plus, I brought you a box of body bags." Joel looked shocked. The chief continued, "Homeland delivered several cases of them to my office last night. I hope you don't need these, but, well, you've got them if you do need them. I gave the boxes to Noah, and he said he would take care of putting them away for you."

"Thanks, Chief. How are your officers holding out?" Joel asked.

"They are doing a lot better now that their families are here with you. I am leaving three of my officers here to support your security team. One is my detective Jennifer Murray. She is pregnant, and I don't think she needs to be out on the streets in town. The other two are rookies who would probably get themselves killed in town but who can be helpful to you. All three are outfitted with weapons, ammo and protective gear."

"We'll take all the help we can get. Thanks." Joel escorted the chief and his officers to the library, and they spent the next hour discussing how the ranch would provide security and how the officers would respond if the ranch called for help. The chief closed the meeting by thanking Joel for the ranch's support and for their willingness to keep the officers' families safe. As the Chief was leaving, Joel stopped him. "Hey, Chief, you know, I always call you Chief, and I'm not sure I even know your name other than your initials FF. Don't you think we're working close enough that you could share your real name?"

The chief grinned. "My real name is Fritz Frederick Muldoon – German mother and Irish father. Now you know why I prefer to be called Chief!"

Joel laughed and shook hands with the chief. "You stay safe in town, Chief. We'll be talking to you soon."

~~~

As planned, right after lunch, the command staff got together, including Stacey and Gwen, and began to outline responsibilities and make assignments. Chase, his son Jason, and Stacey's brother Bill were sent into town to purchase all of the communication equipment and barbed wire they could find. Scott sent Dr. Hawthorne and three of the healthcare workers to town to purchase as much medication and other medical supplies as they could. Most of the guests were quickly involved in various projects, leaving only the children to enjoy planned activities.

~~~

The day progressed quickly, and by dinnertime, everyone looked exhausted and very stressed. Unbelievably, the various teams got all of the critical tasks done and then some. Chase's group was able to buy out a good stock of walkie talkies and radios, enough so that all critical personnel had some means of communications. Frank was happy to see the huge rolls of barbed wire they brought back, and immediately began directing his security team where to place the wire. Dr Hargrove was successful at obtaining a number of basic medications, and he and his team began to interview all of the visitors to determine any pressing medical needs.

The officers' families all got settled into the military tents, and the chief's wife, Sheila, came to let Joel know that there were no problems with them. The heaters in the tents worked well, and since the tents had floors, they were able to set up an area where the kids could play in the tent. Joel reminded Sheila that the kids were welcome to be included in the children's' activities going on, but she said that understandably, the moms wanted their kids close right now. Only two families decided to try to make their way home while they still could. Each family was provided with two gallons of water and a bag of snacks and reminded they could come back if they needed to. Several of the families who lived in town went home to get important items and then returned to the ranch, believing they were safer at the ranch than at home.

After dinner, everyone went out to the field where a number of telescopes were set up. Skies had been cloudy during most of the day but cleared up late in the afternoon. Suddenly, the asteroid was visible to the naked eye. Lines formed at each telescope so people could see Higgens-Moss up close, but many people were content to just sit on the blankets and stare. Scott reminded everyone that if the asteroid appeared to strike in the distance, everyone should sit or lay on the ground until any tremors or air blast passed. Everyone was quite solemn as they watched the asteroid approaching. Suddenly, there was an explosion in the sky, and the asteroid split into several large chunks. All of the chunks turned to fireballs as they entered the atmosphere. The largest chunk flew due west, but several of the smaller ones headed off more to the southwest. It only took a few minutes for the flaming balls of rock to pass overhead. Everything was deathly still for a few moments and people were afraid to even whisper. People were holding their loved ones tight, many with their eyes closed. Suddenly, the earth shook, and a great wind passed over the assembled crowd. The shaking was enough to cause children to cry, but not enough to cause any major damage to buildings. Several people who had been standing fell over, and everyone was terribly frightened. Rachel was holding on to Joel. As the shaking slowed down, she looked around at the people closest to her. Chris and Scott had their arms around each other and around Gwen.

Marcie and Billy were protecting baby William. Liz was crying on Noah's shoulder, and he was gently patting her back. Jimmy Langston was likewise comforting Rebecca as she cried on his shoulder. Stacey was trying unsuccessfully to be brave while holding one of Tom's children. All across the crowd, people were gently comforting each other. Even cousin Ralph was hugging his wife and speaking kindly to her. Rachel let go of Joel as he tried to stand and caught Chris' eye. "We're going to make it, Chris, you know we are," she whispered.

Chris smiled back through her tears. "I know. We're ready for this….." Her voice faded off as she whispered, "I hope to God that we are ready…."

As Joel and Scott stood to address their guests, a sudden gasp went up from the crowd. People began pointing to the west, as a red glow filled the horizon. Several more tremors hit, but people remained sitting on the ground.

Joel picked up his microphone. "Well, folks, now we have our answer as to whether the asteroid would hit or not. If you are on security duty, please report to your stations. Everyone else, please return to your rooms and look for damage. Let us know right away if you find anything broken. Please stay in your rooms tonight unless you have been assigned duties elsewhere. Breakfast will start at seven tomorrow morning, and we will hopefully have more information for everyone then. Come to the main dining room for breakfast unless there is ash or ejecta falling. If that's the case, we'll bring breakfast to you. If anything further happens this evening, we will let you know. Please pray for our safety, for our loved ones, and for the people wherever these things landed. Life may not seem any different at the moment, but our whole world just changed. It is up to us to ensure the new world we create is a positive one."

By now, most of the crowd was in tears, and Joel was having trouble speaking, as his voice was shaking badly. He and Scott stood, arms around each other's shoulders, watching as people gathered their things and headed back to their lodgings.

"Let's get see if we can get anything on TV or the HAM to see if we can at least find out how far these things landed." Scott agreed, and the two headed with their families back to the lodge.

Several more tremors hit as they were walking back. Everyone was alert to damage, but nobody saw anything. They turned on the big TV in the lodge sitting area to see fuzzy pictures of the asteroid calving over Chicago. The scene cut back to the news anchor.

...we are being told that after the asteroid exploded, the biggest piece landed to the southwest off the coast of California. We have no contact with our affiliates in Los Angeles or San Francisco, but the National Oceanic and Atmospheric Administration has put out a tsunami warning for all of the west coast, Alaska, and Hawaii. The smaller pieces landed in coastal waters near Lima, Peru and in the southern Pacific Ocean...

The announcer paused to read a sheet of paper she was handed. She looked shocked.

...We are now being told that most of southern California and northern Mexico has received severe damage from the impact. We are also learning....

Suddenly, the room began to shake with the strongest tremor yet, lasting almost four minutes. The picture on the TV screen shook and jiggled, showing that the tremors extended to the studio in Dallas.

.... Are we still on air? Okay, I'm sorry folks, that was a pretty strong tremor we just felt here in Dallas....

She looked up as a producer handed her yet another bulletin.

...The United States Geological Service just informed us the San Andreas and Cascadian fault lines...this is so hard to believe ... the San Andreas is experiencing a major earthquake rated as over 9.5 on the moment magnitude scale. The Cascadian fault is also letting loose at over 10 on the Moment Magnitude scale. The New Madrid ...

Suddenly, the television screen went black, and the people in the lodge felt more very strong tremors. They could hear items being shaken off shelves and one of the glass panes alongside the fireplace shattered.

Rachel and Chris were sitting on the couch, and both screamed as the window shattered. "I'm so glad we took down anything on a shelf that could fall and break," she shouted to Chris.

"Me, too. I hope we don't lose too many windows, because we don't have all that much replacement glass."

Rachel stood up. "It's time we get all of our command team together. Joel, can you find Frank and Stacey? Have them meet us in the command center." Just then, Frank entered the lodge.

"I was out getting the security teams started. Will and Tom are both taking a team tonight on the perimeter, we've got people at the gate, and the extra lights and barbed wire are all in place." Frank stated.

Rachel nodded at him. "Great. Come on, we're going to meet as soon as Joel gets Stacey."

Ten minutes later, the command team was assembled in the conference room. As soon as everyone was seated, Rachel began. "This has been an absolutely hellatious day, but I felt like we needed to get together tonight to see where we're at in terms of our guests, security, and everything else. Security first. Frank?"

"Security is good at the moment. Teams are out, we've got experienced people in place, and everything seems to be working as planned."

"Thanks, Frank." Rachel then looked at Scott. "Anything with personnel?"

"Well, we had two families leave, insisting they had to try to get home. One family was worried about getting home to see if their house was okay, and the other was worried about some elderly neighbors. We gave each family two gallons of water and a bag with a couple of meals' worth of sandwiches and snacks. We told both families they could come back if they needed to. On a different note, we had three people injured in the earthquakes, none seriously. One of the guests fell and sprained his wrist pretty badly. Dr. Hawthorne checked him out and wrapped his wrist. We had a kid fall and skin both his knees, and another kid got a bump on his head when something fell on him during one of the quakes. Both kids are fine. Nothing else regarding personnel to report at the moment."

"Rachel smiled tiredly at him. "Thanks, Scott. Chris, anything?"

"Nope. Too early for me to have anything to report."

"No news is good news, I guess," Rachel said. She looked at Stacey. "Stacey? Anything to report?"

"Not really. I suspect the New Madrid fault zone just let loose. I was watching the news on TV and just as they were about to talk about it, there was another quake, and the TV went dark."

"We were watching the same program, and I think you're right. That won't have a direct impact on us here, though, will it?" Rachel asked.

"Not directly, but depending on how bad it was, it can essentially cut the country in half, wiping out all crossings over the Mississippi River. That can have a huge impact on us up the road, but not for a while."

"Let's deal with that later. Unless it is going to affect us in the next twelve hours, let's put off discussion until morning." Stacey nodded as Rachel then looked at Joel.

"Joel, how about damages?"

"I'm really not sure yet," Joel answered. "We're going to have to wait until morning to get a handle on it. I do know we are going to have to do something right away about the window next to the fireplace, though. I will hopefully know more at our six AM meeting."

"Does anyone have any other concerns right at this moment? I mean, aside from asteroids, earthquakes and a possible apocalypse?" Rachel looked around and everyone was shaking their heads. "Okay, then let's call it a day. I'd suggest if you can, you should all get some rest. Tomorrow will be a crazy day, I'm afraid. I'll see you all here at six," Rachel said.

Chapter Thirteen

Around midnight, one of the two families who left to go home returned to the lodge with stories of the interstates being backed up for miles, gas stations with miles-long lines, and grocery stores being mobbed. They reported getting in line to get gas at one station when the power suddenly went out. People in line panicked and gunshots were heard in the dark, so the family turned the car around, drove over the grass, and headed back to the lodge. They said going through town, they saw looters at the grocery store in town, and reported all the glass windows and doors on the front of the store were broken. They also reported seeing a number of fires in and around town, and that some streets in town were flooding.

~~~

Throughout the night, several families from town arrived at the ranch, escorted by police officers. Joel had received a call from the chief around three in the morning letting him know the families were on their way and giving him an update on what was happening.

"This town is a mad-house. People are panicking, the grocery store is gone, looted, and set on fire. Same with two of the convenience stores. We closed the two gas stations and I have officers in riot gear guarding them both. Those officers have all experienced fighting and other acts of violence as people tried to get gas before we closed the stations. Fortunately, so far they've been able to keep the underground tanks safe. There are several major fires around town, probably from all the earthquakes. We have several busted water mains, again from the quakes and so no water to try to put them out. I'm sending a couple of families with small kids to you. Their homes are too close to the fires, and they have nowhere else to go. I'm also sending a couple of officers to try to get a little rest before they come back on duty. There's not really anywhere in town right now that they can go that I think would be safe enough for them."

Joel cut in, "What about the police station, Chief?"

"Nope," the chief replied, "It's on fire, along with the firehouse next door and three houses behind us. The fire started in the dry cleaners' shop on the corner and spread to us. Fortunately, we were able to get everything we needed out of the building before the fire reached us. Do you have any problem with us bringing several trucks of stuff out there? Let's just say it will be quite the fireworks display if the trucks were to catch on fire."

Joel chuckled, "You just bring all of your toys here and we'll keep them safe. Just tell the guys to not park them too close to any of our buildings until we can find a safe place for them."

"Thanks, Joel. Hey, tell my wife I'm okay, and let her know it will probably be much later today I get there."

"Will do. You sound exhausted. Maybe you ought to come in and get some rest for a while."

"Man, I'd love to, but it is getting crazy here in town. Let my guys get some rest and some grub, and I'll come in when I can. Joel, I can't thank you guys enough for all you've done, and for keeping my family and my guys' families safe. It means a lot and we all owe you big time."

Joel smiled. "You don't owe me a thing, but you'd best keep yourself safe. We are going to need you and your men here if things keep up like that in town."

"I hear ya, buddy. I'll keep you posted on what's happening in town. If anything changes, I'll let..." Joel looked at his cell phone and saw the call had dropped. Then, he noticed that there was no service. He said a silent prayer for the Chief and his men.

After helping the newest families get settled, Joel headed to the command center in the lodge. Even though it was barely five, the area was busy. He was surprised to see Gwen at the radio, and as soon as she saw him, she waved him over.

"I'm getting some not so good news from north of us," she started. "People in Wyoming and Idaho are reporting a lot of tremors happening around Yellowstone Park, a lot more than they usually feel. They've evacuated the park, and now they are trying to get people in towns surrounding the park to leave. Traffic on all of the highways in that area is crazy, especially with very little gas available." She closed her eyes for a second, then looked directly at Joel. "There was a vulcanologist – I think that's what you call a scientist who studies volcanoes – and he said that he suspects all of the volcanoes in the ring of fire would let loose and explode. He also said he is positive the Yellowstone Caldera is going to erupt, too."

Joel put his hand on her shoulder. "We are far enough away that if it erupts, all we'll get is some ash, and since we are will soon be getting a little bit of ejecta, it probably won't make much difference."

"But think of all the people that will die if it erupts and if all the other volcanoes erupt..." Gwen started, her eyes filling with tears.

"You can't think of that now. Right now, we have to focus on how we are going to survive. As harsh as it sounds, we can't do a thing to help them, but we can help all of the people here and the ones still in town. Keep up with what's going on around the country, but please focus on things that are close enough to affect us. Has there been any word from the government, state or federal?"

Gwen shook her head. "Nothing. I would expect we would have at least heard from Austin, but I haven't heard a thing."

Joel shook his head. "I didn't really expect to hear from them, at least not yet." He turned to leave, but then turned back to her. "I was talking to the chief a couple of hours ago, and the call dropped. There's no cellphone service anymore. Are you able to pick up the police and fire radios?"

Gwen smiled. "Yes, I've been talking to the Chief and to a couple of the officers. They are doing okay, all things considered, but it sounds like town is imploding."

"Thanks. I'll let you get back to what you're doing. If you see Frank, tell him I'm looking for him." Joel left the command center and headed to the kitchen, hoping for a cup of coffee. Rebecca saw him coming and poured him a large cup.

"Thank you, honey. I really need this."

"Yeah, Dad, I could tell. You look like someone rode you hard and put you away wet. Did you get any sleep last night?"

"Not much, but I'll have time to sleep later when I'm sure things are under control."

Joel sat down at a nearby table, and Rebecca brought him a plate with eggs, biscuits, and gravy.

"You've got to eat, Dad. I know you're busy, but you won't be any good to any of us if you don't take care of yourself."

"How....what.." Joel was confused, looking at the plate as though it appeared out of thin air. Then, he noticed the buffet table was set up so everyone could grab a quick breakfast. He smiled at Rebecca. "Good work, honey. Thanks for having food ready so early."

"Well, Scott knew everyone would be up most of the night, so we've been trying to keep enough food ready all night for whoever needs it. The oncoming security team just left a few minutes ago, and boy, were they glad to get something to eat before going out to start their patrols. I expect the off-going team will be in here any minute." Rebecca looked towards the doors, and saw the team coming in, led by Frank.

Joel also saw Frank and waved him over. After stopping to get coffee and a plate of food, Frank sat down with Joel.

"I was looking for you a little while ago. The Chief sent several families over during the night and said it is crazy in town."

"I know," Frank answered. "I've been on the radio with him all night. Our perimeters have been secure all night, and the patrols are doing well. I did have an issue with one of the cops, that pregnant one, Murray I think is her name."

"What kind of issue," Joel asked.

"She wanted to be on patrol last night, and I told her horseback or a four-wheeler is not the place for a pregnant woman, cop or not. She was highly offended and said she could still do her job. I told her I would find something for her that didn't put her, her baby, and the rest of us at risk. I haven't yet figured out what to do with her, though, and she's pretty upset."

"I have an idea, and it's actually why I was looking for you. She would be the perfect person to head this up since she is an experienced law enforcement officer. We've got a lot of people here now, and I think we need to start training everyone we can to shoot. I'm afraid the day is coming when we will need all the help we can get defending this place. A few of our guests can shoot but are unarmed. Then, we have a whole lot of them that don't know squat about gun safety, shooting and defense. If she could organize everyone, assess their competency, and initiate some training, that would be great. We have a couple of older folks who are experienced shooters, but who are not in the best of health to be out on patrol. They could help her. That would solve your problem and would also start to ease one of my headaches." Frank looked thoughtful for a few minutes, then nodded.

"That might work. I know she is a skilled shooter, since she told me she spent ten years as a military police officer in the army. She wants to use her skills, and this might be just the ticket. I'll go talk to her. How are you set for weapons?"

Joel laughed. "Haven't you seen the armory? We're in good shape."

Frank grinned. "Excellent. With all of the stuff the Chief sent over last night, we ought to be able to handle both patrols and training."

The two men took a minute to finish their breakfast and had just stood to leave when suddenly the ground shook violently and they heard an incredibly loud explosion. The lodge was filled with the sounds of people screaming, furniture sliding around, and echoes of the explosion. The shaking went on for several minutes, and then finally ground to a halt. Joel looked around and saw that while a number of people had fallen from the shaking, other staff members were right there helping everyone get back up. Many were in tears, and all looked shocked. Joel waved his daughter Rebecca over and asked her to check on the people who had fallen and let him know if there were any injuries, and to reassure everyone that they were safe. Rebecca solemnly nodded at her father and left to talk to staff.

"What the hell was that?" Frank asked.

"I am betting that was the Yellowstone Caldera letting loose." Joel answered calmly. "Gwen told me just a little bit ago that she was hearing reports that they thought it would erupt, so I am assuming it did."

"Why are you so calm?" Frank asked.

"Well, I figure there's nothing I can do about it, other than manage the additional ash fall and continue to pray. Rachel reminded me the other night that God helps those who help themselves. I figure if we continue with the plan and take care of all of the folks here, that God will handle the big stuff for us. Speaking of taking care of folks, it's almost six. I see Rachel coming this way, and it's time for our morning meeting with General Rachel." He smiled at Frank. "Have faith, my friend. We're going to all be just fine."

"I have plenty of faith, Joel. I just know we also have plenty of challenges ahead of us, but like you said, we've got this."

Chapter Fourteen

Rachel started the morning briefing right at six. "First, before we get everyone's individual briefings, I want to report to you that we have confirmation that the Yellowstone Caldera did erupt. According to all of the research we've done, we do not expect to receive too much ash fall. Projections say we will get up to 10 millimeters, but that is highly variable depending on winds and weather. Coming so soon right after the asteroid hit, there is a possibility that we won't get even that much. We also got reports that there were numerous eruptions of other ring of fire volcanoes, but again, not a significant impact on us at this moment. As I was walking over this morning, I noticed a couple of flakes of ejecta falling. We need to be certain everyone is using their respiratory protection and goggles if they go outside. I was worried about the tent that the police families are using since tents don't usually keep ash out and I didn't really pay a lot of attention to the tents as they were setting them up yesterday. But, when I actually looked at the tent, I saw it was a military hospital tent, and it's set up with a vestibule and a filtering system. Still, I'm worried about some of those little ones that can't wear an N95, though."

Scott spoke up. "I was worried about that, too. We still have two of the single-wides that are not occupied and each one has three bedrooms. I sent a few guys to move the moms with the youngest kids. Rebecca has already come up with a plan to deliver meals to any of our guests with very small kids. With quite a few babies and toddlers, we've also packed up kits to distribute with boxes of diapers, wipes, and other baby needs. We won't start distributing them just yet, because most people have enough to last for a week or two, but we're ready when they start to need it."

Rachel looked relieved. "Thanks, Scott, for taking care of those kids. Since you've already started, why don't you continue?"

"Okay, we've begun our meal service rationing plan. For the next few days, we'll be serving soup and sandwiches for lunch and dinner. Those are pretty easy to transport, and with ejecta now starting, we will begin delivering a very simple breakfast today. We'll still have the buffet tables set up for people here in the lodge and for work teams. The buffet tables will have servers to be sure everyone gets enough, and nobody takes too much. Once the ejecta and ash settle down and people can come to the dining hall, we will resume our usual meal service. . . that is, with the rationing plan in place. So far, while we don't have an exact head count, we are estimating we have around 160 people on the ranch, including those police officers that come and go. There are no reported issues yet with any of our vital functions such as water, sanitation, or medical. I spoke with Dr. Cliburn again last night before the phones went out, and he still wants to stay in town to serve the people there. Dr. Hawthorne agreed to set up a clinic to provide medical care. He is taking care of pulling our medical folks together to do that. I gave him space in the equipment barn, and Joel's guys are relocating some of the equipment that was in the area. I don't have any issues with our guests, most of whom are being extremely cooperative. When we meet tomorrow, I'll have a headcount and will report on the medical services."

Rachel nodded. "Thanks, Scott. Stacey, as G2, you're up next."

"It's early and there is not much to report. We don't have a weather forecast, but right now, it is 46 outside, which is pretty normal for here for this time of year, with winds coming from the north. That's a good thing, I hope, in that it might deflect some of the ejecta from us. Of course, it could also increase ash, so we will just have to watch it. As for activity around us, a few hours ago, my brother Will went into town with one of the police officers to assess what was happening. He observed a lot of criminal activity, including looting, arson, and assaults. In addition, there is quite a bit of structural damage related to fires caused by the quakes, and broken water mains preventing any organized fire-fighting. The Chief is trying to work with local businesses to protect key supplies. They are pulling gas from the two gas stations and filling up a couple of tanker trucks. They are also pulling all of the medications from the pharmacy and also from the hospital. Dr. Cliburn will get some of the medications, but most of them are being loaded onto a box truck and will be brought here for safe-keeping. They had to evacuate the hospital a few hours ago due to earthquake damage and fire. It's a race between the fire and the guys trying to save what they can from the hospital. It's a good thing that all we have in town is a critical access hospital with only 10 beds. Dr. Cliburn has turned his clinic into a mini-hospital, but he only has capacity for four or five patients. Luckily, there were no patients in the hospital who couldn't be sent home. The extra supplies from the hospital will be directed here for our medical teams to use with the understanding that Dr. Cliburn may call if he needs things.

"I mentioned the New Madrid Seismic Zone last night. We now have confirmation via the Ham radio that it did let loose with a major earthquake estimated to be at least a 9.5 on the Moment Magnitude scale. Most of the cities sitting on this fault have had grave damages, and the only way to cross the Mississippi right now is to go north through Wisconsin and Minnesota – and even that is a problem as the Mississippi is behaving very strangely, running backward in some places and following new courses in others. As for the West Coast, there is not much left of California after the San Andreas let go. Likewise, Washington and Oregon were decimated by the Cascadian Fault. Plus, the tsunami came about 25 miles inland – this is more than double what was expected, so apparently it was a huge tsunami. It was big enough that they are not getting any ham transmissions from Hawaii and there is speculation that Hawaii is gone. In addition to Yellowstone, a number of other volcanoes have erupted including Rainer and Mount St. Helen's. There are not any transmissions coming from the West coast of South America, either, or from Japan. One broadcaster on the radio said he suspected casualties are in the hundreds of millions around the world. Oh, and there were major earthquakes up and down the east coast, too, at the same time as New Madrid. There were also tsunami waves along the east coast, not as big as the west, but enough that a number of coastal cities are heavily flooded. All of this is coming from the Ham, and I don't have any confirmations of damages on the east coast yet, so I won't repeat the rumors until I get some validation." Stacey took a deep breath and looked around the room at the shocked faces of her friends. "I think of all of the places we could have chosen to live, we were incredibly lucky to choose right here. I think that is all the intelligence I have right now. Are there other things I should be including in this report?" Stacey asked.

Frank raised his hand. "It might be good to know what our military and homeland security are doing, but that might have to come from Gwen, as she is the one with the radio."

"We are also taking our turns on the radios, and I'll see if we can find out anything about the military. Will and Tom both have connections and have been able to reach a couple of them." Stacey finished her report, and Rachel indicated it was Joel's turn.

"From an operations point, we are in good shape. We had a couple of windows break with the quakes, but all of them except the one next to the fireplace have been replaced. We don't have any glass the size of that big pane, and so for the moment it is boarded up until we can come up with something. We are operating right now on grid power but anticipate that may fail soon. Battery power is at 100% and the generator is ready to be turned on to supplement that and to re-charge the batteries when needed. Wind turbines are still operating without any issues, but with the start of ejecta falling, we will shut them down to avoid any problems. Most of the solar panels were taken down and stored, so I guess once we lose grid power, we will be using the generator a lot to recharge those batteries over the next couple of weeks or so until ash and ejecta stop falling." Joel's voice tapered off, and Rachel looked at him.

"Do you have more to report, Joel?"

"No, I am just worried. I hope that we did enough to make a difference. I mean, I hope we focused on the right things…"

Frank looked at Joel and shook his head. "The right things? You've done that and more. Aren't you glad now that you did all of the preparation you guys did? Can you imagine if you were still back at your home in North Carolina and all of this happened? Your families might have survived, but not like everyone here is surviving now. Think about it, Joel. Because of the preparations you and your group made, you are saving more than a hundred lives. So, there will always be things to think about, and you need to stay on top of things. Just remember that compared to outside this ranch, we are living in paradise here."

"Thanks, Frank. It's hard to comprehend all that is going on, but I am very grateful that we had the means and the ability to do all the preparations we did."

"Sorry, Rachel, I didn't mean to speak out of turn, but you folks need to know that what you've done here is pretty spectacular," Frank explained.

"I guess I'm next," Chris stated. "There's nothing to report from logistics. We have additional food supplies thanks to what the police and other families brought with them. As already reported, the Chief will be sending us two tankers of gas and the pharmacy and hospital supplies. I had a request right before this meeting from Barbara Blake. She'd like to borrow a box truck and a few people and empty the stock from her store. She would also like to get the stock from her husband's shoe store next door to her shop. Both of those are reasonable requests. We have an available truck and people available to help her, plus Frank and the Chief can each provide someone for security. All we need is approval from this group."

"Is there any discussion?" Rachel asked. Seeing everyone shaking their heads, she asked, "All in favor?" All hands were raised, so she continued, "This is approved. When will the group go out, Chris?"

"They're ready to go now. We figured the sooner the better. I'll go let them know and be right back." Chris stepped out of the room and was back less than a minute later. When she saw everyone looking at her, she said, "What? I had Barbara wait right outside the door. I was pretty confident you all would approve. Anyway, that's my report for today."

"Thanks," Rachel continued. "Frank?"

"Security is good. We have roving patrols, sentries at the main gate and all of the cameras are operational. We have round-the-clock monitoring set up for all cameras. Right now, they are digging a number of foxholes, mostly near the main gate and areas that look like places invaders would try to breach. I will be talking with Detective Murray right after this meeting about setting up weapons training for all of the guests on the ranch for defensive purposes. We are collaborating closely with the Chief and his team. As of right now, we have only turned one person away from our gate, and that was a belligerent drunk who wanted to come visit our bar. When we told him the bar went out of business, he left without a fight. No other security issues to report, but it is still early in the game. I expect we won't see any serious issues for at least another week or so – until the crooks in town run out of the food they looted from the grocery store or unless people from other parts of the state move into the area for less-than-stellar reasons."

"Thanks, Frank. Gwen, anything to report on communications?" Rachel asked, looking at Gwen.

"I don't have a lot to report. You've already told them about Yellowstone. The radio waves are going crazy with a lot of rumors, but there isn't a lot of confirmed information. I did hear that most of

Washington DC was evacuated to various shelters to wait out the ash fall and flooding, but I have no idea if that will affect us at all. I guess it is good to know we still have a government of sorts. I am also hearing reports of heavy violence in many of the major cities, again, unconfirmed, although some of the eye-witness reports are pretty unsettling. I've been in contact with the Chief in town, and since the phones are out, he asks that we use my radio to contact him, as the little radios we gave him don't work as well from most parts of town." Gwen looked at her notes. "We've also completed all of our interviews with the guests, and Marcie, Billy, and Toby are tallying the results right now. By tomorrow, we should have information for you on everyone's training and skills. That's about all I have right now."

Rachel nodded and thanked her. "What are our priorities for today?"

Joel was the first to answer. "Once we get a headcount, Scott and I will be looking at housing. We can't have people staying in tents for more than a couple of days. We will need to get an assessment from the Chief of how many more people from town we can expect, and then work to ensure we have appropriate housing. One thing we missed in our rush to get supplies to build additional housing is concrete. Chase is going to try to track down the owner of the concrete plant outside of town and see if we can bargain with him to get two trucks of concrete and begin to pour foundations, even if we don't build on them right away. We did a lot of business with him over the last few months, so hopefully he will agree."

Stacey added, "I want to try to get information today about projected weather patterns. I'm concerned about decreasing temperatures related to Yellowstone and the other volcanoes and the asteroid ejecta. I also want to get confirmation on damage reports from around the country and world."

"Wow," Rachel exclaimed. "We sure covered a lot of information in a very short amount of time."

"Twenty-six minutes!" Joel interrupted.

Rachel looked at him and grinned. "I like short meetings. Let's get busy and we'll meet again tomorrow at 6AM unless something happens between now and then. What was it the Sergeant used to say on the old Hill Street Blues show? 'Y'all be careful out there!'"

As the meeting broke up, Frank called Rachel over. "That was great. Short, sweet, and to the point with no side conversations or tangents. Good job."

"Thanks, Frank. I really appreciate your help. We're all so new to this, but I can see how it's keeping us very organized. I'm putting a white board up in here today so we can keep track of where we are with our priorities, and so we don't get side-tracked or let things fall between the cracks."

"Great idea, Rachel. You might want to save a space on the board for future priorities, too."

"What do you mean by that?"

"Well, it may be early spring now, but we don't know what is going to happen with the weather. A future priority might be to ensure there's plenty of firewood for heating if the temperature doesn't get any higher. Another future priority might be to start teaching basic skills now such as canning. God willing, we will have a productive growing season and a good harvest in spite of the weather, so we need to be prepared to put that harvest up so we can eat next winter. Another future priority is clothing. Clothes will wear out more quickly when people are doing more physical labor, and there needs to be a plan to repair or replace clothes. So future priorities are things you don't need to act on today but need to have in the front of your mind so they don't get left until the last minute, or worse, until it's too late to do anything about them. It helps avoid critical situations and a rush to take care of stuff."

"This is great information," Rachel responded, jotting down notes of what Frank said. "I think at tomorrow's meeting, I will bring up future priorities just to get everyone thinking. For now, though, my immediate priority is to get some breakfast!"

"Great idea," laughed Frank as the two headed over to the dining area.

~~~

As Rachel was finishing her breakfast, Rebecca brought her a fresh cup of coffee and sat down with her.

"What's wrong, dear?" Rachel asked, seeing the look of distress on her daughter's face.

"Other than the world ending, the air not being breathable, and more than a hundred people joining our family overnight, everything is fine," Rebecca answered in a snarky voice. Suddenly, she began to cry. "Oh,

Mom, I'm just scared. I know we're in a pretty good position right now, but I'm worried about the future. How long will it be before all of the violence we're hearing about on the outside comes here to the ranch?"

Rachel put her arms around Rebecca. "Honey, we're all scared, and none of us knows what is going to happen outside our fence. But, I can tell you that we are going to survive, and so is every person here on this ranch. We were ready for this to happen. I'll tell you the same thing I told your father not too long ago. We have to have faith. We are doing everything humanly possible to make sure life goes on here, and we just have to trust God that He will protect us from those things we cannot control."

"I know, Mom, it's just so hard to have faith when I hear people on the radio talking about horrible things happening, or when I listen to the police officers talking about what's going on in town. Jimmy told me the same thing last night, that we just have to stay calm, follow the plan and put our faith and trust in God to keep us strong."

"Jimmy, hmmmm?" asked Rachel, trying to change the subject. "I noticed Jimmy comforting you when the asteroid struck. Anything I should know?"

Rebecca blushed. "Well, Jimmy and I have become good friends, maybe more than friends, I don't know yet. I really like him a lot, and we've been spending a lot of time together when we're not working."

Rachel smiled gently at her daughter. "Jimmy is a good man, and I like him a lot. I'm glad you've found someone to spend time with."

Rebecca looked surprised. "Then you're not mad I've been hanging around with him? I was worried that you and Dad would be mad that I was hanging with the help."

Rachel laughed. "Hanging with the help? For heaven's sake, honey, he's not 'the help'. Yes, he's an employee, but so are you, and for that matter, so am I. The last thing we want to see is a class war here. Some of us might outrank others, but we are all equals. I can guarantee your father feels the same way. Jimmy is an important part of the team, and if you choose to see him, then we are happy for you both. Where in the world did you come up with that idea?"

Rebecca shrugged her shoulders. "I dunno – I guess I was just worried about what you and Dad would think and started making up excuses for why you wouldn't approve." Looking around, she saw Scott stick his head out of the kitchen. "Oh, oh, Uncle Scott is looking for me.

See you later, Mom." She leaned over and kissed her mother on the cheek and ran to the kitchen. Rachel sat thinking for a few minutes, a pensive look on her face, before she, too, got up to start the day's activities.

Chapter Fifteen

Things went well over the next few days. Barbara Blake was able to retrieve all of the stock from her fabric store and her husband Mark's shoe store. She was especially grateful that they were able to dismantle and save her brand new fifty-five-thousand-dollar computerized Gammill long-arm quilting frame and machine. As they were finishing loading the trucks, the Chief came by to tell them that they needed to get the books from the public library, as it was in danger of burning. Some quick rearrangements were done in the trucks, and they were able to load most of the books before the heat and smoke from nearby fires became too intense.

Several other small business owners who came to the ranch for safety also went back to town to salvage what they could of their businesses. Scott's food stock increased when two restaurant owners were able to salvage what was left in their restaurants. Sally Bradshaw, owner of the local feed store, was able to get almost all of her supply of animal feed, along with a lot of other supplies, in spite of the fact that the stores near her were burning and rapidly approaching the feed store. She gave all of the feed and supplies to Dr. Lydia and Jeff Miller to use for the ranch animals.

Ejecta continued to fall for several days. On the fourth day after Yellowstone caldera erupted, there was a large increase in the amount of ash falling, but it only lasted a few days. In the early

hours of the morning on the sixth day after the Event, the power grid failed. As the group gathered to have their morning briefing, Joel noted that with the loss of grid power, the few people left in town would have no power, no water, and no sewer. "That means that shortly, we're going to have a number of people in town with no utilities and no food. They will get desperate quickly. I talked to the Chief right before this meeting as he was headed back to town and told him to watch for people, especially families with kids, who were struggling and would be a good fit here. He'll call us before he sends anyone in."

Scott looked concerned. "We're getting close to our limits here. I think we need to seriously consider starting to build either more cabins or a couple of duplexes or something. I know it's only been a week, but I hate to think of the police families still living in tents. Even if everything was fixed today, there's still nothing for people to go back to in town, as the fires there have been pretty devastating. When Edith Marchant, the owner of the steakhouse in town, moved here, she brought several truckloads of food and stuff from her restaurant, and that extra helped. I think, though, we need to get serious about the housing issue. Chase and I met with the concrete guy, and he is willing to sell us three mixing trucks worth of concrete in exchange for keeping the trucks here and safe. He's going to head to his sister's ranch on the other side of the state but is worried about his equipment. Sounds like an excellent exchange for us. He also said for a week's worth of food for his crew, that they would come pour the foundations for us, too."

Rachel smiled at Scott. "Good work on that. We will vote on it as soon as everyone is here and we can start our meeting."

Most of the morning briefing was taken up discussing the people now filling the ranch. Everyone was surprised and happy to find that most of the former guests quickly transitioned from vacation mode to "everyone works, or they don't eat" mode. The briefing went well, and again, they completed everything in under thirty minutes, including adding several future priorities.

~~~

Everyone was chipping in to help with the many tasks that had to be done every day. Lots of training was happening. Detective Murray had several classes going to teach weapon safety and marksmanship, and even the younger kids were learning the basics. A group of people were working with Steve Porschenko to learn to use the tractors and other farming equipment in the hopes that with the ash fall ending, they would soon be able to ready the fields for planting. With the vegetables from the greenhouse and the large amount of fresh produce brought by Mrs. Marchant from her restaurant, Scott and Chris were teaching a group how to can the veggies.

Rachel was sitting at the desk in the command center going through her notes when Mary approached her.

"Rachel, can I interrupt for a minute?"

"Hey, Mary, come on in. What's going on?" Rachel answered.

"Well, the quilting group is wanting more to do. Right now, they are working on fixing any clothing that needs to be mended, and they are continuing to make quilts for all of the additional people coming in, but they feel like they have a lot more to offer. Eileen has suggested we start basic sewing classes for anyone who may need it. We have a bunch of teenagers here, and we thought we could be working with them to teach them how to sew and quilt. Trina is talking about starting a knitting group too, so we can start getting stuff made in case it stays this chilly. Barbara has patterns in the stuff from her shop to make quilted jackets and hats, too. Plus, before long, we won't be able to mend some of the work clothes and we may need to start making them."

"Those all sound like excellent ideas. Go ahead and get your classes set up, and I'll make sure everyone knows what's going on. Before you start making work clothes, though, let's see what is in storage, what we can salvage, and what people may already have. You may also want to consider making some baby things, as we have several pregnant moms with us, and I don't think there was a baby store in town to salvage."

Mary stepped over and gave Rachel a quick hug. "Thank you so much for bringing Trina and I here. Not only did you probably save our lives, but we really love this place… and you guys, too."

Rachel smiled fondly at her friend. "I'm glad you're here too. Now, you keep those quilters of the apocalypse in line, okay?" Mary grinned and waved as she left the room and Rachel went back to work.

A few minutes later, Joel came into the office. After giving Rachel a quick kiss on the cheek, he sat down next to her and asked how she was doing.

"I'm doing surprisingly well," she answered. "In spite of everything going on, I still can't believe how incredibly well we are doing so far. How are you doing, dear?"

"I'm good. I was just talking to Chase, and he's got a group of people willing to start building as soon as the ash lets up. We've got three places picked out to pour foundations, and we thought we would just build barracks-type buildings or bunkhouses for now, at least to get started. We plan to use one as a school/ kids area, since we now have more kids here than we can accommodate in the lodge."

"That's a good idea," Rachel answered. "We seem to have enough people willing to help with the kids and having three teachers among our visitors is a bonus. They were talking to me last night about getting school going soon for the kids. Can the Chief get them any textbooks and stuff like that from the school in town?"

Joel nodded. "Good idea. I'll ask him. That would surely make it a little easier on the teachers. Oh, and I talked to Jeff and Dr. Lydia earlier. Between you and me, I think there is a little relationship blooming there. The animals are doing well, and they said Alan is doing great with the dog training program, even teaching some of the visitors to work with the dogs."

~~~

The following morning, after the briefing, the group sat at a table in the dining area having a quick breakfast before beginning the day's work.

"It's amazing how well everyone is working together to keep things going," Rachel observed. "I was afraid people would be offended that they were asked to stop being a guest and pitch in, but they've all been great. Even your Uncle Ralph has been behaving himself," she added.

"Uncle Ralph knows he will be booted right out the door if he doesn't behave. I've already had to speak to him a couple of times for complaining about not having any booze. I suspect he has some in his luggage, as he has been fairly easy to deal with. If he does, it will be a problem when he runs out." Joel sighed. "I would hate to kick him out, but I absolutely will if he causes problems. Has anyone had any problems with anyone else?"

Frank spoke up. "I've only had issues with one guy, name is Wally Blankenship. He was giving Jimmy Langston a hard time about the horses. He said he had cabin fever and wanted to take a horse for a ride. He did not understand that horses are now very vital for our security, and that it's bad enough the horses are exposed to ash when they are used for patrols, but to expose them for purely recreational reasons was not acceptable. He came close to slugging Jimmy until several other guys in the barn came over and he backed down. Jimmy called me over to settle the issue, and I warned him that any further issues would result in him being kicked out. He went he went away sulking. We'll need to keep an eye on him for his attitude."

"That's the same guy that Rebecca had to talk to about taking extra food last night. He said he got hungry during the night and needed extra," Scott added. "He had the same portions as everyone else, so it's not like he's being starved. Oh, and I checked. He's not on any of the work details and has been basically cruising from class to class but not getting involved in any of them."

Rachel looked concerned. "Joel, it sounds like you need to have a word with our 'guest' and set him straight. Who is he, anyway? I don't recognize his name as one of our invited guests."

Joel sighed. "He came in with one of the families from town. The Chief really didn't want to let him come, but he was visiting with one of the families whose home burned. The Chief said he was mouthy and was afraid he might become a troublemaker. I'll go have a chat with him and make sure he is either on one of the work details or else is headed back to town."

Rachel reached out to put her hand on Joel's arm. "Honey, take someone with you when you go talk to him. I don't have a very good feeling about this character."

"I'll go with him," Frank said. "He needs to know we are all on the same page and he's not going to try to pull one over on us or pitch one of us against another. Are you ready now Joel? Let's just go get it done." Joel nodded, and the two men headed off in search of their problem guest. They found him in the horse barn, just watching Jimmy muck out the horses' stalls.

"Wally, we need a word, please," Joel called out.

Wally turned to look at the two men approaching him. "Sure, pal, what's up?"

"Wally, we have some concerns we need to discuss with you. Right now, we are in a pretty desperate situation trying to survive, and we need everyone to be on board with what's going on. We've already had to have a couple of conversations with you about the horses, and how you were treating Jimmy, and about taking extra food in the dining room. You've not signed up for any work details, and you're not participating in classes, either. Now we find you out here just watching Jimmy work. I'll tell, you, unless things change, it does not look like you are going to be staying here with us." Joel finished speaking and just stood calmly watching Wally. At first, Wally's face became very red, and he clenched his fists in anger. As Joel and Frank continued to calmly watch him, he relaxed a little.

"Well, geeze, guys, I didn't know I was signing on as a ranch hand when I was evacuated here. I'm still pretty stressed out from watching my friends' home burn and all. I'm just trying to calm down and relax, you know? Trying not to have a heart attack or anything from all of the trauma. You don't know how rough it was, all of the fire and flooding and stuff in town."

Frank looked at Joel and scowled as he turned back to Wally. "Yeah, we do understand. Your friends, you know, the ones who watched their home burn? They are working hard here, in spite of their stress. You need to either sign up on the work details or pack your bags and be prepared to be evacuated back to town."

Wally smirked. "I'd help, but I don't know how to do nothing. Plus, if I work too hard, my back goes out."

Joel could tell Frank was about to explode, so he put his hand on his friends arm to silence him. "I'll tell you what. Since you don't seem to know how to do anything, you can work in the greenhouse. That's not too stressful, but at least it will help you earn your keep. Come with us and we'll introduce you to Steve. He'll keep you busy without you getting your back all worked out."

"Well, fine, but I'm warning you, if my back goes out because of working too hard, I'll wind up being stuck in bed for weeks. That's how I wound up on disability. But if you're going to make a disabled man work…"

"Oh, cut that nonsense out, Wally. You are no more disabled than I am," Frank hissed. "You're just lazy, and lazy won't last long around here. Your back goes out and you'll find yourself recuperating back in town because it won't be here. Now let's get going. Joel, I'll walk him over to the greenhouse and talk to Steve. You go on and I'll get with you later."

Joel nodded and turned away, but not before catching the look of pure rage on Wally's face. "We're going to have to really watch him," Joel thought to himself.

Chapter Sixteen

April 1

On the ninth morning after the event, the leadership team met as usual to review their progress. Joel led off the discussion by reporting they were going to try to pour the foundations later that day in spite of the continuing ash and ejecta.

"Will ash and stuff getting mixed in affect the concrete?" asked Rachel.

"Actually, the concrete guys tell me that as long as the ash is well-pulverized, it will probably increase the strength of the concrete. He said there were studies done after the Mount Saint Helen's eruption that proved this." Joel looked around the table. "I was afraid they were just trying to rush to get out of here, but the three guys doing the pouring said that instead of the week's worth of food they were promised, they would rather stay here and be on Chase's construction team. They feel like they have better chances here than trying to follow their boss. I told them that would be fine unless someone at this meeting had any objections."

"All in favor of allowing the concrete guys to stay?" Rachel interjected. Looking around the table and seeing all hands raised, Rachel continued, "Approved. Joel, please let them know and get with Scott for their housing assignment. Stacey, intelligence report?"

Stacey took a second to refer to the papers in her hands. "As best as we can tell, government has either disappeared or collapsed following the caldera and ring of fire eruptions. There has been nothing broadcast from Austin since the event, and people are reporting that due to all of the tremors on the east coast following the New Madrid quake, that nobody has heard from any federal government officials either. Numerous states have lost their capitals to either volcanoes, earthquakes, tsunamis, or violence. Reports over the ham indicate almost every large city is in flames, with violence soaring out of control. Reports of casualties are in the billions worldwide. Closer to home, the Chief is reporting almost complete destruction of the town. Most of the residents have evacuated – either to here or elsewhere – and unfortunately the people who remain in town are causing major problems. In the downtown area, there are only a few buildings still standing. There is no water, power or sewer. I'll let Frank cover the rest of the information about the town. As for weather today, it is 43 degrees, and guesses on the radio say it might make it to 50 if the wind dies down. The ash/ejecta fall seems to have decreased overnight, but it is still falling a little." Stacey sat and gulped at her coffee, looking down to hide the tearful expression on her face.

"Thank you for that report, Stacey. As harsh as it is and as hard as it is for you to report, it is information we need to have," Rachel said in a soothing voice. "Scott, any personnel issues?"

"Only one, and that is more trouble with Wally Blankenship. He stormed out of the greenhouse yesterday, claiming we were working him too hard. The man has hardly done anything, and all he was doing yesterday was scooping dirt into dixie cups for seeds to be planted. I think he needs to go. He has a couple of guys that he hangs out with, and they are also starting to develop attitudes. I am afraid we are going to have some major troubles if we don't take action now."

Frank interrupted. "I will take care of that this morning and uninvite him from staying here. I'll see if the Chief can take him into town."

"No, Frank, let us talk with him one more time. I hate to condemn someone to almost certain death without being sure he totally understands what is expected of him," Rachel replied.

"I disagree with you, Rachel, but I respect your opinion. Be prepared, though, and I don't want you meeting with him alone," Frank answered.

"I won't. Why don't you bring him to me after this meeting?" she asked. Frank reluctantly nodded in agreement.

Joel reported next. "Chase and I talked to Chris about a scavenging run into town. We need some additional construction supplies with all of the new buildings we are planning."

Rachel looked puzzled. "I thought you guys bought up all of the lumberyards in town?"

"We did," Joel answered, "but we're not looking for lumber. We need stuff to make additional septic tanks and other plumbing supplies. We just don't have enough, and now is the time to get what we need. We planned to take a group of eight of us – six to drive and retrieve supplies, and two for security. We only plan to be gone a couple of hours, and Frank has given his approval for the security part."

SERENDIPITY RANCH

Rachel sighed. "I'm not happy about all of you leaving, but if you think you'll have enough security, then try to go as quickly as you can…and be safe. Frank, anything to add about security?"

"Only what Stacey started to talk about in town. There have been several ranchers murdered and their stuff taken, mostly on the other side of town. The chief is about ready to pull his people in and focus on keeping us safe here, as the areas around town are pretty much done for. He sent a couple of survivors to us last night, and the other ranchers still out there don't want to leave their homes. The town is just about a total loss, between fires, flooding, and looting. He's rounding the last of his people up and they should be here within the next two hours."

Everyone around the table was silent, shocked looks on their faces. Finally, Scott spoke. "Well, we knew it would happen. It's just, well, I didn't expect it to happen this quickly."

Rachel looked at Joel. "If you're going out into that mess, I want you to have a lot more security. At least four, and make sure everyone is properly armed."

Joel smiled at his wife. "Nothing for me to say to that other than 'Yes, dear'." Joel's comment was enough to break the shocked silence, and several people grinned. After a few minutes more discussion, the group broke up to begin the day's activities.

~~~

About fifteen minutes after the meeting broke up, Rachel was sitting at the table going through the days inventory reports when Frank entered the room with Wally.

"Please have a seat, gentlemen. Wally, I need to talk with you, and Frank is going to stay to be sure our conversation stays friendly," Rachel said, trying hard to sound impartial and professional.

"Yeah, whatever," Wally answered, slumping into a chair. "What's the problem this time?"

"Watch how you speak to Mrs. Matthews," Frank growled.

Rachel reached over and put her hand on Frank's arm. "It's okay, Frank." She turned to look at Wally. "I understand you had a problem at the greenhouse yesterday, and I want to know what happened."

Wally shook his head. "They had me filling paper cups with dirt. Do you know how boring that is? I filled more than a hundred cups. There was nobody to talk to except some stupid kids, and they were all singing and acting all happy and it was driving me crazy. I don't need to be hanging around a bunch of kids."

"Well, then, if you weren't hanging around a bunch of kids, what would you rather be doing?" Rachel asked gently.

"I'm disabled. I'd rather be watching TV or fishing and drinking a beer, but there ain't even any beer around here. No TV, nothing to do and everyone is making me work all the time. I went on disability so I wouldn't have to work." Wally's face turned red. "I mean, I had to go on disability because working was too painful, yeah, that's it, it was too painful."

Frank started to speak, but Rachel silenced him with a look. "Well, Wally, you do understand that things have changed, and there is no such thing any more as disability, right?"

Wally looked at her. "What do you mean, no disability? You didn't cure my bad back, so you're expecting me to work in pain all the time?"

"What I am saying, Wally, is that everyone needs to pitch in and help. I certainly don't expect people to hurt themselves, but I do expect that everyone does their part so that we have what we need to survive. That means some people need to fill paper cups with dirt so we can start seedlings. Other people are out working with the crops in the fields, taking care of the animals, helping to cook and clean, teaching the kids, all of that. Everyone needs to be involved. The old ways of sitting back and letting other people take care of you are gone, and that's no longer the way it works. Around here, if you want a place to sleep and meals to eat, you have to help."

Wally interrupted her with a sneer. "So, you're telling me that I need to work if I want to eat. What if I can't work? You'll throw me out?"

Rachel took a deep breath, trying to remain calm. "I'm telling you that everyone is expected to work to the best of their ability. Mrs. Dresher is 92 years old and in a wheelchair. She spends her day every day mending clothes and helping to teach kids how to sew. At 92, she has every right to think she could spend her days sitting on the porch, but she doesn't. She chooses to be useful because she knows it will take every one of us working together to survive the mess we're in. Now, you are certainly not 92 years old, and you can walk just fine, so you don't need a wheelchair. It seems that there ought to be something you can do to contribute and earn your keep."

"What if I don't want to earn my keep? Why can't I just do my own thing? It's not like I eat all that much, and you can certainly afford to feed a poor, old, handicapped man," Wally whined.

Frank could see Rachel was starting to get angry, so he jumped in. "You are not old or handicapped, and just because you were able to work the system in the past, that won't fly here. You will either earn your place here or I will personally take you to town and dump you there."

Wally turned to Frank in a rage. "Why, you…. I ought to tear you apart for that…"

"Stop it, both of you," Rachel shouted and both men started to stand. "Both of you sit down. There will be no fighting here. Wally, you have one choice. You can choose to stay here and contribute to this community, or you can leave, never to return. You have one minute to give me your answer."

Wally looked at Rachel's resolute face, and then at Frank's angry one. "Well, I reckon I'll stay, at least until things get better in town. But I'm telling you that I can't do any heavy work."

"At this point, Wally, you do not get to choose. You've been taking advantage of our kindness for too long. I am sending you back to the greenhouse to work. If you don't like hearing the kids, wear ear plugs or something. This is my expectation. You will show up for your shifts on time. You will do exactly as you are told to do by the shift supervisor, and you will work a full shift every day. Failure to be on time, do your job properly, or to complete your shifts will result in a one-way ticket to town. In addition, I've heard about you stirring up trouble with some of the other men, spreading your negative attitude around. That will also stop now. If I hear of any further incidents with you disrupting life here, you are gone. Do you understand me?"

Wally stared at Rachel, trying to get her to back down. Rachel stared back, with no sign of capitulation. Finally, Wally looked down. "Yeah, I guess."

Rachel did not waver. "You guess what?"

Wally sighed. "I guess I'll follow your rules, at least for now."

"The day you do not follow the rules will be the day you are banished from here, so I think you need to carefully consider your behavior. Town is not a very good place to be right now, especially for someone in your…. ahem…..delicate condition. Frank, would you

146

escort Wally to the greenhouse and inform the greenhouse supervisor of this conversation and my expectations?"

Frank stood. "Let's go, Wally. I'll take care of it, Rachel, and I'll talk to Steve as well as whoever is on-shift as supervisor." Wally stood and stalked out of the room with Frank close behind. Rachel couldn't resist the urge, and called after them, "Have a lovely day, gentlemen!" She was rewarded with a scowl from Wally and a grin from Frank.

Chapter Seventeen

Joshua Rivers and Samuel Thompson crept down the quiet street, staying in the shadows. Around them were the burned remains of businesses, abandoned cars in the streets, and trash everywhere. "This reminds me of Kandahar," Joshua whispered to his partner. "I never thought I'd see an American city look like this."

"Me neither. Let's try to make it through this town so we can find a place to rest," Samuel answered. The two men, dressed in military camouflage uniforms and carrying huge backpacks, continued to make there way down the deserted street. Suddenly, they heard a loud scream, followed by the sound of breaking glass. Several more screams followed, some of them sounding like young girls. The two men looked at each other quickly moved towards the sounds of screams. They came to a large multistory building on the corner of a street. In the shadow of the building, they looked around the corner to see several people standing outside the broken front windows of a shop. A gang of three men were restraining a young girl, with a fourth man holding a gun on two younger girls. There was one more man inside the building. They could hear that man yelling at someone to "gimme the drugs".

Samuel whispered to Joshua, "it looks like only the one guy has a gun, although we don't know about the one in the building. I'll go around behind the shop next door and come out behind the guy with the gun. You go the other way and get ready to get the jump on the three holding the girl. Don't shoot unless you have to, because I don't want to see the kids get shot. Once we have the four outside down, then we can take care of the one inside."

Joshua nodded, and turned to leave when all of a sudden, there was a loud crash and a man flew through the broken window out of the shop. As he landed, the four men outside turned away from their prisoners and headed towards the shop window.

"Let's go," Samuel said to Joshua, and the two men rapidly abandoned their plan and headed across the street, aiming their rifles at the four men standing around the body of the fifth man. "Hands up, don't move," he shouted. "Girls, get out of the way."

The three girls quickly went through the front door of the shop. As Joshua watched the girls safely enter the shop, the man with the gun quickly pulled his weapon up to fire at Joshua. Samuel saw him and fired, killing him. Two of the remaining men attempted to rush Samuel, and both of them were also shot. The man who had come through the window and the remaining gang member put their hands up.

"Hey, don't shoot us, we were just trying to get some food and the guy in there attacked us."

An older man stepped out the front door. "They were not trying to get food. I'm Doctor Riley Cliburn, and these men attacked my family trying to get drugs. They hit my nurse with a metal club and grabbed three of my daughters. They said they would kill all of us if I didn't give them all the drugs we had. They are not really all that smart. If they hadn't tried to assault my nurse, they would have gotten the drugs and escaped."

"How did that one come flying through the window? That was good work," Samuel said.

"He was so busy fighting with Ava, my nurse, that he didn't see me come up behind him. I grabbed him and threw him through what was left of the front window. I guess adrenaline kicked in."

Dr. Cliburn and Samuel jumped as two shots were fired. Samuel turned to Joshua and saw both of their prisoners sprawled the ground. Joshua explained, "The guy on the ground had a pair of pistols in his belt. I saw him pass one to the other guy just as he was trying to get a shot off at you, so I shot them both."

Dr. Cliburn shook his head. "I don't know who you guys are, but thank God you came along when you did, because otherwise they would have hurt my family … or worse."

Samuel reached out his hand to shake with the doctor. "My name is Sergeant First Class Samuel Thompson, but I go by Sam. My partner here is Staff Sergeant Joshua Rivers. Until about a week ago, we were active-duty soldiers with the Army, until our commanding general told us all to go home and do what we could to protect and help our hometowns. Josh and I don't really have a home to go back to, so we were trying to make it to the Gulf coast. We figured that would be a pretty good place to try to settle."

"Well, thank you both for saving our lives. Please, come in and meet my family." The three men entered the shop. Josh and Sam were expecting to see some kind of retail establishment but were surprised to see the shop had been turned into a clinic. Dr. Cliburn saw their surprise, and explained, "When the fires in town started, they were too close to my clinic, and I knew I wouldn't be able to save the clinic if the fires continued to spread . We took over this store – it used to be a dress shop – and set up the clinic here. Between what we were able to save from my clinic before it burned and the stuff they brought us from the hospital, we had a pretty good service going for the people in town. The worse the fires got, though, the more people that left. We had a chance to evacuate to a ranch nearby, but I was pretty stubborn and wanted to stay here to take care of the townspeople."

Just then, several women and girls came into the shop from the back room. "Honey, are you okay?" cried an older woman as she rushed to Dr. Cliburn's side.

"I'm good, Janice, these men saved us. Sergeants, this is my wife, Janice Cliburn, and the three girls behind her are my daughters. Haylie is the oldest. She's 15. Olivia is 12, and the little blonde is Emma. She is 9." He turned to his wife. "How is Ava?"

"She's okay. She's laying down right now because that thug hit her pretty hard. She thinks he may have broken her arm. Her mother is pretty upset, and I gave her something to help her calm down. Ava's dad is trying to keep her mom from driving Ava nuts," Janice explained. Dr. Cliburn looked alarmed.

"I didn't realize he hit her that hard. I'd better go check on her." Just then, Dr. Cliburn heard someone calling his name. He turned to see the Chief of Police entering the store, looking suspiciously at the two soldiers.

"Riley, are you alright, what's going on here?" asked the Chief, pointing his weapon at the soldiers.

"Chief, put your gun away. These two men just saved us from the trash outside. Sam, Josh, this is our police Chief." The men shook hands and introduced themselves, and Dr. Cliburn rapidly explained what happened. "I need to go check on Ava and make sure she's all right."

The chief nodded. Good idea. While you do that, Janice and the girls and I will start packing up everything – and you two can help, too, if you will" he said, looking at Sam and Josh. "Seriously, Doc, I think it's time all of you moved out to the ranch. There's nothing left in town and I'm pulling all of my cops out to the ranch, too."

150

Sadly, Dr. Cliburn nodded. "I should have gone earlier, but I really wanted to be able to help people left in town. Let me check on Ava and her parents and then I'll help you ."

Three hours later, everything was loaded up onto a couple of trucks and the group headed for the ranch. After passing through security, the trucks pulled up to the front of the lodge and everyone piled out. The chief instructed the drivers to take the trucks back to the barn that held the clinic. Joel, Rachel, Scott, and Chris met the group at the door and ushered them into the living room.

"Chief, we're glad you're back safe. Your wife has been really worried about you," Joel said. "Dr. Cliburn, we are delighted you've decided to join us."

"Thank you, Joel. I can't tell you how much we appreciate you all taking us in. We're grateful for your hospitality. Have you met my family? This is my wife, Janice. She is a nurse practitioner midwife, so if there are any expectant moms, she is here for them. Then, there are my girls Haylie, Olivia, and Emma, and my nurse Ava McLaughlin. We also have Pete and Sarah McLaughlin, Ava's parents. Sarah is also a nurse. She was working in Fort Worth until all of this happened, and then she and Pete came to stay with Ava. Pete worked in the stockyards until his accident. He may not be able to walk, but he is a treasure trove of information about raising cattle."

Joel smiled as he greeted the newcomers. "We're really glad to have all of you with us. Why don't you head into the dining room and see my daughter Rebecca. She'll get y'all some dinner, and then we'll figure out where all of you will sleep tonight." Joel waved to Rebecca, who escorted the group to the dining room.

Joel turned back to the chief, but before he could say anything, the Chief said, "Joel, Scott, ladies, I want to introduce these two men to you. I don't know what their long-term plans will be, but I invited them to come for a few days and get some rest and decent food. These guys saved Dr. Cliburn's group from part of a gang that has been terrorizing the town." The two soldiers had been quietly standing behind the Chief. He turned to them and said, "Sergeants, these people are the owners of this ranch. Please tell them who you are and why you're in this area."

Rachel interrupted. "Wait, before we do that, why don't we go sit in the office? I think it will be more comfortable. Chief, would you ask

Rebecca to bring us some coffee? When we're done talking, we can get you both some dinner."

The group moved into the command center, and everyone took seats around the big table. Sam and Josh set their backpacks and rifles against the wall behind them. They both looked around at the many notes on the walls and neat lists everywhere and nodded their approval. Rachel smiled at the two men. "This is a lot more comfortable than standing in the living room. Now, as the chief said, I'm Rachel Matthews, and this is my husband, Joel" She pointed to Scott, and continued, "This is Scott Wilson, and his wife Chris."

"Thank you for allowing us to come. My name is Samuel Thompson, and I'm a Sergeant First Class in the Army... or at least I was until a week ago. My partner here is Joshua Rivers, and he was a Staff Sergeant in the same unit as me. Last week, our Commanding General called all of the troops together and released us, telling us there was no more government, they couldn't pay us anymore, and that we should all go back to our hometowns and do what we could to help the people there. Josh and I didn't really have any place to go, so we thought we'd find some place near the Gulf to try to settle down."

Rachel looked distressed. "Don't you have any family to be with?" she asked.

"No, ma'am. I lost my wife and baby son six years ago due to a drunk driver. My parents and my brother both lived in Los Angeles, and, well, there is no more Los Angeles."

Rachel looked sad. "I'm so sorry for all that you've suffered," she said.

Sam smiled sadly. "Don't be. I'm glad they don't have to try to survive, as messed up as the world is out there. You've got no idea how bad it is – but I can tell you about that later."

Rachel nodded, then turned to Josh. "How about you?"

"Ma'am, my name is Joshua Rivers, and I don't have any family either. My parents abandoned me as a baby, and I grew up in a bunch of foster homes. So far as I know, I don't have any siblings or anything. I'm not married, and don't even have a girlfriend. I really don't have any desire to find any of my foster parents. Sam has been my best friend for several years – in fact, he saved my life twice in Afghanistan, and so I decided I would just hang with him. Like Sam said, we really don't have any place specific to go. We were just headed to the Gulf because it would be warm there and we figured we could get food by fishing and all."

Scott spoke up. "Gentlemen, what were your military specialties?"

Sam answered first. "I was originally trained in infantry. I cross-trained as a medic and eventually became a Ranger with a specialty of Combat engineer. Josh and I were both part of the 2nd Ranger Battalion at Joint Base Lewis-McChord in Washington State. Luckily, our commanding officer there had some prior knowledge that Yellowstone was acting up and might erupt, because he sent all of us packing about 16 hours before the actual eruption."

Scott nodded at Sam and turned to Josh. "How about you?"

"I was trained as a combat engineer to start with, and then joined the Rangers. They just kept me as a combat engineer."

Scott was about to ask another question, when Chris interrupted him. "Scott, these guys look dead on their feet. Can we just get some food into them and let them sleep? You can continue the interrogation tomorrow. I'm sure they have a lot of information we can use, so why don't we bring them into the meeting in the morning?"

Scott laughed and turned to the two soldiers. "As usual, my wife is right. I'm sorry, guys. I wasn't thinking about how tired you might be, I was excited to get information. If you don't mind, we've got a couple of cots set up in the chapel so you can get some rest. They start serving breakfast at 5, and we will meet at 6 right here. I'll take you over to get some dinner and then show you the chapel."

~~~

The next morning, the two soldiers were the topic of numerous conversations. Gwen caught Rebecca away from the kitchen and asked, "What do you think?"

Rebecca looked at her blankly and asked, "What do I think about what?"

Gwen laughed. "About our two new guests, that's what. They are both quite attractive, don't you think?"

Rebecca looked at her dear friend. "Are you nuts? The world is just about ending, and you are busy looking at boys? Yeah, I guess they are good looking. They are nice people, I talked to them a little while they were eating dinner last night."

"Oh, I want to know all about them," Gwen giggled. "Especially the really tall black guy."

"That's Sam. He's older, I think he said he was 31 or 32. The other guy is Josh and he's 29. They were both in Washington State when the event happened. Now, if you don't mind, they are both going to the morning briefing, so you'll meet them then. I'm off to get a little rest before my next shift starts." Gwen gave her friend a hug and headed over to the morning meeting.

~~~

The meeting room was crowded for a change. Scott invited both Dr. Cliburn and Dr. Hawthorne. Frank brought Will Stone with him to discuss a new security initiative, and Joel brought Chase Armstrong to discuss some new housing construction. Gwen sat whispering with her mother while waiting for the rest of the group to arrive. Finally, Rachel and Joel entered, accompanied by Sam and Josh. Will, who had been talking to Frank, looked up and saw Sam.

"Thompson? Sam Thompson? Is that you?"

Sam looked around and saw Will. "Stone! What in the world are you doing here? How did you get here?"

Will laughed. "Hey, Tom Long is here, too."

Sam grinned from ear to ear. "I'm so glad to see you, even under these circumstances." Sam suddenly looked serious. "Is Jenna…."

"Jenna and the kids are here, and so is Tom's family," Will answered.

Frank stood up. "You guys know each other?"

"We worked together in Afghanistan and a couple of other places through the years," Sam answered. "It sure is good to see a familiar face!"

"We'll be talking more," Frank said. Just then, Rachel called the meeting to order.

"We have a number of new faces here this morning, but let's hold introductions for now. First order of business – Scott – G-1"

Scott stood. "I'd like to introduce Dr. Riley Cliburn. He is going to take over the clinic Dr. Hawthorne set up. Dr. Hawthorne will continue to assist and see patients, but he would rather Dr. Cliburn was in charge." Dr. Cliburn stood for a moment to be recognized, then sat down. Scott continued, "Dr. Cliburn brought a lot of supplies and equipment with him last night, including an x-ray machine, so we will be expanding the clinic slightly. He also brought his wife Janice, who is a nurse-practitioner midwife, and she will begin seeing all of our expectant moms, and his nurse, Ava, who will help in the clinic. He tells us there have been a lot of gastric illnesses in town and numerous deaths, mostly he suspects from contaminated water. We'll need to watch closely for any of that here, especially with people we've brought in from town. We also have some housing issues, but I will defer that to Joel for his report." Scott then sat down.

"Welcome Dr. Cliburn, we're glad you're here," Rachel said. "Next is Stacey, G2 report."

Stacey stood. "Weather report for today – it is 39 degrees, and cloudy. Barometric pressure is dropping, so I won't be surprised if it rains later today. Nothing really new on the HAM- just more talk about destruction in the cities. There is still no information at all from state or federal government, and nothing from the military, although since we have members of the military with us today, I guess that's about to change!" Stacey smiled at the two soldiers and sat down.

"Thanks, Stacey, G3- Joel?" Rachel smiled at Joel, and he stood.

"Thanks, honey. From an operations standpoint, all is well. The foundations are poured for three new buildings, and we decided to build duplicates of the bunkhouse, with a few more rooms in each. The current bunkhouse sleeps 24, and each of the new ones will sleep 36, more if people double up in rooms, which they may have to do. Animal services report no issues with the animals, and all systems are functioning well. The only issue is with our septic. Even though it is extremely large, I don't want to over-extend it. I brought Chase with me today to report on our salvage operation yesterday morning. Chase?"

Chase stood. "Yesterday morning, we went to the outskirts of town and were able to get the materials to build four more septic systems. Two systems will be placed to support the three new buildings, and the supplies for the other two systems will be held in reserve to be used as we expand. We also were able to get a lot of plumbing supplies, enough that we shouldn't have to worry about plumbing for a while. One issue we are having is with laundry. With so many people here, the laundry in the lodge and in the vet area are not able to keep up. We were able to get 10 large capacity washing machines on our trip yesterday, and we plan to put up a laundry building out by the bunkhouses we are building. There won't be any dryers because we're afraid that would tax our power systems too much, but we'll also put clotheslines up so when the ash stops completely, clothes can be dried outdoors. Are there any questions?"

Scott raised his hand. "How big a truck did you take to get 10 washers, 4 septic systems and a ton of plumbing stuff?" he asked, laughing.

Chase grinned. "We had a couple of flat beds and commandeered a trailer for each one. It was a heavy load, but we made it."

"Thank you, Chase," Rachel continued. "Joel, anything else?" When he shook his head, she turned to Chris. "Is there a G4 report?"

"Nothing to report except that was are slightly above what we expected to have in terms of food. I would like to recommend a scavenging party soon to find paper products- toilet paper and feminine products especially – and other consumables before everything rots or gets ruined by weather and animals. We can't wait until we are running out of something to stock up – we need to get it now before it's gone. We also need to get more furniture for the three new bunkhouses, and need more school supplies if there is anything left of the high school. I don't have all the details yet – we are still working on it. Probably tomorrow or the next day, I'll present a plan." Chris sat back down.

"Thank, Chris. Frank, you're up with G5."

"Thanks Rachel," said Frank as he stood. "First, I'd like to introduce Sam Thompson and Joshua Rivers. They are both Rangers who happened to be in town yesterday while Dr. Cliburn and his family were being robbed and attacked. They took care of the attackers and saved the Cliburns." Everyone around the table burst into applause, making the two soldiers very uncomfortable. "I also brought Will Stone with me because we were going to talk about a security initiative we are working on. However, until I have a chance to talk to our two newest arrivals, I am going to put that on hold as I think Sam and Josh will have a lot to add to our plan. I would like to make a request, though, of our quilting folks."

Joel started laughing. "I hope you don't want to put the quilters of the apocalypse on security details!" he said, continuing to laugh.

Frank just looked at him. "Hey, Joel, a number of those quilting ladies are already on security details, and they are darn good. I have a request to see if they can make the security teams some tactical vests. We don't have enough to go around for all of our security teams, and I would like each person who would respond in an emergency to be able to have his or her own, already loaded with the proper ammunition and supplies. I've already talked to Chris, and we have enough heavy fabric to make them, and Mary says she has enough people to sew them. She's already made patterns. I just need approval of the council to ask them to go ahead. Oh, and I did ask her not to add any Ohio Stars or Flying Geese to the vests," he said with a smile.

"Yeah, that wouldn't be too tactical, would it," Rachel said, grinning. "Let's take a vote. All in favor?" All hands were raised. "Any opposed?" Seeing no opposition, Rachel told Frank to go ahead with the project. "Last, but not least, Gwen, G6, any communications issues?"

Gwen stood. "We've noticed a number of people we had been talking to in some of the larger cities are no longer broadcasting. We hope it is because they are in the process of relocating, but listening to the horrible reports, well, it doesn't sound good for them. I've also asked Reverend Arnold to talk to two of my radio operators because they've been really upset listening to the graphic reports being given over the radio. We need to hope none of that comes near us, because it is truly hell on earth out there in some places."

Seeing Sam and Josh nodding agreement, Rachel interrupted Gwen. "Unless you have more communications issues to report, I'd like to turn the floor over to Sam and Josh for them to tell all of us their story."

Gwen sat, and Sam stood. "First of all, Josh and I want to thank you for your hospitality. Last night, we slept better than we have since before the asteroid hit. As I told you when we got here, Josh and I were stationed at Joint Base Lewis-McChord in Washington state. The night before the asteroid hit, command called all of us together and warned us that there was a good probability it was going to impact the earth, although they weren't sure where. They let a number of guys go to take care of their families and told the rest of us to stand by for further orders. Josh and I talked and decided we would be ready to go if needed, so we filled up both tanks on my truck with gas and loaded as much stuff as we thought we'd need into the back of the truck. Just in case, you know? We put together a plan that if it hit, unless the army had a mission for us, we would just head down to Texas to the gulf. It would be warm there and we could probably survive whatever happened. Then, when the asteroid did hit and they were forecasting tsunamis, the army tried to evacuate everyone. They got out almost all of the families and a lot of the troops, but there were a lot of us left behind. We moved inland to Yakima, and that was a sight- a huge convoy of military and civilian vehicles. When we got to Yakima, I think the Commanding general had some inside knowledge that Yellowstone might erupt because he turned us all loose, told us all to go home and try to be a force for good in our hometowns. He didn't have to tell Josh and I twice. We were out of there ricky-tik. We were two hours south of Salt Lake City when Yellowstone erupted, and we kept driving until we reached Lubbock. Thank goodness for the panty hose we had purchased, as it kept the air filter in my truck clear once the ash started. Anyway, we ran out of gas just south of Lubbock, and couldn't find anyone that would sell us any. Everywhere we tried, they were saving gas for the police and emergency services. Well, we couldn't argue with that logic, so we decided we would start walking until we got to the ocean. Thankfully, the Rangers taught us to carry heavy backpacks, and so we were able to bring a lot of our necessities with us. We started out with a game cart to carry some stuff, but around twenty miles south of Lubbock, the wheel fell off. It's just as well, because the longer into this emergency we went, the more destruction, disease, and death we saw. We went through one small town where everyone died. It looked like the entire town came together and committed suicide Jonestown style, because there were paper cups everywhere. There were a few families in the middle that had been shot – we figured those were the ones that didn't want to go along with the town's plan. There was another town we went through that the only living people were four women who had been raped and badly beaten. They said a gang came through, killed everyone except the women, girls, and a few young boys. After they were done abusing them, they left them all for dead. The four women were the only ones left alive by the time we got there, and even though we tried to help them, two of them died from their injuries. The other two committed suicide because they said they had nothing left to live for. It was horrible, and even my tours in Iraq, Afghanistan and Somalia did not prepare me for that. We snuck through other towns where gangs were rife, destroying property and killing people. It's as though when all of this catastrophe started, it released millions of evil demons or something. I've never seen so many acts of plain old evil in all my life. Everywhere we went, we saw chaos, violence, anarchy, and destruction. When we got to your town, we were going to just sneak our way through until we could get back out into the countryside and rest. There was just something about hearing the screams of those young girls, though, we couldn't *not* stop and help." Sam's voice faded off and he looked at the ground. "I think I speak for

Josh and myself when I say we will have nightmares for the rest of our lives for the things we've seen right here in our own country. It has made us stronger, though, and it has given us a resolve to not let that happen to other good people. You are the first group we've seen that have banded together and are working for the good of the people. It helps us to restore our faith in humanity after the atrocities we've seen. We talked last night, and if you are willing, we would like to stay here and help you however we can. Knowing that Will and Tom are here confirms for us that you must be good people." Sam finally stopped talking, and everyone in the room was silent. Finally, Rachel stood and walked over to the two men.

"Sam, Josh, we would be so honored to have you join us."

The two men looked at Rachel and began to smile. Suddenly, everyone in the room was on their feet and applauding. With tears in his eyes, Sam looked around the room. "Thank you, folks. Josh, it looks like we finally have a home."

Josh just smiled; his eyes full of tears. "Thank you all," he said, choking up.

"Don't thank us yet, you don't know how hard we all have to work to keep this place running," Joel said with a smile.

"We're not afraid of hard work – if the result is families happy together and safe, it's worth it," answered Josh. "Put us wherever you need us."

"We are assigning you two to Frank. He's in charge of security, and I know he will be able to use you both. Now, is there anything else we need to discuss before I adjourn this meeting?" Rachel asked. Seeing no response, she ended the meeting and sent everyone off to their assigned tasks. Frank and Will took Josh and /Sam with them to introduce them to the rest of the security team.

Chapter Eighteen

April 23

Rachel and Chris were sitting in the living room with Mary and Trina from the quilting group after dinner, all of them working on finishing the bindings on quilts they made for new arrivals. "It's hard to believe it's been a whole month since the asteroid hit," Chris commented.

"Yes, and it's hard to believe how much our lives have changed as a result," Rachel answered. "I mean, I got the quilting retreat I wanted for so long, but its not exactly the way I thought it would be."

Smiling, Chris said, "Well, so it's like a 24-hour-a-day quilting party, right, with just a little drama thrown in."

Rachel rolled her eyes. "Don't jinx us. The last two weeks have been relatively quiet, I'm just waiting for the other shoe to drop."

As everyone laughed, Chris smirked, "Why? What do you think will happen next? Alien invasion? Attack of the murder hornets? Geeze, we're running out of good apocalypse ideas, I'm afraid."

Trina giggled. "Chris, really, don't jinx it. My nerves are finally starting to settle down after all we've been through. Let's just pray for quiet."

No sooner had Trina finished speaking, and they could hear someone yelling outside. Everyone looked at Chris and Rachel quipped, "You had to tempt fate, right?" Chris shrugged and went back to her sewing. A minute later, Joel, Scott and Frank came through the back door into the living room, followed by a crying woman.

"Ladies, have any of you seen Margaret lately?" asked Frank.

"Which Margaret?" asked Chris. "We have about five Margarets here."

"Teenager, 16 years old, long curly brown hair, a little on the chubby side, wears braces, likes the horses..." Scott answered. "This is her mother, Sarah. She said Margaret disappeared after dinner and she can't find her. We're putting together search parties to look for her."

Rachel stood up. "We have a protocol we wrote for a missing person. I'll go get it, so we have some structure and organization to this search. Chris, can you maybe get Sarah a cup of tea and help her relax a little?"

As Chris walked the distraught woman over to the dining area, Rachel quickly retrieved their book of emergency protocols and opened it to the page for missing persons. "I'll start calling people to come to the command center. We'll need all of our G officers available to coordinate each area. Frank, get your search teams ready and have them report here before they go."

Rachel quickly contacted the others on the command staff, and within a few minutes, they came running into the command center. Rachel pointed at Gwen. "Gwen, you will be running the radios. Get a couple of helpers, and make sure each search team has a working radio set to the correct frequency. Scott, put the medical team on alert. Do we know if Margaret has any health issues like diabetes or seizure disorder?" Seeing blank looks, she added, "Get Dr. Cliburn over here to interview the mother, just in case."

Stacey walked up with her sister-in-law Jenna. "Rachel, Jenna is great at working her son's drone, and it has a camera. We can use her to look for anything from a distance and if she sees anything, she can help direct the searchers."

Rachel nodded. "Perfect. Frank, coordinate with Jenna please. Do we have a description of what Margaret was wearing when she disappeared?"

Frank responded, "Mom says she was wearing a green sweatshirt with a pink tee shirt and blue jeans. White tennis shoes, and she's not sure about the socks. She also had on a green ball cap that said 'John Deere' on it. We'll get that description out to all of the search teams."

"Thank you," Rachel added, looking at her list. "Joel, I need you to conduct a check to see if anyone else is missing, especially other girls or adults who could have taken her. Trina, Mary, can you both help Joel do that?" Both women nodded, and Joel opened his laptop to print off lists off all ranch occupants to check against.

As the search groups formed, Frank gave instructions and the groups set out after checking their radios with Gwen. Finally, it was just Scott, Rachel, and Stacey at the big table.

Scott stood up. "I hope she's okay. I'm going to go get Rebecca and start getting food ready for the searchers. I don't want to lose any of them to hunger."

As Rachel reviewed the list, she suddenly stopped and looked at Stacey. "Go tell Jenna to start the drone searching the entire fence line.

That will help us to know if the missing kid is on the ranch or if somehow she left. Tell Frank what I told you to tell Jenna, too."

Stacey ran outside to find Jenna and Frank, and Rachel walked over to the radio desk. "How can I help you, Gwen?"

Gwen handed her a list of call signs. "Every five minutes, we are doing a radio check with each search team. You'll call out 'radio check' and their call sign and they will press the talk button two times if everything is okay and three times if they need help from Frank. If they need help, tell me and I'll relay it to Frank."

Rachel nodded. "Okay, break squelch two times if okay and three times to get help. When should I start?"

Gwen smiled and said, "Now."

After twenty minutes of radio checks among the five search teams, Frank suddenly came over the radio. "All search teams, the drone has spotted a hole cut in the fence at sector north 326. Teams three and four, report to that area. Teams one, two, and five, continue in your assigned search areas, but be prepared to move on my command." The next hour was tense. Finally, Frank came back onto the radio. Teams one, two and five, return to base. Base, please switch to command frequency."

Gwen looked at Rachel with a frightened expression on her face and switched to the frequency set for the leadership team. "Frank, you've got Gwen and Rachel, go ahead, over."

"Roger, Command. We found the hole in the fence with a ripped piece of green sweatshirt stuck on one of the cut chain links. About 20 yards up the trail, we found the John Deere hat. Either the kid snuck out or she was taken. Judging by the footprints we found, it looks like she had help from an adult male. Find out from Joel if anyone else is missing, over."

"We will contact Joel and get that information. What are your plans, over?"

"The Chief is with me, and we plan to follow the trail and see where it goes. Will and Sam are both coming with us, along with a couple of guys from team four. I'm sending the rest back to base to increase security just in case this is a diversion. The guys I am sending back will fix the fence and the cameras and lights – it looks like the wires for both the camera and lights were cut. You might want to check recordings for this sector to see if you can tell who cut the wires. We'll contact you in 30 minutes. Over"

Rachel was shocked. It took her a minute to collect her thoughts, then she told Gwen she was going to find Joel.

"Rachel, it's okay. Take a deep breath. I'll call Joel on his radio and have him meet you here."

Five minutes later, Joel arrived at the command center. Rachel told him of her conversation with Frank. "We're almost done, and so far nobody is missing. Let's get Billy over here to help. He's a whiz on the computer and I'll bet he can look at the sector films faster than anyone. If he sees anything on that sector, we'll have to check all the video for the other sectors at about that time as well."

"Great. If you'll get Billy going on that, I'm going to go check on Sarah and Chris and let Sarah know what we've found out so far." Rachel sighed. "Just an hour or two ago, we were having a quiet night and saying how happy we were that things settled down..." Joel gave Rachel a quick hug.

"We'll get this resolved quickly and then maybe things will calm down again," Joel whispered.

Rachel just smiled sadly as she walked out of the command center.

~~~

When Sarah saw Rachel coming, she jumped out of her chair. "Did you find her?" she cried.

"Not yet, but they did find some clues. Has Margaret ever talked about wanting to leave the ranch?" Rachel asked.

Sarah shook her head vehemently. "No, as a matter of fact, she told me just this morning how she loved it here, and that even if it meant the world outside ended, she was glad we were here."

"Did she have a boyfriend?" Rachel asked.

.

"No, Margaret is a little shy around boys. She's self-conscious about her braces and her weight."

"Would she tell you if she found someone? I mean, what if she found someone she didn't think you'd approve of, would she tell you?"

Sarah looked shocked. "I cannot imagine she would hold anything back from me. Ever since her father died last year, she and I have been very close, and she tells me everything."

Rachel tried to look calm as she asked her next question. "Is there anyone who has been paying particular attention to Margaret? Maybe visiting with her or talking to her more than other girls? Maybe

163

someone older that she might look up to or whose company she might enjoy?"

Sarah's eyes opened wide. "You think someone might have taken her, don't you." She began to cry. "I can't think of anyone who has shown her more attention than anyone else. Of course, there's Wally and his buddies. They are always fawning over all the girls, but not any one girl in particular. Several of the other girls' mothers and I have told that bunch to stay away from the girls, but I've never seen Margaret singled out among them." As Sarah continued to cry, Chris led her to one of the couches in the living room, exchanging a serious look with Rachel.

"I'm going to check in with Joel," Rachel said, as she went back to the command center. Billy had just arrived, and Joel was giving him instructions on what to look for. As soon as he was done, Rachel related what Sarah told her. Joel began muttering under his breath and checked his list.

"No, Wally was sitting on the front porch of his bunkhouse along with his buddies. They were all accounted for." Joel shook his head. "But, I swear, I will bet money that he is involved somehow."

A few minutes later, the radio blared, and they heard Frank's voice. "Base, we are returning with our objective. Have Dr and Mrs. Cliburn meet us in the command center, over."

Rachel grabbed the microphone. "Frank, is she okay? Is she hurt?"

Frank answered, "We're on our way and will be there in 30 minutes, Frank out."

While Gwen got on the radio to get the Cliburns, Rachel hurried out to let Sarah know she was found.

"Oh, thank God," Sarah cried, falling to her knees. "Is she hurt? Is she all right?"

Rachel gently helped Sarah to her feet. "We don't know. Frank wants Dr. and Mrs. Cliburn to see her when they get back, but we don't know why. It's going to take them some time to get back, so we will just have to be patient and pray that its nothing serious."

Sarah looked at Rachel with a terribly sad expression. "After the loss of my husband, I didn't think anything worse could ever happen to us. Now I'm not so sure. I am going to wait in the chapel. Please let me know when she is here." She turned with as much dignity as she could muster and walked into the chapel.

"That poor woman," Chris whispered. "I just can't imagine what she's been through."

"Let's just pray that they need the doctor and the midwife as a precaution, not because anything has happened to the child," Rachel whispered back.

While they were waiting for the return of the search team, Rachel decided to check on Billy's progress.

"I know you only started a few minutes ago, but have you found anything?" Rachel asked.

"Actually, it only took me three minutes to find the video of where the wires for the camera and lights were cut. Here, let me show you." He pressed a few keys on the computer, and Rachel watched as a person completely covered in a large blanket poncho wearing a ski mask, sun glasses, and rubber gloves moved over to the fence. The person obviously knew exactly where the wires were, because he quickly reached up and cut them, at which point the video went black."

"I wonder why nobody saw the video go black?" Rachel muttered.

"I'll tell you why. There are over 500 sectors, each one with a camera. At first, we tried putting all sectors on the screen at a time, but even with two large screens, each sector was too tiny to really see any details. Then, we hooked it up to show random sectors, and if anything was triggered by the motion sensor lights, that sector would be displayed. Again, there was a problem with that. The motion sensors picked up birds, butterflies, leaves, animals, and sometimes even the wind itself would trigger, so we had lots of sectors flashing. Finally, we set it up so that we would have 30 sectors displaying, and it would change sequentially every two minutes. That seemed to be working, but with so many sectors displayed and changing so often, nobody was paying attention to the numbers of each sector to notice the missing one. It just skipped the one that wasn't connected. I think I have a solution, though. Once I print out pictures of the person who cut the lines, I am going to work on the programming for the sector displays. I think I can set it up to alarm when a sector either goes offline or when the camera view is obstructed. I'll add a third screen that will display the alarms, and also sectors that are triggered by the motion detectors. Using a third screen will keep the alarms from affecting the display on the two main screens. It will probably take me a couple of hours to do this, and we'll need to add another person to monitor the extra screen, but that's a lot safer than the way it is now. Of course, that's if you guys are okay with me doing that."

Rachel smiled at her son-in-law. "Marcie sure found a treasure when she found you! You are a genius. By all means, please make your changes, and I'll let the rest of them know what you're doing. Thank you for figuring it out."

"I'm happy to help," he answered, blushing. "Here, take these pictures and give them to Frank and Joel please," he said, pulling several sheets from the printer.

Rachel took the sheets and patted Billy on the shoulder. "Don't stay too late doing this, dear. You can always finish it in the morning."

"Oh, it's no problem. Marcie has already gone to bed, and I'd like to get this done so it doesn't happen again." Rachel watched for a minute or two as lines of computer code ran across the screen of the computer.

"I'm glad he knows what that says," she thought to herself as she headed back to the command center.

A few minutes later, the search team entered the command center with a crying Margaret. They were followed by Dr. and Mrs. Cliburn and Sarah. Sarah rushed over to Margaret, and the two embraced, both crying. Dr. Cliburn got everyone's attention and spoke. "I need everyone to leave the room except Margaret and Janice while we do a rapid exam. Sarah, I know you want to stay, but we can do this faster if you'll just step outside for a few minutes."

Margaret looked at her mother and nodded. "It's okay, mom, I'm okay." Sarah gave her daughter one more hug and left the room with everyone else. It seemed like only five or ten minutes passed before the command center doors opened and Margaret came out, followed by the Cliburns.

"Sarah, you may take Margaret home. She has some medications she needs to take, and Janice will go with you to explain them. I would like to speak with just the council, please," he said, as he turned and went back into the command center. Rachel, Chris, Joel, Scott, Stacey, Frank, and Gwen followed him back into the room and shut the door behind them. They sat around the table looking at Dr. Cliburn expectantly.

"Well, the good news is she was not raped. She was assaulted, though, and roughed up pretty bad. The man who took her was from the town. She said after dinner, she went over to the horse barn and was watching the horses when someone came up behind her and grabbed her. She tried to yell, but he gagged her right away and pulled her behind the barn into the woods. She tried to fight him going through the fence, which was already cut, and ripped her clothes on the fence. The man got mad and smacked her around pretty good. He told her that it was a good thing that he was being paid a lot of money for her, because otherwise he would just have his fun with her and kill her. Apparently, there is a brothel in town, and they are paying well for fresh 'employees'. The guy bragged to her that she was the fourth girl he was bringing in, and that he had an inside connection to get a lot more from the ranch. Oh, and he bragged that they paid a premium for younger girls that were, let's say inexperienced." Dr. Cliburn looked around at the shocked faces. "He would not tell Margaret who his inside connection is, but Margaret said she wouldn't be surprised if it was a group of men who seem to have nothing better to do than follow her and her friends around."

Frank swore under his breath. "I'll bet its Wally and his gang."

Joel looked at Frank and nodded. "I agree. Go get Wally and let's ask him a few questions." As Frank left, Joel turned back to Dr. Cliburn. "Is Margaret going to be okay? What can we do to help her?"

"Honestly, I think her physical issues will clear up without any problems. The girl is utterly terrified, though, and I think she is going to need counseling for a while. Janice seems to have formed a bond with her and is talking to her and her mother right now about setting up some sessions. I am also concerned for all of the other young women here. If there is an inside person, other girls are also at risk. When Frank gets back, we need to talk about how we can provide additional security until we resolve this issue."

"Thank you, Dr. Cliburn. I'm so glad they found Margaret and that you and Janice were here to help her," Rachel said. "I think Scott, Joel, Chris, and I will wait for Frank to bring Wally back. You ought to go get some rest, as its getting late."

"Thanks Rachel. Call me if you need me," he said, as he picked up his medical bag and left. The group sat around the table looking at the pictures Billy printed and talking about the changes he was making to their surveillance system. After about twenty minutes, Frank called on the radio.

"Wally is not in his room, and his buddies said he went for a walk and should be back soon. I'm going to just hang out here by the bunkhouse and wait for him. The rest of you ought to just go home and I'll call you all when he shows up. I can have security watch him tonight and we can interview him in the morning."

Joel hesitated for a minute before answering Frank. "I'd rather talk to him tonight, but it is getting pretty late and everyone's tired. Just make sure once he gets back that security sits on him until morning." He turned to the others. "Frank is right, we all are exhausted, let's just go to bed and we'll interrogate him in the morning."

~~~

It was almost three in the morning, but Billy was happy. His programming changes worked, and the system alarmed when cameras went out for any reason. He had one of the security team at the front gate test it several times and it worked perfectly. He was exhausted, but very glad he was able to contribute something special. Working as an accountant was good, and he knew he was invaluable to Chris in terms of keeping up with the inventory, but he was really happy he was able to add something nobody else had the skills or training to do. As he was walking home, he thought to himself that they needed to add solar lights, as the path to the housing area was pretty dark. Just then, he heard noises coming from the side of the path he was on. When he stopped to look, he saw Wally Blankenship and a young girl walking towards the woods beyond the housing area. The girl looked like she had been crying, and he noticed Wally was holding her tightly by the arm.

"Wally, what are you doing out here with her? Why aren't you in your room asleep? Who is the girl?" Billy asked, rapid fire as he grabbed the girl by the arm and pulled her away from Wally.

Wally let out a roar and pulled a knife.

"I'll teach you to interfere with my business," Wally yelled as he lunged at Billy with the knife.

Billy screamed at the girl, "Run! Go to the front gate and get help!"

Wally lunged again, this time stabbing Billy in the abdomen. As Billy fell to the ground, Wally disappeared into the darkness. Billy put his hand to his stomach and pulled it away covered with blood. He could feel himself passing out but fought to stay awake. Finally, the guard and a hysterical girl appeared at his side. The guard pulled out his radio and called for assistance.

"Who did this to you?" the guard asked.

Billy could barely speak. "Wally…" he whispered as he finally passed out.

~~~

Two hours later, Dr. Cliburn and Dr. Hawthorne opened the door to the command center. They had used the room as a makeshift operating room. The two doctors looked exhausted.

"We've done everything we can. We think he is going to make it, but it is going to be a complicated recovery."

Marcie was being held up by Joel and Rachel, and she burst into tears at the doctor's statement. "Thank you for saving him. I only found out yesterday I am pregnant again, and I want my babies to have a daddy," she sobbed.

Dr. Cliburn smiled at her. "Congratulations on your baby. We are going to do everything we can to be sure he is around for the birth, ok? A lot of things will have to happen between now and then. He lost a lot of blood, but he is young and healthy. Luckily, we have plenty of IV fluids to keep him hydrated. We don't have blood to give him, but we think he will be able to replenish his own blood supply over the next few days. Our biggest worry is infection. His bowels were cut and so his entire belly cavity was contaminated, but we have him on some pretty strong antibiotics. Right now, we are going to move him from here to the clinic where we will be better able to take care of him."

"Can I see him?" Marcie asked timidly.

"Just for a minute now, and then you can come to the clinic in the morning. If anything changes, we will come get you, but it is important you get some rest tonight, especially now knowing you are pregnant." Dr. Cliburn escorted Marcie to see Billy.

At the same time, Joel was pacing back and forth, torn between rage and grief. Rachel had to physically hold him back to keep him from running out to look for Wally.

"Joel, stop," Rachel finally said. "Frank and his crew are out looking for him and you would only be in the way. You need to calm down because all of this rage is not going to solve anything. It won't help Billy, and its not good for Marcie to see you like this." Rachel continued to hold onto Joel's arm with one hand while rubbing his back with the other. "Frank will find him. Meanwhile I need you to be strong. I can't do this without you, and you're going to make yourself sick or give yourself a heart attack."

Finally, Joel calmed down. "I'm sorry, honey," he said, tears pouring down his face. "I just feel so guilty. We knew Wally wasn't where he was supposed to be, and we still went to bed. We should have hunted him down last night. We almost lost another little girl, and we might still lose Billy."

"But we didn't lose either one. Right now, that little girl is talking to Sam and Gwen, and Gwen is radioing the information to Frank's team." Rachel looked at Chris. "What do we know so far?"

"Well, the little girl is Elizabeth Sevier, and she is the daughter of one of Chief's police officers. She lives in the big tent for now and went outside to use the porta-potty when Wally grabbed her. She identified two of Wally's friends– Les Stenton and Jared Crimmons – as being part of Wally's scheme, and security has gone to pick the two up. The girl is fine, other than a bruise on her arm where Wally was grabbing her."

Suddenly, an alarm went off on the computer screen. The girl who was watching the monitors called out, "The camera on sector 312 just went offline."

Rachel quickly grabbed her radio and called Frank to tell him. Frank responded quickly.

"I know, I'm right behind him. He just cut the fence here. We're going to try to catch him, but I suspect he is headed to town. If that's the case, we won't follow him into town because we're not prepared. Frank out."

~~~

Three hours later, an exhausted Frank and the Chief returned to the lodge with the searchers. They had followed Wally to a house on the edge of town, where Wally was met by several men. In the interests of the safety of his team, Frank decided they needed to return to the lodge to plan an assault on the house.

"How's Billy?" Frank asked when he saw Joel.

"He's holding his own for now," Joel answered. "We've got a present for you two," he said, pointing to several men in the living room. "Security brought them in a little while ago. These are Wally's accomplices."

Frank and the Chief were happy to see the two men sitting on the couch in the living room, tied up and guarded by two guards. Frank looked at them with disgust and instructed the guards to bring the men into the control center.

"Joel, Rachel, and Scott, you can stay for this if you want, but you may not participate in this interrogation. I would rather you all didn't stay, because it might get a little messy. I'd rather it was just the Chief and I."

Rachel stood. "We don't need to be here. Joel, Scott, come on, we have other things to do right now."

"Thanks, Rachel. Can you all check on the young lady from tonight? I asked Sam to question her and then write down what he found out. Also, please get on the radio to the security teams and tell them I said to initiate Code Scarlet."

Rachel nodded, and she left the room with Joel and Scott, shutting the door to the command center behind her.

"I wonder what Code Scarlet is?" she asked.

"I think it is something he and the chief put together to confuse those two men, but it might also have to do with increased security," Scott guessed.

"It might also be a code to let the team know he's back and to expect trouble," Joel added.

Rachel smiled tiredly. "Whatever it is, Joel, go call the security teams. I'm going to look for the girl and Sam. She turned as she heard Chris calling her from the Chapel.

"Rachel, we're in here," she called.

Entering the chapel, Rachel saw the girl sitting with Chris and another lady Rachel assumed was Elizabeth's mother. "Are you okay, dear?" she asked the girl.

Elizabeth nodded and put her head back on her mother's shoulder. The mother, who had obviously been crying, tried to smile at Rachel. "Your son-in-law is a true hero. He saved my daughter's life, and we will forever be indebted to him. Is there anything we can do for him or for his poor wife? I feel so bad that he was hurt saving Lizzie."

Rachel smiled and patted the woman on her shoulder. "I'm just glad your daughter is okay and wasn't hurt." She turned to Chris. "Where is Sam? Frank wanted me to get something from him."

"Sam… and Gwen… are in Gwen's office, supposedly writing down the results of their conversation with Elizabeth," Chris said.

"Supposedly? You think there's more to it than that?" Rachel said with a grin.

"Well, let's just say that Gwen has been looking at Sam with starry eyes ever since he arrived. I haven't decided if that's a good thing or not," Chris answered.

"Stop being such a Mom. Your daughter is a very smart adult, and I'm sure she can make perfectly good decisions for herself without your help right now," Rachel scolded.

The two women found Sam and Gwen in Gwen's office talking. When Gwen saw then, she picked up a typewritten report and handed it to Rachel. "Here's what we found out talking to Elziabeth. We were just about to bring it to Frank."

"I'm sure you were, dear," Rachel said with a smile as she picked up the report.

Gwen rolled her eyes and grinned at Sam. "I told you one of my two mothers would make comments."

Chris grinned. "Hey, that's what mothers are for."

Sam laughed; a healthy belly laugh that made everyone smile. "I can assure you, Chris, I have no evil intentions towards your daughter, but I'll tell you that she is a lovely and interesting person, and I hope you will allow me to spend time getting to know her better."

Chris looked shocked. "Um, well, when you put it that way, of course," she stuttered. "Come on Rachel, let's take this report to Frank," she said as she made a quick escape from the room.

Rachel put her arm around her friend's shoulders. "Take a deep breath, Chris. Everything will be fine. Sam seems to be a great person and Gwen is a big girl. Let's go get some coffee while we wait for Frank to finish his interrogation."

Chapter Nineteen

April 25

Joel, Rachel, Scott, and Chris spent the night dozing on the couches in the living room. Every so often, Joel would walk over to the clinic to check on Billy, who seemed to be stable every time he checked. The door to the command center remained ominously closed, although every so often, they were startled by yelling from the room. Frank and the Chief interrogated the two men all night. Finally, around five AM, they opened the door to the command center and announced they were finished talking to the men. The Chief instructed the two security guards who remained outside the room all night to lock the two men up in the cage in the back of the police van and to stay with them until he and Frank decided what to do with them.

As the guards led the two men away, Scott went to the dining room and brought a tray with coffee over to Frank and the Chief.

"You all might as well come in and find out what we learned," Frank said wearily. As everyone took seats, the Chief closed the door and Frank poured himself a large cup of coffee. He took a minute to savor a sip and then looked at his friends around the table. "This is a huge problem. The gang that took over the town is not just running one brothel. They are also selling young girls, women, and even boys to gangs in nearby towns. They're not using money- they are trading for drugs and supplies to make meth. Wally had friends in town who remembered Wally came here. They were able to set up contact with him early on, and he has been relaying details of the ranch to them. Their ultimate goal is to take over the ranch for their operations, and, of course, use all of the women, girls, and little boys to feed into the business." Looking at the shocked faces around the table, he added, "I think they can make life difficult for us, but I don't think they have a snowball's chance in hell of taking over the ranch. It does mean, though, that we are going to have to take this group on."

The Chief interrupted Frank. "We're going to have to institute a few more security precautions. It will take us a few hours to identify the best way to protect everyone, so for now, we want to keep people inside as much as possible. Nobody leaves the ranch for any reason, and nobody goes anywhere on the ranch alone. The two idiots we interrogated tell us that they have about 40-some odd men in their group. I am guessing we are going to have to send out some people to get more information about them before we can make any decisions."

Frank looked deep in thought. "We have four highly skilled soldiers with us right now. Two are rangers and this is the kind of thing they are trained to do. I am thinking we could probably send at least Sam and Josh out to do some surveillance with Will and Tom to back them up. We need hard information to make any decisions on what we are going to do. I agree, Chief, we need to keep everyone indoors as much as possible for the next day or two and make sure people only move in groups."

"I'll take care of initiating that right away," Joel said. "You two focus on what we need to do to keep the ranch safe, and we will take care of making sure people are following your instructions. By the way, what was with the Code Scarlett?"

Frank smiled. "That was something we came up with to let our folks know not to relax until we told them otherwise. It increased security, especially on the perimeter and the front gate. As much as I want to take a nap right about now, I need to meet with our four soldiers and get a plan set up. Chief, I am worried that with what those guys told us, they may try to attack us before we get our surveillance completed. I suggest we get our guards ready to repel an attack. Break out some of those toys you brought. I think at a minimum, our perimeter guards are going to need grenades and heavier weapons than what they've been carrying. We also need to be sure everyone is wearing ballistic protection. If we can keep our non-combatant personnel inside and away from the perimeters, that will help. Also, we need to be sure the fire truck is up near the front gate in case they throw incendiaries over the fence. We need to be prepared for just about anything."

"I'll take care of that, Frank. You go get our guys ready to sneak into town and I'll take care of preparations here." The Chief yawned. "Maybe once we are sure everything is buttoned up, we can catch a few minutes sleep."

"What can we do?" Scott asked.

"Have food ready for the security people and get everyone but security to stay inside. No farming or construction today and keep your eyes out for anyone acting suspiciously. The two men said they were

Wally's only helpers, but I've got someone talking to all the girls to see who else was hanging around with those three and security will detain anyone they identify, just as a precaution. Joel, you might also want to be sure people you trust who are not on security details but who are competent are armed. It would help to have armed people bolstering security in the areas where people are congregating like here, around the cabins and bunkhouses, and around the clinics and barns. I know Jennifer Murray has been training people – have her help deploy people to critical places since she knows their skill levels. You might also want to make sure more ammunition is easily available from a central place. We have a lot of it in the trucks we brought, and I can have a few officers bring a bunch here and stay to guard it." The Chief looked at Scott and added, "You remember we talked about making some major weapons like Napalm and homemade claymores? You might want to think about getting the ingredients for those things together. If they try to assault the ranch, we will need every dirty trick we've got."

Joel frowned. "We can take care of that. I think we will also try to gather as many people as we can here in the lodge. I'll have Noah and Dr. Lydia shut all the animals into the barns and then congregate here. Likewise, I will have the health clinic moved over here. I think Billy and the Cliburns will be a lot safer in the chapel than out in the clinic. We've got this, you go do what you need to do."

As Frank and the Chief turned to walk out the door, they heard someone yell, "Wait!" They turned to see Mary and Trina each pulling a large wagon. Trina was out of breath, but she told the men, "These are all the tactical vests we're gotten made so far. We modified the pattern a little. We didn't have ceramic plates or Kevlar, but we put a bunch of layers of heavy fabric fused together in the front and back to give at least a little bit more protection. We tried it and it resisted being stabbed with a knife. It probably won't stop bullets, but at least it will be a little protection. We hope this helps." Frank hugged Trina and then Mary. "Thank you, ladies, these are excellent, and you may have helped save someone's life with these. Can you keep making more?"

"Of course, we've got our quilters working on them right now."

"That's awesome," The chief said smiling. He thought to himself how great it was that everyone on the ranch with a few exceptions worked so hard to help.

~~~

SERENDIPITY RANCH

Eight hours later, the four men who snuck into town were back and seated at the conference room table in the Command Center along with Joel, Rachel, Scott, Chris, Frank, and the Chief. Frank and the Chief, both having been able to get a few hours sleep, were anxious to hear what the four had to say.

Sam began the narrative. "We took the electric four-wheeler to a point just outside of town and hid it. Then, while Will and Tom provided overwatch, we went in and found a good observation point not far from the houses where this gang is staying. They've taken over three houses on a cul-de-sac on the south side of town. One house must hold the women and kids they've taken prisoner, because there are several guards on the doors. The other two houses look to be where everyone is staying. All three houses look filthy with trash everywhere. There were about thirty guys we saw in the driveway of the biggest house. They have a bulldozer, and they're welding steel plates to the front and sides."

Joel interrupted. "I thought that was just something in the apocalyptic fiction!"

Sam looked at Joel and frowned. "Apparently, they've read the same books. Most of the guys were passing around bottles. There was a bunch of whooping and hollering about how they are going to come here and take over the ranch and kill all the men. They plan to move their operations here once the ranch is theirs and then take over the state, if not more. I did smell the distinct smell of cat urine, so I suspect they are also making meth someplace close by, although we didn't see anything." He pulled out a cell phone. "Here are some pictures I was able to get of the houses, the bulldozer and the guys. As you can see in this picture, Wally is there with these guys, talking to two men who seemed to be in charge. Here's a close-up of the two guys he was talking to."

The Chief looked closely at the picture. "Oh, crap. That's Dwayne Huxley and his partner is Seth Heath. I've arrested both of them several times and I thought they were both still in prison. I guess that answers another question I had if the prisons were still working and holding prisoners."

"Well, if you look at the pictures of these guys, a lot of them have what looks like prison tattoos," Sam replied.

The chief looked closely at the pictures. "You're right. I recognize a couple of these guys as people we put away, mostly for drugs, although Huxley and Heath were doing long sentences for attempted murder, rape, and child endangerment."

"So, what's Wally doing with a bunch of prison escapees?" asked Joel.

"Seth Heath is his brother-in-law. Wally was married to Heath's sister until she died a few years ago," the Chief answered. "How did they act towards Wally?"

"Like he was part of the family," answered Sam. "Thanks for letting us use the police parabolic microphone- we could hear Wally telling them all kinds of things about the ranch. One thing I heard that is good for us is he told them it is best to assault the front gate, because even though there are guards there, it is a softer target than the side fences with the eight-foot stone fences, and also the cameras and lights. He said since that is the way he escaped, he expected we would have really reinforced the fences, but that we wouldn't think about the gate."

Rachel looked shocked. "How is it good for us if they attack the gate?" she asked. "They can just run the bulldozer right through," she cried, tears in her eyes.

Frank reached over and patted her arm. "It is good, Rachel, because we are more vulnerable along the fence line, and it looks like we might have some time to reinforce the main gate. We can do all kinds of things to stop the bulldozer long before it gets anywhere near the gate."

Sam continued. "Wally also said it would be better to attack at night since we only have a couple of guards on at night and everyone is asleep. Finally, he made a point to tell them he knew where all the young girls and women lived and would lead a group to capture them while the rest of the gang was busy killing off the men and old women."

Joel muttered. "We should have just killed Wally when we could. It was a mistake to give him more chances."

Frank turned to Joel. "Don't waste time worrying about the 'shoulda coulda wouldas'. We will take him out, along with the rest of his gang." He then turned back to Sam. "Good job, guys. What did you see for weapons with these guys?"

Josh answered. "A bunch of hunting rifles, a few ARs and AKs, and about half of them had visible handguns. There was also a guy playing with a flame thrower in the driveway, so we can only assume they plan to try to use that. The only thing I saw that is worrisome is it looks like they built some kind of cannon that they were mounting on top of the bulldozer. I have no clue if it will work, but it could be a little…er… problematic for us if it does."

Sam laughed. "I'm betting the first time they try to shoot it, it tears the top off the cab of the dozer. It looked like the breach end was welded shut, which means somebody has to climb onto the top of the dozer to reload it – if it survives the first shot. It looks like a chunk of steel pipe about 6 feet long with the breech end welded shut. They made some kind of metal base for it that was welded to the roof of the dozer, and they were welding the pipe to the contraption. I couldn't see that they would be able to aim the cannon except by the direction the dozer was facing, and it didn't look like they could change the elevation of the pipe, so while it can be dangerous on that first shot, it is not going to be a particularly accurate weapon, and we'll just have to plan to take it out before it can fire."

Frank nodded thoughtfully. "How about vehicles? Other than the dozer, what did you see?"

Josh shook his head. "Other than a couple of pick-up trucks, one SUV and three motorcycles, I didn't see anything. I also didn't see any gas or diesel storage tanks, although they could have a bunch of gas cans hidden in one of the garages."

Frank turned to the Chief. "Okay, here's how I see it. We think their houses might hold prisoners, so we don't want to bring the fight to their houses to protect the prisoners. We also don't want to fight them here at the ranch. I would suggest that we set up a couple of traps for them on both ends of the road off the highway leading to the ranch. Joel, I want you to grab a couple of guys and start covering all the windows on the front of the lodge with plywood, especially the big stained-glass window. Chris, how many canning jars can you spare?"

"We have several hundred cases, so how many do you need?" Chris responded, with a confused look on her face.

"Let's say 4 cases for now. I want you to bring them, and a bunch of fabric scraps down to the parking area near the front gate. We'll need a couple of people and about 3 gallons of gasoline. You're going to make Molotov cocktails to toss at these guys. Also, do you still have all those Styrofoam coolers that you use at picnics? Can we use about half of them?

"Yes, we have about 30 of them. I also have at least 25 big sheets of Styrofoam – they're like 36' by 48" and about four inches thick. They came with some of the equipment I ordered. I saved them to use for crafts," she answered.

"Those would be perfect, better than the coolers. Bring them to the parking area, too. We'll need a few people to help cut them up into pieces." Frank turned to Scott. "Have you still got those glass gallon jugs for cider making?"

Scott smiled. "I sure do. Shall I bring them and a few gallons of diesel to the parking area?" He turned to Chris. "We're going to make napalm, honey!" Chris rolled her eyes and shook her head.

Rachel piped up. "I feel left out but let me tell you what the quilting group and I did while you were sleeping. We sewed up a bunch of burlap tubes, like the kind you see put on the side of the road to prevent erosion. We filled them with gravel, broken glass, and sheets of tannerite. If we put them along the road, all it will take is someone to shoot into them and they will explode."

Frank laughed. "I will never see the quilting group as a bunch of mild-mannered ladies with needles again! You gals are ferocious, and I love it! Alright, here's what we are going to do. We're first going to dig two large trenches that go completely across the road about 150 feet down on either side of the main gate. We'll cut some rebar so the ends are pointy and bury them, pointy side sticking up about two feet, into the bottom of each trench. Then, we'll cover the trenches with sheets of plywood painted black and scatter leaves and dirt on top of them. We'll line the road on either side with Rachel's burlap tubes. Tom and Will, we'll need both of you up high enough so you can see the tubes to shoot them. We will also hang glass jugs filled with napalm from the big oak trees that hang over the road. We'll spray paint the jugs green and put an infrared dot on each jug so our snipers can see to shoot the jugs. Guys, use tracer rounds to be sure the napalm ignites."

"What about the Molotov cocktails?" Chris asked.

"We'll save those for if they get closer to the gate." Frank told her. I suggest you find out who your best pitchers are so they can throw them where they need to go. Chief, I want you to gather together a defense force who can line the inside of the fence on either side of the gate. Anyone who is an accurate shooter can be part of this force. We need to have a second group who can respond to any attempted breaches in other areas of the fence. Make sure they have enough ammo and give them some of those grenades, too. We also need to be certain that every camera on the fence is being monitored and any movement is immediately reported. We need to be sure all the kids, the elderly folks and people who are unable to fight are put somewhere safe- maybe the storage room in the basement of the lodge? Its 1400 now, so we only have a few hours. Let's go!"

Everyone dispersed to accomplish their tasks. Since Scott was busy, Rebecca took over the kitchen, making sure there were plenty of sandwiches and snacks available. She gathered a group of the teenagers who wanted to help and had them distribute the food to the various working groups.

Chris gathered a few of her quilting friends to make the Molotov cocktails. Mary, as usual, brought her sense of humor with her. "I'm glad we're using up these nasty scraps. I never did like this shade of green or that orange. Isn't it fun to be able rip them into strips and then watch them burn?"

Chris laughed. "Let's hope we don't see them burn – hopefully they won't even get used if we can stop all of them a ways away. But even if we do use them, if we can see them burning, we're too close!"

Across the parking lot, Scott finished the last jug of napalm. The infrared dots were tested and were easily visible to the snipers. The Chief arrived with a group of police officers and several game carts loaded with rope, ladders, and Rachel's burlap tubes. "Joel's guys have the trenches dug, so now we just need to get these things put out."

By five that evening, all of the portable traps and weapons were in place, and all of the defenders were ready. Frank called them all together for last-minute instructions. "You all need to be at least 50 feet away from the fence. If you see anyone trying to climb over the fence, shoot them. Do not hesitate, and do not shoot to wound." He looked over the group and was surprised to see Rachel and Chris among the shooters. "You, two. I want you in the lodge. Both of you are too valuable to be out here."

Rachel looked at Frank angrily. "That's bull and you know it. We are both excellent shooters."

Frank put his hands out to calm the two women. "Okay, that didn't come out right. I know you are good shooters, but you two have other valuable skills. Rachel, you are going to coordinate radio calls for medical assistance. Since you know every person staying on the ranch, you can help get them help and get their family to them as needed. Chris, I need you to coordinate radio calls for supplies. You know better than anyone what we've got and can get it to wherever it needs to go faster than anyone else. I want both of you near the radios."

"Fine," said Rachel as she and Chris stormed into the lodge.

At the main gate, the Chief arrived carrying a large rifle case. "Hey, Frank, here's my secret weapon." He opened the case to reveal a Browning Springfield .30-06 rifle and a bag of armor piercing rounds. "I plan to take out the bulldozer with this," he said. Frank smirked and commented, "Nice toy! Good luck."

~~~

When Rachel and Chris entered the lodge, they saw Toby, his wife, and several other people manning the cameras at the reception desk. "Why are you doing that from here and not from the Command Center?" Rachel asked.

"There's another group manning the cameras in there, too. We don't want to take a chance on missing something," Toby answered.

"Good idea," Rachel answered. They entered the Command Center, and the first thing Chris noticed was Stacey manning the radios.

"Where's Gwen? Why isn't she at the radio?" Chris asked.

Stacey looked a little nervous answering. "Ah, she asked me to run the radio, and she's out front with the Molotov crew."

"She What?" Chris yelled, turning and running for the front door.

"Chris, wait," yelled Rachel, following her friend. Chris was a fast runner, and Rachel didn't catch up until they were at the staging area for the Molotov group.

"Gwendolyn Marie Wilson, you get yourself up to the lodge and to your station at the radio, young lady." Screamed Chris.

Gwen calmly turned to her mother. "No, Mom. They need the best pitchers to make sure these things get on target, and all those years of me pitching for little league are about to pay off. Stacey can handle the radio just as good as I can, and I am needed here." Gwen took a resolute stance and Chris knew it would be useless to argue with her.

Seeing everyone staring at her, Chris backed down. "You had best do everything you are supposed to do, and don't you dare get hurt," she said.

Suddenly, in the distance they heard a gunshot. Rachel grabbed Chris and pulled her along. "We've got to get back to the lodge, it's starting," she screamed.

Chris turned back to Gwen. "I love you baby, stay safe," she yelled as the two women ran back to the lodge.

~~~

The next three hours were a nightmarish medley of gunshots, explosions, and screams. There were surprisingly few calls on the radio for medical assistance, and only a couple for supplies. People were told to stay off the radio unless they had something urgent to report. Doctors Cliburn and Hawthorne set up an aide station in the living room of the lodge, and there was a constant trickle of people coming in for minor injuries – burns, falls, and one person who had a powder burn from his partner's weapon. After three hours, the noise began to taper off. Finally, the sounds of gunfire stopped. Frank called on the radio for Chris and Rachel to meet him, the Chief, Joel and Scott on the front porch.

When Rachel and Chris walked out the front door, Joel and Scott ran to them, each embracing his wife tightly.

"Oh, my gosh, Rachel, that was the worst thing I've ever seen," Joel cried.

Frank cleared his throat. "Ladies, the war is over and there were no survivors from the enemy group. I am now taking a group over to town to rescue the women and kids from the gang's hideout." Frank was starting to report on the battle when all of a sudden an ATV wheeled up to the front porch and Sam got out, carrying a bleeding Gwen.

"Quick, help me get her inside," Sam called out.

"What happened? Is she okay?" Chris cried, as Scott moved to help Sam. Everyone followed Sam as he called out for Dr. Cliburn.

Sam gently laid Gwen down on the examination table and told the doctor, "She's been shot, I think in her shoulder." Chris pushed past Sam to be near her daughter.

"Gwen, I told you not to get hurt," she cried. Scott gently pulled Chris away.

"Give the doctor some room," he whispered to Chris.

Gwen's eyes fluttered open. "Sam? Mom? Dad? What's happening?" she asked. Dr. Cliburn stepped up to the exam table.

"Gwen, you're going to be okay, so just stay calm." He turned to the crowd forming around Gwen. "I need all of you to stay back and give us room." Two nurses pushed a folding curtain around the exam table, blocking everyone's view of Gwen and the doctors.

"Sam, what happened?" Scott asked.

"We were on our way back to the lodge, and I went over to where the Molotov brigade was. We actually had to use Molotovs towards the end to help finish off the last few. They had reinforced the pickups with steel sheeting around the beds, so our bullets weren't getting through, but they forgot to cover overhead, so they threw a few jars on them, and that solved the problem. Anyway, I was looking for Gwen, and she wasn't with the others. I turned around and saw her lying behind one of the bushes. It looked like she passed out after getting shot. I saw she was still breathing and had a strong pulse, so rather than do field first aid, I picked her up and started carrying her back to the lodge. Sean came by on the ATV and drove us the rest of the way." Sam looked very anxious. "I hope she's okay."

Scott looked closely at Sam and could see how genuinely upset he was. "You really care a lot about her, don't you." Scott said softly.

"Yes, sir, I do. Gwen is a very special lady, and, well, let's just say I have strong feelings for her, and I think she does for me, too," answered Sam quietly.

"We can't do anything for her now, let's go get a cup of coffee while we are waiting. Chris, are you coming?"

Chris looked at Scott guiding Sam by the elbow with a puzzled look. "I guess I am?" she answered questioningly. The three sat at a table and one of the kitchen workers brought them all coffee.

Sam smiled timidly. "This seems so strange, not too many minutes ago we were fighting for our lives, and now we are sitting here drinking coffee." He looked across the dining room and saw Frank. Suddenly, he stood up. "I gotta go," He mumbled. "Hey Frank, are we ready to go to town?" he called.

"You are not going to town, and neither am I. The Chief took a contingent of officers and Josh, Will, and Tom to go rescue the victims. You need to stay here and wait to hear about your lady." Frank turned to Scott and Chris. "Are you two okay?" he asked. "I saw Dr. Cliburn working on her, and he called out to me that it's going well."

SERENDIPITY RANCH

Chris closed her eyes and said a silent prayer. "I hope so. We're trying to be patient and wait for word. Hey, what do you mean, Sam's lady?"

Scott smiled at his wife. "Honey, Sam and Gwen have gotten very close over the last couple of weeks, and that is a very good thing. You are going to be calm and happy and be glad Gwen and Sam have found each other in these troubling times."

Chris, who was not only exhausted from the battle, but emotionally overwhelmed by Gwen's injury, began to cry. "I'm losing my baby," she sobbed.

Scott put his arm around her as Sam looked like he wanted to be anywhere but sitting at the table with Chris. "Honey, you are not losing Gwen. Sam is a good and honorable man and if he wants to spend time with Gwen, he has my – our – approval. And if it leads to more than that, we will happily welcome him into our family." Scott looked at Sam. "Why do you look like you're about to be tarred and feathered?" he laughed.

Sam let out a sigh of relief. "Thank you for saying that. I was a bit worried, there for a minute."

Scott let out a belly laugh. "You'll get used to Chris! But I've got to warn you, Gwen can be just like her mother."

Sam grinned. "I think that is one of Gwen's charms, being like her mother."

Chris reached over and punched Sam in the arm. "Quit trying to suck up. Scott said we approved." She laughed. Just then, they heard Dr. Cliburn calling them. They hurried over to his makeshift aid station.

"Your daughter is incredibly lucky," he began. "A bullet went through her shoulder, but missed all of the nerves, blood vessels and organs. She has a clavicle fracture and two wounds- an entry and an exit wound, that will need care. Otherwise, she is fine. I've sedated her and she is being moved to a bed in the chapel to rest, but you can see her when she wakes up."

Chris hugged Dr. Cliburn. "Thank you, thank you for saving my little girl," she exclaimed.

Chapter Twenty

April 27

The morning after the battle, the command staff gathered in the command center. Rachel stood up and started the meeting. "Before we rehash what happened yesterday, I want to thank Frank and the Chief for everything they did. Without all of your planning, knowledge, equipment, and guidance, who knows what would have happened. We are incredibly grateful.

"Early this morning, our rescue group returned with twenty-two women and children that had been held prisoner by the gang. Right now, they are at the medical clinic with the doctors getting checked out." Rachel choked up for a second. "Some of them are in really rough shape. They've all been through a lot. All of them asked if they could join our community." She looked around and saw everyone nodding their agreement. "We'll deal with that once the doctors clear them. Frank, let's start off with a description of the battle. We all know bits and pieces, but I think you are the only one who was right on the front lines throughout."

"Thanks, Rachel. I'd like to say these guys were just a bunch of drunk druggies, but they did have some idea of tactics. Of course, they also did some really stupid stuff, too. We heard the bulldozer before it got close. The up-armored dozer was a great strategy, but what they did wrong is they had a few guys out in front of it. Those guys started shooting as soon as they could see the gate. That was pretty dumb, because they didn't have any targets. Of course, they made great targets, and the snipers took care of them pretty quickly. They also only came from one direction. When the dozer crossed the trench covered with plywood, the plywood collapsed, but the trench wasn't quite wide enough, so it just got stuck. The Chief did a great job with his Springfield taking out the dozer driver and the "cannon" on top of the dozer. He actually did them a favor because looking at the cannon afterwards, I am positive that cannon would have exploded if they tried to fire it. Anyway, the rest of the gang with the exception of three guys who stayed back to guard the prisoners and the houses all piled into three pick-up trucks and followed the dozer. When the dozer got stuck, they all jumped out of the trucks and swarmed forward. One guy actually managed to fall into the trench. It wasn't pretty what that rebar did. They tried moving forward along the side of the road, but those burlap quilter rolls exploded quite nicely when we shot at them. Give the quilting group my compliments!" Rachel and Chris grinned and high-fived each other.

"The quilter rolls took out a few of the guys. Our shooters behind the fence took out most of the rest. A couple got close enough that the Molotov brigade deployed several jars, which didn't hit any of them, but it was a good deterrent. The group that was left changed directions, and that was when we shot one of the napalm jugs. Again, I don't think it actually hit anyone, but it did cause them to change direction again. Two of the guys tried to surrender, and they were shot in the back by their leader... about thirty seconds before we killed the leader. There was another guy who must have been ex-military because he was also calling out orders of which direction to go and where to shoot. After we took him out, the remaining guys basically just shot at anything that moved and made themselves excellent targets of opportunity.

"I am really proud of all of our people. Everyone stayed calm, stayed on their posts, and practiced excellent firing discipline. For a bunch of people who had never fired at anything other than a target, they were amazing. On a side note, I spoke briefly with the doctors and with Reverend Arnold a few minutes ago. I am afraid as the adrenalin of battle wears off, some of our folks may be in need of some counselling to help them deal with what happened.

"When the battle was over, we went out and counted 39 bodies. We used our dozer and created a mass grave on the other side of the road, out past the dozer trench. Some of the guys are working on their dozer right now to see if it can be salvaged. If nothing else, it will be good for parts.

"On our side, we had very few casualties. The worst one was Gwen, and I suspect she was hit with a ricochet, listening to the doctor's description. There were a number of people hit with flying debris, one guy got too close to his partner and wound up with a powder burn, a couple of falls with sprains, and a few people with lacerations from falling or getting hit with stuff. Again, pretty amazing for a bunch of amateurs! Chief, you want to talk about what your guys on the perimeter saw?" Frank sat down as the Chief stood.

"I want to echo Frank's praise of our people. I had a contingent of mostly police patrolling the borders. We split up into several teams, and they were in constant contact with the folks on the cameras. When the first few idiots in front of the dozer started shooting, one of my teams was nearby on horseback. They were the first to start shooting back. Once the majority of shooting started, only that group moved closer to the gate. The rest continued to patrol just in case the gang tried to flank us. Other than a couple of elk, a javalina and a few birds, the guys on the perimeter didn't see anything."

Scott smiled. "Were they disappointed?"

The Chief looked very serious. "No, actually they were happy they didn't see anyone. Remember, if they did see anyone, it would have decreased our odds of winning by a lot."

Scott looked embarrassed at his question as Frank stood up again. "Scott, don't feel bad asking. Just remember that the guys on the perimeter were mostly law enforcement who have already had their share of gun battles. It wasn't a novelty to them." He turned to face the rest of the group. "Now let the Chief tell you about what the men found when they went to town. Chief?"

"I took a bunch of law enforcement officers, Josh, and Will with me to town. It was a very short battle. We told them to put their weapons down and they shot at us. So... we shot back. It only took two minutes to take all three down. Once they were down, we spread out and did a complete search of the area. One of the three was still alive, and he confirmed there were 42 members in the gang- the 39 at the ranch and the three left behind."

"Did you bring that guy back as a prisoner?" Joel interrupted.

"No, he did not survive his injuries," the Chief answered flatly. "Of the three houses, the big one was home to the gang leaders, it looked like. There were three women chained up in that house. It was a filthy, disgusting mess. The second house was worse. That was where the rest of the men lived. The third house was where the prisoners were kept. All I am going to say about what we found there was that it will feed our nightmares for many years to come. That gang was pure evil, and what they did to those women and kids was ..." He stopped and took a sip of water. "It was indescribable. Please do not ask the victims to describe the torture they endured. Just know that entering that house was like entering the gates of hell." After another short pause, he continued.

"Behind the third house, we found a large, detached garage that was being used as a meth lab. Once we were absolutely sure we had removed all of the victims, both the living ones and the deceased ones, we used grenades and destroyed all four buildings. When their prison house exploded, quite a few of the victims cheered. We stayed long enough to be sure the buildings were destroyed and would not pose any kind of fire hazard or other danger to the land around them, and then we brought the victims back. There are a couple that are pretty critical and I'm not sure they will make it."

There was silence around the table. Finally, Rachel spoke. "I have a few ideas on where we go from here. Frank, I think you and the Chief need to put a group together to go out and visit the other ranchers and anyone else who survived all of this. We need to start making alliances so that this never happens again. I also think we need to take a serious look at housing for everyone. We keep adding, but families can't live in bunkhouses. Joel, I think you need to get with Chase and come up with a plan to expand our community so everyone is comfortable and safe. Maybe look in town and see how many manufactured homes are still in the sales lots that we could drag here. Frank, listening to you, I would really like you to form a militia with regular training so we have a force ready to go. You'll need to get with Chris to inventory weapons, ammunition and other force multipliers (Ha, bet you thought I forgot what that meant!) Who you put into the militia will depend on any alliances we make with our neighbors. Chris, we need to get some salvage teams together. Now that the gang is gone, let's see what is still available in town to help the folks here before something else happens or more bad guys come along. We know there are still bad guys out there because of what those two friends of Wally's told us about selling women and kids to other gangs. We need to be ready for them if they come this way."

The Chief smiled. "You're right, Rachel, we cannot get complacent. We also need to have an active law enforcement present in this area. I have already started making plans of how we can do that. I'm glad you mentioned Wally's friends. They are still locked in the back of the police van under guard. We need to decide what to do with them."

"I say we just shoot them and be done with it," Joel muttered under his breath.

"No, dear, that is not the answer," Rachel said. "There has been enough killing. They've already confessed to helping Wally get information about the ranch, so we can't just set them free, and if we release them, they could just join up with another gang. They need to serve a sentence, but it bothers me to think of us feeding and taking care of them for years and getting nothing in return. I think we need to have a work gang. The guys are locked up when they are not working. We can put them out working in the fields or something so we get something back from them and they can repay their debt to the community."

"Sounds like you're talking about a chain gang, Rachel," said the Chief. "That is pretty much what I had in mind. If all of you are okay with it, I will see that that gets done. We'll need to come up with a jail of sorts so we can get them out of the cage in the van. I'm sure Mr. Stenton and Mr. Crimmons will appreciate your mercy."

Suddenly, the door to the command center opened and Gwen entered, accompanied by a protective Sam. She had her arm in a sling and looked a little wobbly, but everyone was happy to see her up and around.

"Gwen, honey!" Chris shouted, running to embrace her daughter. Scott was right behind her, followed by everyone else.

"I'm okay, Mom, Dad. Dr. Cliburn released me a few minutes ago, but I have to take it easy for a few days. I'm still on pain meds and will be for a few days. Once the wounds and my clavicle heal, I'll start physical therapy. Thank goodness we invited a real physical therapist to our opening! Meanwhile, I'm headed home to get some rest, and Sam is insisting on coming with me to be sure I really do rest."

Sam jumped in, "You know the doctor said you are not to be up running around for at least a week. My job is to be sure you follow the doctor's rules."

Gwen smiled and put her good arm around Sam. "Come on, then, my guardian. I feel woozy and want to go home." Chris and Scott both kissed their daughter on the cheek and watched as Sam and Gwen slowly left.

"That is such a relief," Chris said with a sigh. "Rachel, I forgot to ask amidst all of this fighting and all, how is Billy doing?"

"He's doing better. Dr. Cliburn let him move over to his house this morning. He'll be on bedrest for a few weeks, I suspect. Marcie is fussing over him, and Dr. Cliburn is sending a nurse over twice a day to give him his antibiotics and other medicines and to take care of his dressings. The doc says he thinks Billy will make a full recovery as long as he avoids getting a major infection." Rachel sighed. "And all I wanted was to open a quilting retreat and spend our days sewing. Who would have thought we'd go through all of this?"

Joel hugged Rachel. "Well, now that we're past this, maybe you'll have time to do some sewing… at least until the next crisis happens!" Everyone started laughing, and Rachel swatted Joel's arm.

"Don't tempt fate," she laughed. "Let's get back to business. We still have a lot to talk about."

Chapter Twenty-One

September 7

Scott looked around the dining room with pleasure. The harvest was excellent, and they just finished a massive canning operation. He admired the stacks of freshly canned vegetables cooling on the tables before being put away for use this coming winter. He taught a large group of people how to safely can, and every day for the last two weeks, they prepared and canned the bounty of the harvest. They spent an additional week canning meat, mostly for trade with other survivors.

"Wow, it looks like they canned even more today than yesterday," Chris said, as she walked into the dining room and hugged her husband.

"They have certainly been busy. It was an incredible amount of work, but come this winter, we'll be glad to have everything. I'll tell you, though, even after working as a chef all these years, I've never seen so many bushels of veggies. Green beans, peas, corn, squash, potatoes, turnips, greens, okra, asparagus, carrots, beets, tomatoes, peppers, cabbage, oh, my gosh, and the list goes on...and that's not even including the fruits! Or all the herbs we dried. How did you know to get so many quart and half-gallon sized canning jars? I expected to have the pint jars, but boy, was I surprised to see the big ones!"

Chris grinned at her husband. "You may be the chef, but I am the supply expert. We do have lots of the pint-sized ones, and we've been using them to make jams and jellies. I knew, though, if we were going to be feeding a hundred or more people, we wouldn't be doing it with pint-sized jars – that would be an incredible waste of lids!"

"So, what about next year? Will we have lids for then?" Scott asked.

"Well, of course we will. We still have thousands of jars in storage and several hundred thousand lids, so we will be in good shape for the next several years. Hopefully, we'll find a factory or warehouse with more, or else we'll learn to make our own by then. Plus, don't forget everything we dried in the freeze-dryer. I've got scavenging teams looking for a couple more of them."

Scott smiled wistfully. "Yeah, I wish I thought about getting a couple more of them when we could just order them and wait for delivery. But I'm glad we have the one we have. Did you know that for the last few months, at the end of every meal, Rebecca has been packaging any leftovers and freeze-drying them? I didn't realize she was doing that until a couple of weeks ago, and I'm jealous I didn't have that idea first."

"We've all had some pretty good ideas, and they sure have paid off." She leaned her head onto Scott's shoulder. "Now how about making a cup of coffee for your tired wife, and after we drink that, I'll help you get these jars into storage."

"Sounds like a deal to me," he said, kissing Chris on the forehead before walking over to the coffee pot.

~~~

After the battle last April, the ranch command group sent out teams to find other survivors. Although Serendipity Ranch was by far the largest and most successful ranch around, there were other ranches that also were able to salvage crops and livestock. Many escapees of the town found refuge on some of those ranches and set up small enclaves where they could live safely in exchange for working on the ranch. It was a good system, and the other ranches seemed to also have good harvests.

As they met with the other ranchers, the Serendipity Ranch staff were quick to share equipment, ideas, support, and friendship. On numerous occasions, Dr. Lydia went with the teams to deal with animal health issues in outlying areas. At other times, some of the medical staff went to help with human illnesses. Sam found his niche as the leader of these expeditions. As the other survivors got to know Sam and his team, they learned to trust each other. Before long, they were sending representatives to meetings at Serendipity Ranch to develop ways they could all help and support each other. By early August, Rachel became the elected leader of a coalition of survivors that encompassed several counties. She immediately appointed Frank and the Chief to oversee security and protection for the entire area. The other ranchers were delighted to have the leadership and guidance to keep themselves and their neighbors safe and were active members of the new militia and sheriff's department. One of their first combined missions was to clear the entire area of criminals and troublemakers. It took time, but by the time the mission ended, the area was clear of people who would cause problems. The militia set up routine border patrols of the entire area, and manned roadblocks to keep potential problems out. The Chief, who absolutely refused to be called the Sheriff, set up routine law enforcement activities. A jail was built on the property across the street from the ranch's main gate, and other than housing a few belligerent drunks from time to time, had very little use due to the thoroughness of the earlier mop-up operation.

Joel entered the command center to find Rachel sitting at the desk working on the agenda for the weekly rancher's meeting that afternoon. "Are you ready for the meeting?" he asked.

"I will be shortly. I asked Steve Porchenko to talk to the ranchers about what they can use to condition their fields this winter to be ready in the spring for planting. We want to be sure everyone has enough seed for winter cover planting."

"We probably have enough to share, I would hope," said Joel thoughtfully.

"I'm sure we do, but we want to see what they have, first. We need to have a discussion now while there's still time to go out and look for stuff before the cold weather really sets in. I don't want to be an enabler. We'll share, but only as a last resort. It benefits everyone to make sure everyone has a good harvest every year," Rachel added.

"Don't the ranchers already know this stuff?" Joel asked. "I mean, they've been doing it a long time."

"Not all of them," she countered. "Remember, quite a few ranches were abandoned and now are being run by people who have never done it before. So, it pays to help them learn. I'd rather teach them than feed them." She paused. "Oh, speaking of teaching, did you hear my good news?"

Joel looked at her and shook his head.

"When Stan Willetson and his crew come for the meeting this afternoon, they are bringing a few women who want to learn to quilt. They heard about our quilters and all the great things they've been able to make for us, and they want to learn to do the same for their own ranch. Mary and Trina are so excited, as are all of our quilting group." With a huge smile, she added, "See, we really do have a quilters' paradise here – even in the middle of an apocalypse."

Joel laughed. "Rachel, you and your quilters of the apocalypse! They have certainly earned their keep. I'm glad you got to see your dream, even if it's a bit different than you planned!"

Chapter Twenty-Two

October 18

Rachel and Chris finally finished hanging the last of the white drapes on the grape arbor in the lodge back yard. Chris took a step back and looked at the arbor. "It looks perfect. We need to get ready if we don't want to be late to our girls' weddings."

Rachel laughed. "I am not the least bit surprised that when they each started planning weddings, that they would decide to have a joint wedding. We'd best hurry if we want to spend any time with the girls before the ceremony."

Two hours later, almost the entire Serendipity Ranch community turned out to watch Rebecca marry Jimmy Langston and Gwen marry Sam Thompson. A lovely ceremony, conducted by Reverend Arnold, was followed by a huge barbecue. Also in attendance were representatives from a number of surrounding ranches. Rachel was happy to see that all of their hard work developing alliances with other survivors in the area paid off, and now many of them were not just allies, but friends as well.

Once dinner was done, the dancing started. Rachel, Chris, Joel and Scott sat off to the side watching the brides dancing with their new husbands. "They look so beautiful, and so happy," Rachel whispered to Chris.

"I'm so happy for both of them," Chris answered. "There were a lot of times I wasn't sure if we would ever see this day, but here we are. I wonder if they will like their wedding presents?"

The two laughed. Long ago, long before they ever won the lottery, Chris and Rachel bought some amazing fabric at the local North Carolina quilt shop. They intended to make matching birthday quilts for their daughters, but never got around to it. Instead, they resurrected the fabric when the weddings were announced and made each couple a matching double-wedding-ring quilt. The various shades of blue with metallic silver threads interspersed made two very striking quilts.

"Isn't it funny? A few years ago, a double wedding like this would have costed a fortune. We would have had to order flowers, cake, caterers, photographers, and a venue. Then, there would be the wedding dresses and all the bridesmaids dresses and stuff. The happy couples – or their parents – would have had to spend tons of money on a honeymoon. There would have been all kinds of drama with bridesmaids and groomsmen. Then, the guests would have to worry about fancy clothing, wedding gifts, travel, and all of the other old trappings of what we used to call civilization. I like this so much better." Chris gestured to the crowds of happy people dancing and eating. Most were dressed in their everyday work clothes, and all were happy and smiling. "This seems so much more real. I think the catastrophe really distilled life down into just what is important. Family, friends, safety, hard work, and genuine fun."

Rachel smiled at her dear friend. "I know exactly what you mean. Life is a lot harder now and the future is uncertain, but right now, it just doesn't get any better than this."

Just then, the DJ put a slow song on the player, and the two ladies and their husbands went to dance and enjoy the music. For most of the residents of the ranch, the hours passed with laughter, good food, and a lot of love. Even the guards, deployed around the ranch to keep everyone safe, were rotated out so they could each enjoy the festivities, too. The dancing kept up until the early hours of the morning. Even though most everyone would have to be up early to do their morning chores, events like this just didn't happen very often, and most wanted to take advantage of every minute.

Sometime after midnight, the two bridal couples were about to leave the festivities and head to their homes when they heard the jingle of bells on the ranch buggy. Out of the darkness, Joel and Scott pulled up to the two couples, driving the buggy. "We're here to drive you folks home," Scott announced. Amid much laughter and delight, the four climbed onto the well-decorated buggy for the short ride back to their houses. After dropping them off, Joel and Scott took the buggy back to the barn, chatting while they untacked the horses and cleaned up the equipment.

"I'm so happy everything went so well tonight," Scott sighed.

"I know. We can't count on it always being this peaceful and happy, but I'm really glad our girls got their dream weddings without any drama getting in the way," Joel answered.

"Well, if we can keep up our activities with the other ranchers, maybe it will stay pretty peaceful. Funny, I was a little worried that without the government in place, we would see anarchy. Not one word after all this time from Austin or Washington, and things are going really well. I hope the old government is gone for good, and we can continue to run things the way we are. I mean, look at what we have. Everyone works, there are no handouts except for our oldest and most infirm, and even they contribute in their own ways. There's no racial strife, no worries about taxes, no stupid bureaucratic laws, just good old-fashioned common sense. Our kids are getting a good education, and we are even starting college level courses without all of the hoopla and big bucks that go with college education. I'll tell you, I am tired every night, but I go to bed happy for a good days work and for the life we have." Scott yawned. "Are you done? I'm about ready to just lay down here in the stall and go to sleep," he laughed.

"I hear ya, man, and I agree with everything you just said. I'm done, let's go. And don't forget to add a few thank yous to your bedtime prayers tonight- I know I will."

Epilogue

July 17

Today was a big day. After months of discussion and meetings, Rachel was being named the Regional Governor of the new state of West Texas. The winter was hard, but because of the alliances forged the year before, all of the ranches and communities in their region not only survived, but thrived. The alliance made a number of salvage runs outside of their area, and found conditions were not good. The salvage teams found many supplies that the alliance needed, and also found abandoned factories and the equipment needed to make a number of supplies. They also found people who survived, but who were living in abject conditions. They brought in those people who agreed to follow their simple rules and were able to start several communities in areas that had been abandoned after the asteroid hit. Those communities were set up to be able to barter goods and services with other communities. All of the ranches around had their own communities as well. One of the refugees brought in was the former president of a local Christian college. He was asked to oversee the educational system being developed to ensure kids were being taught things that were important for their continued survival, but that they also were taught history, literature, music, and other subjects that would contribute to a civilized future.

Rachel was nervous. She, Joel, Chris, Scott and Stacey were getting ready to leave for the swearing in ceremony, and Rachel was having some last-minute jitters. "What if I can't handle such big responsibilities?" she moaned. "What if I mess up and make mistakes?"

Chris laughed at Rachel and put her arm around Rachel's shoulders. "Girlfriend, you've been running all of us for years now, and you've done a fine job. This is no different, except you've got a whole lot more help now. You've got the support of hundreds of people around us, and everything will be fine. Besides, look at all we've accomplished under your leadership. We're off to a brand-new church that was built in town because you insisted we all needed a place where people could come together and worship as a community instead of just on the ranches. We'll have the swearing-in ceremony and reception there, but you get to still work from home. All the times we talked about minimal government, and you've made that happen. Quit being nervous and enjoy the day!"

Joel and Scott laughed and started clapping. "I nominate Chris for Secretary of State," Joel quipped. "Now, can we all just get in the car and go so we're not late?"

Rachel was even more nervous when they arrived at the church. There were hundreds of people in throngs around the church. When they saw Rachel, they started to cheer. The Chief and his officers cleared a path for Rachel's party, and they entered the church. Every pew was filled, and there was such a positive happy attitude among all the people, it was palpable.

The ceremony itself was brief and to the point. Following the ceremony, a reception had been prepared on the front lawn of the church. As people settled down after getting something to snack on, Rachel was asked to say a few words. She began by introducing her cabinet. First was Deputy Governor Roger Armstrong, owner of a ranch a few miles from Rachel. Next was the new State Supreme Court judge, Stacey Bennett. She introduced Frank as Commander of the State military forces, and the Chief as the Commander of law enforcement. People were surprised that she didn't have a lot more cabinet members. "I know who to ask when I need help with something, but that doesn't mean we need to inflate the size of government by adding all of those extra positions." She explained. "I also want to say that all of us are serving without a fancy salary or lavish living expenses. The state's funds will be used for the people of the state, and we will be true community servants, the way it was intended to be from the beginning. Nobody in my administration will get rich from their office," she explained as people cheered. "We are all in this together. We all have choices. I choose to try to make our state the best place to live. I want us to be safe, healthy, and successful. It will take a lot of work to get there, but look what we've accomplished so far? All by working together. Let's keep it up so we have something wonderful to give to our children and grandchildren. Let's not go back to old ways of being greedy. Let's continue to love our neighbors, and to honor and respect each other. I want us all to be happy and to live with dignity, peace and prosperity. We can do that, my friends; I know we can." Rachel sat down to tremendous cheering from the crowd as her family looked on proudly.

Later that night, Rachel was sitting in the living room with some of the people most important to her: Joel, Chris, Scott, and Stacey. She looked at each of her dear friends, and finally spoke. "Can you believe it has only been just over two years since we all sat around a table together for the first time and created Paratus, Inc.? Look at all that has happened since then. We've been to hell and back, it seems, but we did it together. I am so grateful for all of you."

Chris frowned at her. "Rachel, if you get all mushy and make me cry and ruin my makeup, I'm going to smack you, governor or not!" she laughed. "Geeze, first time I get to wear makeup in years and you're gonna make me get all weepy."

Stacey jumped in. "I just want to say how glad I am that Scott called me that day to help all of you. I can't tell you how much better my life has been since then- in spite of all the negativity, I've never been surrounded with so many loving and kind people."

Rachel reached across the table to pat Stacey's arm. "You've been invaluable to us, and you feel like a sister to us. We're so glad you decided to hang with us."

"Poor Rachel," Joel chuckled. "All she wanted was to open a quilters' retreat and sit and sew all day with her fellow quilters, and now she's the governor. I was trying to be funny when I called y'all the quilters of the apocalypse, but that's exactly what you all became. These last two years have been exciting, exhausting, frightening, and redeeming. I can't wait to see what the next two years will bring for all of us."

Just as Joel finished talking, Gwen and Rebecca entered the dining area, accompanied by a grinning Sam and Jimmy.

"I can tell you two things the coming year will bring," Gwen said.

Rebecca added, "Yes, and I hope you stocked lots of diapers for your new grandchildren!"

SERENDIPITY RANCH QUILT BLOCK

To make this block, you will need:
- 74 green half-square triangles
- 18 purple half-square triangles
- 2 red half-square triangles
- 2 gold half-square triangles
- 3 red squares
- 3 gold squares
- 3 purple squares
- 3 green squares
- 36 background squares

All half-square triangles and squares should be the same size. Using 4 ½" unfinished squares (4" finished) will give you a 48" square block. This pattern will work with any size square, as long as all squares and half-squares are the same size! To assemble, lay out all pieces as shown above. Stitch pieces into rows, then stitch rows together to make the block above. Alternate the direction of seam allowance in each row to help all seams nest together.

THE COMPLETED SERENDIPITY RANCH QUILT
(Made in batiks and hanging in the Serendipity Ranch lobby)

To complete this quilt, you will need:

- One completed Serendipity Ranch quilt block
- Green border (2-4" wide, depending on the size of each square in the block)
- Background border 1 ½" wide
- 32 purple flying geese (same width as each block)
- Background border the same width as flying geese
- Second Background border 1 ½" wide
- Green binding

To assemble:

- Apply the green border, first to sides, then to top and bottom of block
- Add the 1 ½" background border the same way.
- Stitch 8 flying geese together as shown in the illustration (make 4 units of flying geese).
- Attach background border to flying geese units and trim to the size needed to fit.
- Attach this border to 1 ½" background border
- Once attached, then stitch on final 1 ½" background border.
- Add batting, backing, and bind with green binding.

www.ingramcontent.com/pod-product-compliance
Lightning Source LLC
Chambersburg PA
CBHW072354020726
47506CB00004B/1116